The Rescue

Book One of the Timestream Travelers Chronicles

Sher J. Stultz

First paperback edition December 2021
Second paperback edition September 2023

Cover art by Vivien Reis

ISBN: 9798455440540 (paperback)

https://www.timestreamtravelerchronicles.com/

This story is dedicated to all my brave students.

Timestream Travelers Chronicles Who's Who

Fall 2015

Entwistle Family

Archie (Father)

Miranda (Mother)

Socrates (Older Brother)

Aeneas (Middle Son)

Persephone (Youngest & Daughter)

Willoughby Family 1

Charlie (Father)

Sakura (Mother)

C.J. (Son, Cousin to Tabitha, Sadie and Seth)

Willoughby Family 2

George (Father)

Martha (Mother)

Tabitha (Daughter, Cousin to C.J. and Sadie)

Seth (Younger Brother, Cousin to C.J. and Sadie)

Willoughby Family 3

Catherine (Mother)

Sadie (Daughter, Cousin to C.J., Tabitha and Seth)

Carl Hoffsteder (Dad to Sadie, Ex-husband of Catherine)

Also Appearing

Harold Torkelson (Entwistle Housekeeper/
   Eleanor Caregiver)

Eleanor Meachum (Widower)

Everett Veltkamp (Teammate of Aeneas)

Bethany Purvine (Classmate to Tabitha and Aeneas)

Mr. P. Schmidt (Middle School Geometry Teacher)

Bob North Sky (Time traveler, Shaman, Mentor to Aeneas)

Spring 2053

Cassie Entwistle (Daughter of Aeneas)

Lux Entwistle (Twin son of Aeneas)

Tor Entwistle (Twin son of Aeneas)

Missi Entwistle (Daughter of Socrates)

Thena Entwistle (Daughter of Socrates)

Keniah Collier Entwistle (Mother of Missi and Thena)

Sheila North Sky (Daughter of Bob North Sky)

Sandra North Sky (Cousin of Sheila)

Mini Bios of Main Characters

Aeneas

Birthday: September 23rd, 2001

Parents: Archie Entwistle and Miranda Freeman Entwistle

Siblings: Socrates and Persephone

Pets: Sput the dog-share

Ancestry: English, Irish and African American

Favorite Foods: Breakfast Burritos, Enchiladas, Pizza, Fish Chowder, Peanut Butter Pancakes

Favorite Book: *The Call of the Wild* by Jack London

Sport: Soccer

Cassie

Birthday: September 18th, 2028

Parents: Aeneas Entwistle and ?

Siblings: Pollux and Castor

Pets: None in 2053

Ancestry: Scottish, English, Italian and African American

Favorite Book: *The Sea Runners* by Ivan Doig

Favorite Foods: Sushi, soup, anything from a bakery

Sport: Soccer, Bowling, Swimming

Persephone

Birthday: January 21st 2006
Parents: Archie and Miranda Freeman Entwistle
Siblings: Socrates and Aeneas
Pets: Giant Hissing Cockroach colony
Ancestry: English, Irish, and African American
Favorite Foods: Curries, Pizza, Soups, Popcorn
Favorite Book: *Silent Spring* by Rachel Carson
Sport: Swimming

Socrates

Birthday: June 16th, 1998
Parents: Archie Entwistle and Miranda Freeman Entwistle
Siblings: Aeneas and Persephone
Pets: None, but likes dogs and cats
Ancestry: English, Irish, and African American
Favorite Foods: Steak and frites, Curries, street food
Favorite Book: *Genius: The Game* by Leopoldo Gout
Sport: Racketball, Ping Pong, Pool

Harold

Birthday: March 12th, 1987
Parents: Robert and Clara Addison Torkelson
Siblings: None
Pets: None, but likes to taste test with Sput; not a cat person
Ancestry: Scandinavian and Irish
Favorite Foods: Name it and Harold will cook it or eat it
Favorite Book: *Hyperbole and a Half* by Allie Brosh
Sport: Frisbee Golf

C.J.

Birthday: February 6th, 2003

Parents: Charlie and Sakura Nishimoto Willoughby

Siblings: None

Pets: Sput the dogshare

Ancestry: English, Scottish and Japanese

Favorite Foods: Japanese dishes, Pepperoni Pizza, Dry snack foods

Favorite Book: *The Twelve Kingdoms Series* by Fuyumi Ono

Sport: Biking, karate

Tabitha

Birthday: November 1st, 2002

Parents: George and Martha Borrelli Willoughby

Siblings: Seth

Pets: Fish

Ancestry: English, Scottish and Italian

Favorite Foods: Thai dishes, Pizza, Sushi, Oatmeal cookies

Favorite Book: *The Daughter of Time* by Josephine Tey

Sport: Bowling

Sadie

Birthday: February 14th, 2001

Parents: Catherine Willoughby and Carl Hoffsteder

Siblings: None

Pets: Cat named Elvis

Ancestry: German, Irish, English

Favorite Foods: Anything wrapped in a tortilla, street food,
Indian, Mexican
Favorite Book: *Juliet, Naked* by Nick Hornby
Sport: Miniature Golf

Sput

Birthday: Unofficially September 15th
Ancestry: Blue heeler, mutt (according to pet DNA test)
Favorite person: C.J.
Favorite snack: Anything Harold will let him taste
Favorite Book: *Harry the Dirty Dog* by Gene Zion
Sport: Squirrel stalking

For more details about the characters:

https://www.timestreamtravelerchronicles.com/

・ C H A P T E R 1 ・

Not Your Average Entwistle

Entwistle Farm, Walla Walla, Washington, July 1986

WILLIAM'S WHOLE BODY SHOOK, causing his teeth to chatter in his head like a jackhammer. He was freezing, even though it was summer. William picked himself up off the hardwood floor and leaned against his upstairs bedroom windowsill. Heat shimmered over rows of crops in the fields behind their house.

"Not this again," he groaned. William had been caught in a stream of energy, trapped in his own memories of the past. When he was inside the stream, he would wish with all his might he was home, and an unseen force would jerk him back.

A familiar sound reached his ears. His brother Archie was calling him to come downstairs. Archie and Larry were going out to the barn to test Larry's new invention, a small remote controlled plane with a camera attached.

William yelled back to his brothers, "I'm gonna shower."

William tried to walk, but his legs were like jelly. He stumbled into the bathroom, gingerly stepped into the shower and turned the nozzle. He rested his head against the tiles and let warm water fall over his body.

~

West Seattle, Washington, October 2015

Aeneas Entwistle stretched his legs and glanced down at his feet. Two different socks *again*. He pulled off each sock, carefully examined the patterns and thought back to the night before. He'd stayed up late finishing his geometry homework, but he was certain when he went to bed that his socks had been green, with the Seattle skyline etched in white. Yet attached to his feet were a bright red sock scattered with blue dots and a black sock with a pattern that looked like falling snow.

The decision before him now was whether he wanted to make a mad dash for the bathroom without changing his socks and risk a sighting by his younger sister or his older brother or stash them at the bottom of his sock drawer. In a house full of geniuses, any unexplained phenomenon like waking up with socks of unknown origin was bound to cause suspicion, invite comment, or draw, as it were, too much unwanted attention to oneself. One of the geniuses might even take it upon themselves to hook up a machine to monitor his REM cycle or tag him with a tracking device. Aeneas had to be vigilant to escape their notice.

Having just turned fourteen, Aeneas wanted less, not more, attention from his overachieving siblings. With this in mind, the socks were kept secret from everyone except his two best friends, Tabitha and C.J.

Aeneas was not a genius like the rest of his family. He was a bright, funny, athletic teen who loved games of all kinds and played for the sheer fun of it rather than to win. His parents were shocked to find after several different IQ tests were administered that genetic diversity had endowed their middle child with only above average intelligence.

Miranda confided to Archie, "Surely there must be some mistake. Aeneas can't just be *above average.*"

Archie smiled and replied with a shrug, "What about my younger brother William?"

Miranda sighed. There was no arguing that. Archie had two brothers, one a genius and the other, not.

Miranda and Archie were scientists holding Ph.D.'s in both chemistry and chemical engineering. After their wedding they decided to settle in Seattle's Industrial District and hired an architect to help them retrofit an old warehouse into a state of the art laboratory. They were considered innovators by their peers and frequently published scientific articles in prestigious academic journals. Soon after Aeneas's older brother was born, Archie decided to convert the adjacent warehouse from a spare laboratory into a livable loft, because their family was beginning to grow. For a few years they resided there quite happily.

From the time Aeneas could walk, he loved to play soccer and spent hours a day practicing inside the loft when it was too rainy for his mom or dad to bundle up his baby sister and take them to the park. However, after a series of mishaps involving broken glassware, a small explosion and loss of power for two city blocks, Aeneas at the tender age of four suggested to his father that they buy a house near a park where he could practice soccer without causing a blackout.

Aeneas was beloved by his parents even though he wasn't brainy like his siblings. He was, in fact, quite astute in ways his parents began to appreciate. One day Aeneas had spotted a house for sale a few blocks from Hiawatha Playfield in West Seattle when he was attending a birthday party of a friend from Montessori school and insisted his father go see it. Archie took one tour of the house and decided that his young son was shrewd about practical matters. They were a family of five now and a home was needed. Archie called the realtor, offered a good cash price and the Entwistle family moved in a week later.

Archie and Miranda had always had enough money to buy a home, a very nice home, but their priorities were occupied with testing chemical compounds that would reduce carbon dioxide emissions and serve as sustainable fuels, so buying a house simply never crossed their minds. Throughout his life, Aeneas assisted his parents in practical ways, such as buying a house, and even later when the whole family became extremely busy, proposing a housekeeper to prepare regular meals and tackle their mountains of laundry.

But Aeneas was keenly aware that his interests and the interests of his family were diverging, so he kept a few secrets. Some were small, like his stash of comic books hidden under neatly folded hoodies at the top of his closet and others were big, like waking up with two different socks. And the socks... Well, they didn't need to be up for scrutiny.

CHAPTER 2

Not My Socks

AENEAS SENT AN URGENT text to C.J. and Tabitha asking them to meet him at their usual hangout, Freshy's, the neighborhood coffee shop just across from Hiawatha Playfield. He snagged a table next to the window and spied C.J. walking up the street, his cousin Tabitha next to him wearing a hoodie, her long auburn hair piled under a blue and white Fair Isle beanie.

Aeneas had been a little edgy, but relaxed when he saw his friends approaching. The bell chimed loudly as the door flew open and C.J. and Tabitha sat down at the table, their favorite drinks already ordered and waiting for them. C.J. was distressed as he carefully unwound a Seattle Seahawks fan scarf knitted for him three years ago by Tabitha.

C.J. started watching football when he was seven years old, the same year Pete Carroll was hired as the Seahawks head coach, and he hadn't missed a game in four years. C.J. Willoughby was a "twelve" even though he was only eleven years old and "twelves" (devoted Seahawks fans) all owned pieces of fan gear that were special to them. The item, cherished above all things, was a scarf with a hawk's beak overlaying the Olympic Mountains. C.J. handed it to Tabitha. "Can you fix this by Saturday?" he asked anxiously.

Tabitha glanced at the scarf and quickly reached into her bag. "I always keep a pair of size 10 knitting needles on me," replied Tabitha calmly. She was used to his worries over the scarf. In under a minute the dropped stitches were repaired.

"Thanks, Tab. You're the best!" C.J. smiled appreciatively and gave Aeneas a nod of acknowledgement as if he, too, had been worried about the scarf.

Aeneas looked at him, shaking his head with exasperation. "Bro, you've got to let this thing go. It's about skill, not scarves."

"Every time I take off that scarf the Seahawks lose. After what happened last year at the Super Bowl against the Patriots..." C.J. stopped, overcome with emotion. He hated to relive the last few moments of that fourth quarter. It was unbearable. He'd even written an apology letter to Pete Carroll, explaining his culpability in the loss.

Aeneas shook his head, sipped his chai tea and glanced at Tabitha for support. Tabitha had briefly left the conversation and was making a mental note of a niche market for her future counseling business: sports grief and sports superstition disorders.

Relieved that his scarf was repaired for the next Seahawks game, C.J. took a bite of his oatmeal cookie then a swig of hot chocolate. Tabitha was still lost in thought tapping the lid of her latte when Aeneas leaned in and whispered, "Hey...I woke up with two different socks again."

In the last few months, the friends had worked feverishly to determine why Aeneas would sometimes wake up wearing different socks. The most obvious reason, proposed by Tabitha, was a practical joke by one of his siblings, but after C.J. installed a video camera in Aeneas's bedroom that hypothesis was ditched. No one had ever entered his room, pulled back the sheets and changed his socks; however what they did see completely dumbfounded them.

Frantic with excitement they huddled around C.J.'s camera to watch the high-speed video playback from the previous night. All three friends were stunned into silence when at 12:27 a.m. the sheets went slack and Aeneas was gone. Then everyone gasped as a zombie-like Aeneas reappeared, climbed in through his bedroom window at 1:44 a.m. and headed straight back to sleep. Clad to his feet were not the socks he'd worn to bed.

They focused on those eighty minutes and after weeks of discussion there was a small breakthrough. After scouring the internet for anything unusual that occurred during that date and time, C.J. recalled a database his science teacher had shown his class when they had studied earthquake hazards called the Pacific Northwest Seismic Network. This helped direct his discovery. His text message read:

Hey Aeneas, I think I found something unusual. There was a 5.6 earthquake just south of Victoria. It hit at 12:26 a.m. Could be a coincidence. But we should investigate.

Since then, the friends had found consistent evidence to correlate Aeneas's nighttime disappearances with seismic activity in the region.

All the sounds of the bustling coffee shop filtered into white noise as the table of friends fell silent. C.J. started to ask something then choked on his hot chocolate causing him to clear his throat several times before he spoke.

"Did anyone at home see you wearing those socks?"

"Nope," said Aeneas. "I changed into my slippers and hid them at the bottom of my sock drawer for safekeeping."

"Were they your socks, ones that you currently own or owned in the past?" asked Tabitha. She'd already unraveled several pairs of the unusual socks searching for clues about how or where they were made, but all she could determine was that the yarn was a wool blend.

"I didn't recognize either and I checked Dad's sock drawer," replied Aeneas.

C.J. ran his fingers through his hair and muttered, "What about your brother?"

Tabitha shook her head. "Aeneas memorized all his pairs the last time."

"I'm sure Socrates updates his footwear," said C.J. curtly, giving his cousin an annoyed glance.

Aeneas shrugged. "Both socks were unique, C.J."

Tabitha asked even though she already knew the answer, "Did you check the P.N.S.N.?" Since they had managed to correlate earthquake activity to Aeneas's disappearances all three friends regularly consulted the Pacific Northwest

Seismic Network. "Any activity near the Juan de Fuca plate?"

Aeneas nodded. "3.1. Yesterday afternoon."

"Only 3.1? That's not consistent with your past disappearances," said C.J. frowning.

The three prior disappearances had all occurred with seismic activity along the Juan de Fuca Plate, but with more energy. The range was between 4.2 and 5.6. This new data didn't fit the previous trend. If Aeneas was susceptible during lower energy events, his disappearances could increase, which might not go unnoticed. So far he'd been able to keep this a secret from his family and considering his little sister Persephone was freakishly observant, this had been no small task.

Something else was still bugging C.J. as he finished his oatmeal cookie. All the times Aeneas had woken up with unusually patterned socks, it had been nighttime. This seemed odd to C.J. because Aeneas was fond of his naps. In fact, he napped on weekends and every day in the summer and often after soccer practice.

"Why does this always happen at night? Why not during one of your naps?"

Tabitha raised an eyebrow. "That's a good point, C.J." They both turned to Aeneas expectantly and his expression changed from bewildered to helpless in a matter of seconds.

"I dunno," he replied, thumping his fingers on the table, his brain registering this new piece of the puzzle brought forth by C.J.

Aeneas first noticed that he slipped in and out of locations just after his parents bought the house in West Seattle. One day while playing in his bedroom, young Aeneas realized his favorite plush toy—a soccer ball with googly eyes had been left behind at his parents' laboratory in the Industrial District. This occupied his young mind off and on for several hours.

Thinking back, Aeneas remembered bounding down the stairs, wishing he had his ball. A moment passed and he was still bounding down the stairs, but these stairs were in the laboratory. He saw the ball, grabbed it, then started back down the stairs. Except this time, he was back at home.

While he was aware of these spatial shifts, at five years old Aeneas had no way to articulate these events to his parents. Other events, like waking up with different socks left him perplexed, even a little concerned, which is why he'd confided in Tabitha and C.J. They were his best friends and he enlisted their help to figure out why he sometimes woke up wearing strange socks. And they did not disappoint. C.J. found the link between his disappearances and seismic activity and Tabitha had first alerted him to the fact he was wearing different socks.

Later that day, determined to find a connection from the recent information Aeneas shared, C.J. tapped his feet as he scrolled through recent data from the P.N.S.N. He was searching for anything that might explain Aeneas's recent disappearance. The network only covered the Pacific Northwest earthquakes, so he loaded his U.S.G.S (United States Geological Survey) page and searched there as well.

A list of recent earthquakes showed no significant activity along the Cascadia Subduction Zone. Stumped, he tapped his feet some more then glanced over at the Seahawks schedule posted on the wall. The October 22nd game against the San Francisco 49ers caught his eye.

When his brain was sluggish, C.J. knew a surefire way to get his neurons back up to speed. He poked his head out of his bedroom door and listened carefully for his parents. His father was playing the violin downstairs in the music studio and his mother was busy in the back garden trimming away dead summer flowers. In a house where classical music was king, he preferred not to divulge his secret playlists to his parents. Once he was sure the coast was clear, C.J. grabbed his MP3 player, maxed the volume and immersed himself in the sounds of Bollywood, practicing dance moves he'd seen on YouTube.

Well into song number three on his playlist, C.J. glanced again at the Seahawks schedule and the October 22nd game. He grabbed his tablet and loaded the Berkeley Seismological Lab page and checked their database. Sure enough, there had been a series of small earthquakes off the coast of northern California. They were too small to be noted by the P.N.S.N. or U.S.G.S page, but the earthquakes had occurred in succession, just before midnight, a closer match than the 3.1 earthquake earlier that day near the Juan de Fuca Plate.

C.J. studied the page. The earthquakes had been close together and registered 2.9, 2.0, 1.7 and 1.2 on the Richter scale. Then there was the distance. These had occurred over five hundred miles south of Seattle. Normally the earthquakes linked to Aeneas's disappearances were nearby, all within one hundred and fifty miles of his location. This new evidence seemed to indicate that Aeneas could be affected by less powerful earthquakes even as far as Northern California.

・ C H A P T E R 3 ・

The In-Between Dreams

AENEAS WALKED HOME FROM the coffee shop with his mind wandering in a thousand directions. He stopped to watch some kids play a pick-up game of soccer at Hiawatha Playfield and wished he could join in, but he had work to do at home.

Aeneas Entwistle, not normally a list maker or documentarian, had been secretly trying to unravel the unusual nighttime events that had begun to distress him over the last several months. Although he could've asked either of his siblings or his parents for help, he wasn't comfortable becoming a science experiment for his family.

Aeneas had experienced some weird dream-like scenarios during the missing time, but kept these from C.J. and Tabitha because they were hazy and tough to explain. And also because they frightened him a little. He knew Tabitha would press him on this and he wasn't sure how deep he wanted to go just yet. Plus, he felt their longstanding friendship was changing. When Tabitha sat down across from him at Freshy's he noticed how flushed her cheeks were, how her auburn curls fell to her shoulders when she took off her hat and that unsettled him. The distractions, the things that were confusing him seemed to be piling up.

The last few times he'd returned to his bed, bizarre memories had lingered. He scribbled these in a journal he kept in his backpack with a decoy cover on it titled, "Soccer Moves for Defenders." Just to keep it all legit, he actually sketched and labeled the first few pages with moves for defenders and made notes for himself.

The most prominent recollection that lingered was of his best friend, C.J. His gut feeling was that C.J. had somehow gotten him back home and had even taken care of him. Aeneas mumbled to himself as he walked up the steps to his house and opened the front door.

"The old dude that gave me a sandwich looked just like C.J. And then I swear he said, 'Can you see it? Look for the sparkling lights and wish that you were home in your bed...'"

"Sounds like something from the *Wizard of Oz*," said a small voice.

Aeneas leapt to one side and let out a breath, his heart pounding. His little sister Persephone, whose hair seemed to be the biggest part of her body, bobbed up from the corner chair that he'd walked past. Her golden Afro had swelled with the humidity so she appeared to have a halo, but that was definitely deceptive. Persephone was anything but angelic.

"Hey Seph," said Aeneas cautiously.

What an idiot I am, thought Aeneas to himself. *Persephone is like a ninja, popping up everywhere.* He knew it was prudent to never say anything to pique her curiosity or else she would dog his every footstep.

"What were you mumbling about?" asked Persephone, setting aside her ecology textbook.

"Ah, nothin' much," replied Aeneas lightly, trying to throw her off. His grumbling stomach sent him towards the kitchen to grab a quick snack.

Aeneas snagged a bag of trail mix from the pantry and headed to his room.

"I'll be upstairs doing some homework if you need me, Seph," Aeneas called back as he ascended the stairs. Persephone usually left him to it if he said he was doing homework. He grabbed some colored pencils from his desk drawer and plopped into a bean bag chair. He sketched the sparkling lights, the colors like a thousand Christmas lights and the face of the man who looked eerily like C.J.

"Geez, Clint. I must be losing my mind," said Aeneas softly. Clint referred to Clint Dempsey, forward for the Seattle Sounders and Aeneas's favorite soccer player. The poster of Clint was the only decoration in Aeneas's bedroom besides his own soccer photos which his mom had framed to adorn his empty walls. Clint never answered back, but Aeneas spoke to him often.

Aeneas sighed and kept sketching, all the while shoveling handfuls of trail mix into his mouth. Concentrating to recall the details, he drew a sort of swirling tunnel with pinkish golden light and pictures of his life, some parts clearer than others. He pulled C.J.'s school picture from his desk drawer and taped it in his journal using it to recreate the man's face. The eyes were the same color and the chin had a dimple. Aeneas stopped and scrutinized his sketch.

"That old dude has got to be C.J.," murmured Aeneas to himself. "It kinda looks like the pictures we made last year on the age simulator at the science center. Same chin dimple."

~

Cassie Entwistle's Condo, Ballard, Washington April 30th, 2053

Cassie paced her living room, sighing with anticipation as she stepped around boxes of broken picture frames that had fallen off the walls. She was waiting for her father. She'd been waiting for him for days. Amidst all the other chaos from the earthquake, her father Aeneas had vanished and her mother was becoming more and more anxious by the day. Cassie had searched the timestream several times. It wasn't difficult. Given the aftershocks, the timestream seemed to be permanently open. Everywhere she looked the sparkling lights caught her eye and even though it seemed inappropriate given the fact that people everywhere were dealing with the aftereffects of a natural disaster, she found herself smiling.

The greater Seattle metropolis was reeling from the 7.2 earthquake that had struck along the Birch Bay fault line days before, leaving a path of destruction along the Puget Sound. Luckily long standing predictions of the "big one" had given western Washington counties time to prepare. Yet there had been significant damage, and some loss of life while the aftershocks continued, keeping people on edge. Cassie assumed Aeneas had been swept into the timestream during the earthquake, but it had been four days and there was still no sign of him.

CHAPTER 4

Jack of All Harolds

AT AGE TWENTY-FIVE HAROLD Torkelson found himself homeless. Growing up in Chimacum, a small community on the eastern Olympic Peninsula, Harold skipped several early grades, graduating from high school at sixteen and proudly finishing his degree from the University of Washington at just twenty. After graduation Harold was on fire. He'd opened his own consulting business and was on the fast track to becoming a wealthy young techie, but in less than five years his start-up had gone bankrupt, forcing him to foreclose on an expensive condo in Seattle's trendy Fremont district. Nearly everything he owned was repossessed by the bank leaving Harold with seven hundred dollars to start his life over again.

After bouncing from friends' couches and spare rooms for a few weeks, Harold saw an ad for a housekeeper in West Seattle. This appealed to him greatly for several reasons. First, Harold did his best work when he was cooking and cleaning. The serenity of these menial tasks freed his mind to solve complex coding problems. Second, he didn't have enough money to start his own company again and, because of his idiosyncratic work habits, few employers wanted to hire him. A programmer, no matter how brilliant who requires a fully stocked kitchen, is considered too much of a prima donna even in a progressive city like Seattle. Harold was offered a job in Portland, where the employer was willing to convert the staff lunchroom into a kitchen, but the space was not to his liking. It contained only a tiny electric stove (he preferred gas), a single door refrigerator, and two microwaves and lacked adequate counter space, not to mention the shallow sinks.

When Harold came for the interview, Aeneas's parents, Archie and Miranda took an instant liking to him. Archie's culinary skills were relegated to making a bowl of cereal, but he loved homemade food. Miranda, too, liked fresh wholesome meals but was mediocre in the kitchen, despite being a world class biochemist. In contrast, Harold was a gourmet cook who could provide their family with two nutritious meals each day. Harold's expertise in the kitchen thrilled Miranda because all the Entwistles, including young Persephone, were hearty eaters.

Miranda also had more personal reasons for liking Harold. He didn't infringe upon her mothering. Though Miranda worked outside the home, there were maternal undertakings that she felt were her domain, such as illnesses, trouble with friends, back to school shopping, and holiday planning. Many other applicants for the job made her feel squeezed out of her role as mother to her three children. Harold, unlike other more nurturing candidates, left the mothering to Miranda. He was hopeless at first aid and wasn't inclined to give the best advice regarding childhood conflicts, having been an only child himself.

Harold arrived at the Entwistle home promptly at 6:00 a.m. each morning and began preparing bistro-style breakfasts, a requirement Aeneas insisted his parents add to the job description because they all loved big breakfasts and in this respect Harold never disappointed. Eggs Benedict, homemade waffles, quiches, scones, oatmeal on the coldest rainy days, served with sausage or bacon and fruit salads all summer were regular menu items at Chez Harold. Harold was also tasked with the major chores like laundry, dishes and floors as well as packing lunches, and leaving a homemade dinner ready for the family. Although some parents wouldn't consider hiring a housekeeper based on the suggestion of their ten-year-old child, Aeneas's argument proved convincing and Harold meshed into their family life with ease.

After Harold left the Entwistles' house around two o'clock, he took the bus across the West Seattle bridge over to the Queen Anne neighborhood and started his second, but smaller dinner preparations for his other client, Eleanor Meacham. While he enjoyed the bustle of a busy home with children, Harold's work at Eleanor's house was much different. Harold appreciated a quiet evening where he could make tea, bake the odd pound cake, walk Maizy the golden retriever and read the latest Janet Evanovich novel in between his freelance programming work. The pace was slower and allowed him to relax after a busy day in West Seattle.

Eleanor Meacham was eighty-six-years-old and required less of everything. Harold's main job was to give Eleanor peace of mind. After her husband's death, being home alone, especially at night, made her uncomfortable. Maizy also needed the occasional midnight stroll, being an old gal dog, which was where Harold's younger legs came in handy.

Maizy was adopted by Eleanor from the King County Animal Shelter to keep her company now that she was a widow. At eight years old, Maizy had lost her home because of a human divorce; the family having been split up into new homes that didn't allow pets. Her daughters, Charlotte and Lorraine were skeptical. Maizy was a big dog that would require daily walks. They thought a small dog with less exercise needs would be more appropriate, but Eleanor walked into the shelter, took one look at Maizy, asked a few questions and requested to adopt her.

Eleanor and Harold got along well. She liked his cooking, enjoyed his company and felt secure in his presence. Harold was also pleased with the arrangement. He had a huge upstairs bedroom to himself, his own bathroom and the freedom to come and go in the early evening hours to various social engagements.

Eleanor's days were quite full. She breakfasted at a local café, reading *The Seattle Times* and visiting with neighbors. She and Maizy would go for short walks, and Eleanor would eat lunch at various restaurants throughout the week. She was well known throughout the Queen Anne neighborhood.

Usually when Harold arrived in the afternoon, Eleanor was napping in her chair with a novel or knitting, giving him more quiet time. This all suited Harold perfectly. He wasn't homeless, but lived in two homes and had the company of people he liked. Harold had plans though. He wanted to start a new company again, but that required significant funds. At the present, he'd saved around two hundred thousand dollars from his freelance work, but that was only a fraction of what he needed.

Of course, there was another reason. Deep down Harold had become attached to both homes and the people and pets within. They formed a stable matrix of daily habits that was so productive and gratifying Harold worried that even if he saved enough money that leaving them would be impossible.

Not My Laundry Data

HAROLD SAT AT THE small kitchen table and paged through his vegetarian cookbook searching for inspiration for the evening's dinner. Persephone had asked him if they could go meatless once a week since the resources required to produce one pound of meat seemed excessive compared to the resources needed to grow vegetables. Persephone was studying sustainable systems and in her mind, sustainability should start at home.

On first meeting Harold, Persephone was intrigued and a little shy to talk with him. He was a person that lived between two homes and seemed to be happiest when he was cooking and coding. Persephone knew enough about software to understand it was created by coding, a computer language of directions and rules that a person had to be quite bright to learn and use effectively. Given this, she was not sure why someone like Harold would be making her waffles and washing her clothes.

Aeneas explained it one evening in terms he hoped her nine-year-old genius brain could understand. Seated in their modern, brightly furnished living room, Aeneas planned to keep it short. Persephone could often draw him into long conversations that exceeded his communication quota.

"Seph, Harold has to really focus when he's coding, so he gives his brain a break when he cooks or does laundry... it's like his brain is napping a bit and then he can get back to coding."

Persephone thought about this.

"Aeneas my brain works all the time and I don't have to give it breaks. Why does Harold's brain need breaks?"

Persephone's golden brown Afro haloed her face. She looked at her brother with sincere curiosity, which made Aeneas smile gently at his baby sister who helped him with his geometry homework. Aeneas cleared his throat. "What about your documentary collection on the cloud?"

Persephone was known to spend hours watching documentaries, so much so that her documentary time was regulated to six hours a week. She also liked to watch the giant hissing cockroach colony contained in an old, repurposed aquarium on her desk. Often she would have to be pulled from in front of the colony by her brothers when it was time for their evening meal, which their mother, Miranda insisted they eat together.

Persephone narrowed her eyes, wondering. *Is it the same thing I do sometimes?* Persephone patted Aeneas on the cheek and hustled off to the roach colony. Aeneas smiled to himself. That was a record, under two minutes.

Harold paused from the cookbook to resume his coding. His mind was blank. He had no ideas for dinner. His coding, too, was sluggish. Normally paging through a cookbook sparked inspiration and once that happened his coding took off.

He gazed out the kitchen window. The sun peeked in and out of clouds and since there was a light breeze, Harold cracked the window over the large farmhouse sink in the Entwistles' cheerful buttercup colored kitchen. It was cooler today and autumn had made its presence known. It was a favorite season for Harold. He liked the cooler mornings, the leaf change, and creating anything with pumpkin and winter squash. Squash was not a favorite of Archie Entwistle and Harold was quite sensitive about his cooking, so he took great pride in cooking squash dishes that Archie would eat.

After five minutes, amounting to little progress on his coding project, Harold grabbed the cookbook and walked past the laundry room on his way to the bookshelf above the stove. He stopped and noticed a blue clothes basket tucked just inside the door with a note attached:

Harold,

Could you please wash my violet leggings? I slipped in a puddle as you can probably see from the stains. I've also included some other items so you can do a full wash.

Thank you, Persephone.

Harold smiled at the note and pushed the basket inside the door. He stayed there for a moment, gazing into the laundry room. Something was amiss. He sniffed the air, but despite being filled with laundry from all three children, the odor in the laundry room was tolerable. He shrugged and closed the door and thought it best to get out of the house for a bit to see if he could shake off whatever strange feeling he'd had all morning.

Harold decided to take a walk over to PCC Market and browse the vegetables. Sometimes seeing the ingredients before he cooked helped his thought process. He gazed at the produce, all colors of fall that he loved. He pulled back for a moment and saw them as a woven pattern like a quilt of veggies. Harold gasped. A mother and her small children looked at him with concern.

Harold gave a weak smile and said, "I know the answer now."

The woman gave him a tentative nod and turned her cart. Sometimes Harold forgot that he wasn't speaking to someone who knew how his brain worked.

Harold made his way back home. He dropped off two delicata squash and a bag of shallots on the granite countertop. He turned and entered the laundry room, pulled down the missing sock basket and stared at it. All of these socks had matches somewhere because Harold had seen them before at some moment in time inside the Entwistles' house, but these two new missing socks were just that, *new*. The socks in question had come from the bottom of Aeneas's sock drawer. Eventually Harold was able to re-pair all the single socks as the other matches would appear except, in lost circumstances. But even then they had made previous appearances through the wash cycle and were recorded in Harold's eidetic memory.

Socks of unknown origin, thought Harold. Socks that suddenly appeared without any previous existence in the laundry cycle. Harold was a master at finding anomalies in data and now one had appeared in his very own laundry room, slipping into his mind like a tiny piece of gravel in his shoe. It would bug him until he'd solved the puzzle, but then Harold had always been that way, restless and persistent when there was a puzzle to solve.

~

Seattle, Washington, May 2nd, 2053

Cassie sipped a green smoothie while she waited for Harold to finish his conference call. Harold was seated around a large oblong table conferencing with a consortium of landowners from Arizona that was pitching him an investment opportunity for a solar farm. Each person was represented by a different holographic screen and Cassie marveled at how this scene compared to conference calls of the past that she'd watched in old sitcoms.

"Well you were right, Cass. They have a great idea going, but there are still some hiccups to work through before I can invest."

Harold made this comment with a nod of respect. Cassie had been working for him for two years now and it was clear she had a knack for finding promising business opportunities and also had a knack for knowing when they were not quite prepared to be launched.

Cassie shrugged in return, too distracted to care much about the solar farming consortium or Harold's compliment. Her dad had been missing for nearly a week.

"Still no sign of him?" asked Harold with a sigh.

"Not a one. And my mom is frantic with worry," said Cassie wearily.

"Even when he's been injured, Aeneas has always shown up within a day or two," said Harold absently scratching the gray stubble on his chin.

"I don't know where else to look. I've scoured his timeline," said Cassie, twisting one of her curls tightly around a finger. She felt like her insides were as twisted as her curls.

Harold shook his head wishing he had an answer. His mind was still quick, but not like it was when he was younger... He mumbled something to himself and Cassie raised an eyebrow.

"Say something?" asked Cassie sharply. She detested his mumbling, but he was her employer and an old family friend so she refrained from eye rolling.

"Oh, I just said that I wish I could ask my younger self to help us find Aeneas. You know, back in the day when my brain whizzed along at top speed, I was quite the problem solver, if I do say so," replied Harold as he leaned back in his chair reminiscing about his late twenties.

"Well I can easily hustle back thirty or so years and ask your younger self," deadpanned Cassie, trying to shake her bad mood.

A sudden tingle creeped along the back of her neck. Cassie snapped her fingers and pointed at Harold, excitedly. Her spidey senses as her dad jokingly called them were sending her a message.

"Hey Harold...that just might work. I'll go back and ask you!"

Harold's eye's bulged and he started shaking his head before words could leave his mouth. "No, no, no. Not a good idea," said Harold walking over to the sink to refill his water glass. Cassie followed and was closing in on his heels. She was tall and willowy like all the Entwistles and her long legs could cross a room in three seconds.

Harold knew that once Cassie had an idea she wouldn't relent until she gave it a chance. As soon as she was upon him, Harold turned to Cassie, and held up his hands. His expression was serious.

"Cassie, I'm not certain this is the solution to finding Aeneas. Besides, I've changed a lot over the last forty years. The version of me you'd meet will require some convincing of who you are and why you need his help and even then he might think you're a nutcase."

Cassie patted Harold's cheek smiling.

"Don't worry. I can handle the younger version of you."

Harold frowned. "But can you ensure that your visit won't impact the present? It's risky, Cassie and I don't think Socrates will go for it."

Cassie scoffed. "I'm a pro, Harold. I know the rules."

Then her expression softened.

"I've gotta find Dad. My family will fall apart without him."

Harold sighed. It seemed like a whim. And not much to be gained by it. Still, there was a possibility that his younger, nimble intellect might help Cassie find a clue.

"You'll have to convince your mother and Socrates before you zip back to the past," replied Harold sternly.

Cassie shrugged and fought back her tears. "Things are getting desperate. They won't say no."

CHAPTER 6

Space-Time
Sandwich Revelation

AENEAS AND HIS OLDER brother, Socrates were sprawled on either side of the living room couch waiting for their parents who were supervising their younger sister in the kitchen. It was NOVA night at the Entwistle home and an educational documentary was on the evening agenda along with Persephone's special popcorn.

Socrates was doodling in his journal while Aeneas was watching replays of the latest Sounders game on YouTube. Socrates looked up when a notification ping broke the silence. A message from Tabitha had popped up on Aeneas's screen, followed quickly by another ping. This message was from Sadie about her upcoming visit for Tabitha's thirteenth birthday. Aeneas winced, ignoring both messages, but not before Socrates noticed his reaction.

"Who's messaging you, little brother?" asked Socrates, scrutinizing the subtle change in Aeneas's expression. "Uh, just Tabitha," said Aeneas dismissively.

"I heard two dings. Who else messaged you?" Aeneas gave his older brother a glare. Socrates chuckled and gave a playful kick to Aeneas's outstretched leg.

"Girl trouble?" teased Socrates, raising an eyebrow. Socrates was seventeen and already considered himself an accomplished dater.

"Not really," said Aeneas trying to appear nonchalant. There wasn't really trouble, but rather his own uncertainty. Tabitha and he had been close friends since first grade and even though she'd tried unsuccessfully over the last two years to set him up with girls from their school, he wasn't sure dating her cousin Sadie would go over very well. While Sadie's interest in him was flattering, his own internal barometer towards one of his two best friends was increasing. It felt like a huge muddle, then on top of all that those strange socks started showing up causing Aeneas's usually easy going manner to fray.

NOVA night wrapped up and the family dispersed to have the remainder of the evening to themselves. Aeneas climbed the stairs to his room, wondering about Albert Einstein's intuitive thought experiments that set him off on his lifelong quest. Should he embark on his own thought experiments? Aeneas was anxious to decode the foggy memory of a man giving him a sandwich and telling him to look for the sparkling lights. After saying goodnight to his parents, Aeneas situated himself in his bean bag chair, his decoy journal and pen by his side. Taking some deep breaths and closing his eyes, Aeneas let his mind wander back through the memory that felt like a waking dream.

"Aeneas, you can't stay here, buddy," said the man kindly, handing him another half of a sandwich packed with pastrami and sauerkraut. Aeneas felt ravenous and was taking huge bites, chomping down with an intense urgency to get nourishment into his body.

"Finish up and then we'll walk around and look for the sparkling lights." The man handed him some type of electrolyte lemonade then whispered to someone nearby. The person seemed to be on a floating screen.

"Can't I just go home?" asked Aeneas groggily, talking with his mouthful.

"Sure buddy, you can go home, but you have to use the sparkling lights to get there," said the man patiently.

"Why can't I just walk back?" asked Aeneas looking out the window at a familiar neighborhood.

The man shook his head. "You took the sparkling lights highway to get here, you have to take it back home."

Aeneas snapped out of the memory and whispered excitedly, "If time and space are relative then..." He quickly grabbed his journal and began scribbling about the Einstein documentary and the man with the sandwich. It was all converging into one very unbelievable idea.

∼

Sadie Willoughby-Hoffsteder was checking Snapchat when a message popped up that caused a flutter in her stomach. It was a picture from last October, Tabitha's twelfth birthday party, a reminder that soon Sadie would be taking the train up to Seattle. She loved spending time with her cousins Tabitha and C.J., and of course she loved seeing Aeneas too. Maybe sometimes more than her cousins.

Sadie played the cello like her Aunt Sakura, C.J.'s mom, but she also played the electric guitar. Her cello playing was progressing nicely according to Auntie Sakura, but no one in her family paid much mind that Sadie played the electric guitar. Most Willoughbys were classically trained and had no interest in rock music.

Sadie's favorite playlist on her MP3 included several Neil Young albums as well as The Rolling Stones, Led Zeppelin, Pat Benatar and even some Van Halen songs. Currently, she was rehearsing a classic Neil Young song, "Cinnamon Girl," for Tabitha's birthday party. The arrangement needed some fine-tuning to fit her voice and Sadie had spent hours reworking it. Sadie longed for a deep, raspy voice to belt out certain lyrics, but she was content to be a mezzo soprano with a three octave range.

Sadie sent a response to her cousin:

It's almost here, Tabby!! I'm leaving in three days and Mom says I can miss school the day before too, and take the early train up Friday to Seattle. Can we facetime for a bit?

Tabitha jumped up off her bed and opened the app.

"So you'll arrive on Friday October 30th? That's perfect. We can make plans for that night, just the two of us."

Sadie didn't respond immediately and Tabitha sensed something else was to be said. Then Sadie replied casually, "What about Aeneas? And C.J.? Did you want to invite them too?"

Tabitha shrugged. "Not really. I spend a lot of time with them at school and at home. I'd rather it be just us."

"Oh," said Sadie, hesitating. The thing she couldn't say to Tabitha was that lately she and Aeneas had been in contact via Snapchat and there were some feelings, which she hoped were mutual, but definite feelings.

"If you'd like them to come then that's fine with me," said Tabitha, breaking the stalemate. She adored Sadie and if Sadie wanted a group outing, then Tabitha would let her have her way.

CHAPTER 7

Beecoming Tabitha

JACQUELINE TABITHA WILLOUGHBY WAS born on November 1st, 2002, just barely. The time stamp called by the obstetrician was 12:01 a.m. The day before, her mother Martha had been filling in for a music teacher at a downtown elementary school who was, ironically, out on maternity leave. It was Halloween and with all the school festivities, she was dressed in her maternity pumpkin costume complete with a handmade tulle orange jack-o'-lantern skirt, black tights and a green knitted cap which the students loved.

After a long day at work, Martha was starving so she waddled over to her favorite pizzeria. Working her way through a mushroom, cranberry and goat cheese pizza with extra sausage and rosemary was the only way to satisfy herself and the hungry baby. Seattle's infamous Serious Pie, the premier place for an eclectic pizza, never asked any questions of Martha regarding her unusual culinary requests.

As Martha finished her pizza—a sixteen-inch pie, all by herself—and began the walk to catch a bus back to West Seattle she felt a twinge, followed by another. Later, Martha realized she wasn't the first pregnant woman to have her water break on a King County Metro Transit bus.

The driver said, "Hold on, folks. We're taking this lady to Swedish over on Cherry Street."

A few minutes later the driver cheerfully deposited Martha at the emergency room entrance as George rushed to meet her at the hospital.

Once she was old enough to capitalize on the adjacent holiday, Tabitha preferred to celebrate her birthday on Halloween. November first was such a bland day to be born in the United States. In Mexico, it was the first day of Día de los Muertos— Day of the Dead. In Ireland and Scotland and some parts of England they celebrated Samhain, a Gaelic harvest holiday. It was also International Vegan Day, but Tabitha was not a vegan and had no affinity for the other festivities celebrated that day. In fact, her personality was somewhat daring and mischievous, so Halloween suited her best.

Each year there was a terrific party with pizza that most children would never eat and pumpkin treats of all varieties. Lots of toppings were picked off over the years, but Martha would not relent.

"Cheese is not a topping, Tabitha. It's the base for the toppings."

Tabitha tried to explain to her mother that most children wouldn't eat green olive, pineapple, bacon and goat cheese with peppercorns on their pizza. Aeneas was the only exception.

"Aeneas loves the pizzas I order, sweetheart," said Martha with finality. Because of this, she insisted on going with her father George to collect the pizzas and every year Tabitha, with money she carefully saved for this day would purchase three pepperoni pizzas for the party, inserting them onto the buffet table while her mother Martha was occupied in the kitchen.

Her cousin C.J. only ate pepperoni pizza. This was a sore spot for her mother who detested picky eaters, but Tabitha didn't see it as a necessary position to take on the matter especially because C.J. loved all Japanese food that his mother Sakura made. Tabitha often pointed out he was only really picky about American food. However, Martha would not be swayed; she and Tabitha were occasionally at odds when it came to Martha's views on food choices.

"Sakura and Charlie baby him too much," Martha complained to George in front of Tabitha and Seth. "The child was practically raised on chicken parts mashed together and fried."

"They're called nuggets, Mom," offered young Seth, who had secretly consumed them with his cousin C.J.

Martha huffed, shaking her head. "Children need to eat what their parents eat. We have a whole generation of children whose entire diet consists of macaroni and cheese, chicken nuggets, pre-cut peanut butter and jelly sandwiches and sculpted carrots."

George stayed silent as his daughter Tabitha gave him a wink. He knew they would be sneaking in pepperoni pizzas to the party again this year.

As Halloween neared, Tabitha searched the racks at Value Village. She'd been a witch of sorts every year at her party, reworking her costume as she aged, but this year she wasn't feeling witchy. She was feeling different. Tabitha was going to be thirteen, a year younger than most girls in eighth grade. Still, it felt like time for change.

A costume caught her eye. A bumble bee costume, not for a little girl, but for a young woman. The girl in the photo looked glamorous, confident, at ease with herself, and she filled out the bust region of the costume. Tabitha felt like growth in that direction was slower than she'd like, but perhaps it was time to give her chest a try with more mature clothing.

Martha caught up with Tabitha, Seth in tow behind her holding a used but well preserved dragon costume.

"A new look this year?" she asked.

"I like this bee costume, Mom. What do you think?" asked Tabitha eagerly.

Martha smiled. "It's charming. I like it."

Tabitha had kept the same costume for years and Martha was determined to be supportive, even if she felt a little concerned. Tabitha was growing up. Of course she would want to look older and Martha was worried that would mean shorter shirts and lower necklines.

"Can I get some fishnet stockings too?" giggled Tabitha, eyebrows wiggling up and down cheekily.

Martha paused. She wanted to say no. She wanted to say that Tabitha wasn't old enough, but she remembered her own mother holding her back in such odd ways that made her feel inadequate, so she smiled again and said, "Those will finish the look perfectly."

"And my black high tops," replied Tabitha brightly.

Martha's anxiety eased a bit. Black high tops were youthful, not grown up. Tabitha wasn't asking to wear black high heeled boots.

Back at home, Tabitha tried on her purchase with the fish-net stockings, high tops, wings and bobbling antennae. She gazed in the bathroom mirror. The chest could be more filled in, but overall the costume fit well. Seth popped his head in, "Can I come to the party, Tabby?"

This was expected. He asked every year and every year she said no. She loved Seth. He wasn't as annoying as other little brothers, but he was only in third grade and she wanted her privacy. "Not this year Seth. Maybe Sunday we can go bowling."

Seth smiled. "Now you're talking! That sounds much better than a costume party."

Tabitha knew Seth just wanted some time with her and bowling was his favorite. Seth wasn't much for sports, prefer-ring music or chess, but he excelled at bowling. Tabitha made a note of this since the sport he managed to be really good at required skill and agility with a ball, but that only applied to bowling. He was hopeless at soccer and worse at baseball. Seth was too young for a league, but it was only a matter of time. Tabitha thought it would be rather ironic after all those hours of practicing the trumpet that Seth would have a career as a professional bowler someday.

Tabitha glanced at her reflection one last time, shuffled her bosom around, stepped back and smiled. The bee costume hugged her torso and the skirt flared perfectly around her hips. It was quite a transformation and one that she'd wished to happen. Tabitha was a year younger than her peers, but she never felt that way in her mind. Now her body was catching up.

CHAPTER 8

A Boy and His Dog-Share

SPUT LET OUT A yawn, did some stretches, scratched his left ear and smelled his groin region. He trotted over to Aeneas and licked his cheek. Aeneas shifted a bit and rolled over, so Sput jumped on the bed, and gave an even bigger lick making sure his very cold nose hit Aeneas's left eyelid blasting morning breath right over his face. This was the final measure Aeneas couldn't ignore. He groaned, as dog breath assaulted his senses.

"Sput, buddy, your breath smells like old leftovers." Sput yipped back in affirmative and Aeneas sat up.

"You need to go out?" Sput replied with two strong barks and Aeneas stood and looked over his floor to see where he'd last left his squirrel slippers.

Sput, as he was affectionately known, was actually named Pete Sputnik Wilent and he was a dog-share. Sput was a medium sized, brown, scraggly canine that showed up at the park where the boys played after school. At the time Aeneas was in seventh grade and C.J. in fifth and for as long as either boy could remember they'd both wanted a dog.

Aeneas's parents had said no because raising three kids and running a research laboratory didn't leave much time for a dog. The Willoughbys declined because Sput was a music lover himself and when C.J. first brought him home his mother, Sakura was playing her cello and Sput joined in, much to the delight of C.J. and the horror of Sakura.

"Look at that, Mom," declared C.J. "He likes the cello too."

Sakura stopped and took one look at soon-to-be-named Sput and returned his friendly stare with one of skepticism. Both sets of parents thought Sput should be taken to the animal shelter even though Aeneas and C.J. had promised to take care of all his feedings, and walks, plus pay for his vet bills.

In the end, it was C.J.'s downcast face that proved to be too much for Tabitha. She got the idea from Harold. Harold lived in two houses each day, didn't he? Couldn't Sput live in two places as well? Both families had fenced back yards with plenty of Sput-space and were only a short five-minute walk apart.

Tabitha set up a schedule where Sput was shared between both houses with times to be agreed upon by parents and subject to change if one family took a vacation. Then Sput would stay at the other home. Tabitha explained in her presentation to the families this would also save them money on pet boarding. This would give both boys a dog, and both sets of parents less Sput-time.

Persephone was thrilled to have Sput around. She instantly began replicating Pavlov's experiment, ringing the bell each time she fed Sput. However, Aeneas and C.J. put a quick stop to her work. C.J. was adamant, saying "If you want to conduct experiments, then get your own dog, Persephone. Sput is a boy's dog. He's meant for games, walks, scaring off burglars and chasing cats." Aeneas and C.J. were in complete agreement about that, but Sput's name took a few days.

C.J. insisted on "Pete" being the dog's name since he was very bright, friendly and could sniff out a treat no matter where it was hidden, but mostly because he wanted to name the dog after his idol, Pete Carroll, head coach of his beloved Seahawks. When Aeneas balked at the idea, C.J. called an emergency meeting to settle the issue. The two were hunkered down in Aeneas's room and had been going back and forth for fifteen minutes.

"C'mon, bro, Pete, for the dog's name?" Aeneas was eyeing C.J. as if he'd finally gone off his rocker with his sports obsession.

"Pete's a great name for a dog, Aeneas. I mean look at him, he's a 'Pete' for sure," said C.J. cupping the dog's face. The dog edged forward and licked C.J. on the chin. "See, Aeneas. He likes the name."

Aeneas shook his head. He wanted a name that reflected the dog's energetic personality. "What about Spunk?" suggested Aeneas encouragingly.

Socrates stopped by as he was passing Aeneas's bedroom.

"Nah. It sounds too much like 'punk'," said Socrates, dismissively much to the delight of C.J.

"Your brother is right, Aeneas it *does* sound too much like 'punk.' And look at this guy. He's definitely no punk." C.J. leaned in and the dog nuzzled him playfully.

The youngest Entwistle with her keen hearing wandered down the hall.

"Are you talking about Sputnik?" inquired Persephone cheerfully. She'd recently watched a documentary about the Russian space program and was eager to join the conversation.

"We are trying to name our dog, Persephone," said C.J. curtly. He was wary of Persephone's involvement in the caretaking of their dog.

"Call him Sputnik," she said enthusiastically.

"That would be a great name for a dog! Don't you think so, Aeneas?" She caught her brother's eye, hoping he would include her in his decision, but this was not the case.

"Seph, were you eavesdropping again?" asked Aeneas with a you-know-better tone which made Persephone seethe. Socrates turned and gave Persephone a disappointed older brother look.

"No. I just was walking past your room," hissed Persephone.

She glared back at her brothers then grumbled through clenched teeth, "I was only making a suggestion."

Socrates could see she was fuming. "Okay, Seph. Thanks for your suggestion," said Socrates. Persephone stalked back to her room mumbling about always being excluded.

Socrates leaned down and petted the dog, who eagerly returned his affection. "You know, Persephone is right. Sputnik isn't so bad and you could call him Sput for short," he offered.

"Hmm. I like 'Sput,'" said Aeneas. He glanced over at C.J.

"It's a unique name, but I still prefer Pete," said C.J. with a downcast expression.

In the end the dog's chosen name was to pay homage to Pete Carroll and the Russian space program of the 1950s. While C.J. was a huge Seahawk's fan, his greatest respect was reserved for the head coach, who C.J. felt made all the success possible by encouragement and hard work. Plus, he was a friendly and energetic coach and their new dog was just that as well. And so Pete Sputnik Wilent was adopted as a dog-share.

~

Aeneas and C.J. walked Sput near Me-Kwa-Mooks Park. Sput liked to take walks near the seashore and the boys always made sure to take him there at least once a week. "We're closing in on Tabby's thirteenth birthday," said C.J. excitedly.

Aeneas chewed on his thumbnail lost in his thoughts. He knew that this year was going to be different. Tabitha looked different. Her face was thinner. She was taller and curvier too, but he didn't say these things to C.J. "What did you have in mind?" asked Aeneas.

C.J. gleefully hopped up and down the stairs leading to the shoreline while he outlined the plan. "Sadie is coming and bringing her guitar. She's working on a playlist for the party. I thought maybe we could get a dance floor, hang up some of those tiny pumpkin lights, rent a fog machine and have a disco ball."

Aeneas smiled. This was actually a great idea. "High five, bro. That sounds perfect."

C.J. beamed a mouth full of braces back at Aeneas. "Thanks. I thought a dance party would make up for last year's snafu."

"Snafu?" yelped Aeneas, laughing so hard he plopped down on a step, gasping for breath.

"The poop earrings party," he wheezed.

C.J. scowled at him. "I didn't realize when the cake flipped out of the pan the earrings would be on the opposite side. My parents are musicians, not scientists. I didn't spend my toddler years in a science lab."

Each year, C.J. tried to insert something unusual into his cousin's party. The year before he'd baked a cake and had hidden a tiny pair of earrings inside it as a surprise. Unfortunately, Tabitha didn't get that piece of cake and another party guest had accidentally eaten the earrings. Once they finally appeared a few days later, Tabitha declined to receive them. "Don't be upset, C.J., but I can't put anything in my ears that has passed through someone's colon."

Aeneas knew the great thing about C.J. was that while he could blunder, and blunder big at times, those mistakes were immediately fixed and he didn't make them again. So this year's party was sure to be memorable.

Aeneas threw up his hands and exclaimed, "Where can we rent a fog machine?"

• CHAPTER 9 •

An Enigmatic
Entwistle

IN THE PACIFIC NORTHWEST autumn comes in two ways. Days can be breezy, cool, clear, with abundant sunshine, boasting leaves of bright red, orange, and yellow, the shades of nature winding down, or the wet, windy, cloudy, gray days that remind all that winter is coming.

Thursday, October 29th was one of those clear, sunny days. Harold was headed back to Queen Anne for the evening, but before leaving West Seattle, he dropped into one of his favorite shops, The Swinery, to purchase some smoked turkey breast for Eleanor's sandwiches. Eleanor loved to have soup and sandwiches for dinner as the weather cooled, but her tastes in meat were fatty and salty, both of which were forbidden by her naturopathic doctor. Harold discovered the wonderful meat shop and often dropped in for a pulled pork sandwich.

Upon encouragement from the shop owner he tried the smoked turkey breast and seized on it as an alternative for

Eleanor. She loved it. Harold made toasted turkey on rye with Swiss cheese, pickles, lettuce greens and his own homemade garlic mayonnaise. This was served with his cream of broccoli soup and Eleanor had declared it a favorite.

Waiting to be served, Harold noticed a beautiful woman looking at him from a table in the corner of the shop. There was something familiar about her, but he dismissed it as he placed his order. Collecting the turkey and some salami for himself, Harold turned back to look again, but she was gone. He sighed. It seemed his love life was one missed opportunity after another.

Harold walked to the bus stop and waited. He sniffed the air and smelled an aroma that seemed to waft through West Seattle in the fall—pumpkin spice latte. He turned slightly left and saw, a few feet away, the same woman from the corner table sipping the pumpkin spice latte. She smiled. Harold returned the smile.

The bus arrived and they boarded. She sat directly behind Harold, who felt quite cheered by his good luck at another chance to meet her. He waited for the bus to start moving before turning to face her. She was looking directly at him. Harold felt a little unsettled by her forwardness.

"Harold, I need your help," she said evenly. Harold didn't immediately reply. Instead he quickly scanned her features, activating his eidetic memory. Her eye color, the green, was so familiar. The long, thick, dark brown curls tied behind her head were luxurious. Her race was not obvious. Her hair suggested African ancestry. Her skin tone was light but not Caucasian. The shape of her face and nose reminded him of someone. He knew her from somewhere, but for the moment his only question was how she knew *his* name.

Cassie waited for Harold to reply. She'd been watching him for several hours, anticipating an opportune time to make contact without bumping into her parents. Harold surveyed her face again and decided it was possible they'd met before given the wild parties he used to throw at his old condo in Fremont.

Trying his best to channel some charm Harold replied smoothly, "Pardon me. I can't recall your name, but we've met before, I think?"

Cassie smiled sweetly at Harold. She'd met Harold before, definitely *before*, but more like after. "You're a friend of my mother's."

"Ah. And your mother's name is..." Harold paused for Cassie to respond, hoping the name would spark his memory.

"My mother prefers to remain anonymous at the moment."

Harold was perplexed. "I'm not sure I follow."

Cassie took a deep breath. "My father is missing and my mother has sent me to get your help."

"Hang on. Who's your father? For that matter, who are *you*?" Harold was starting to feel uncomfortable with this whole encounter.

"My father is Aeneas Just Entwistle. My name is Cassiopeia Valentina Entwistle."

Harold carefully scrutinized Cassie's features trying not to react. Her resemblance to Miranda *was* uncanny, but at his core Harold was a skeptic, so his response was nothing short of what Cassie had expected.

Dispensing with any attempt at charm, Harold responded flatly, "Lady, Aeneas Entwistle is fourteen years old and unless I've entered a time warp of some kind, you being his daughter is impossible."

Cassie flashed her gorgeous smile then laughed.

"Maybe the person who's entered the 'time warp' as you call it, isn't you, Harold, but me."

CHAPTER 10

Excitedly Northbound to West Seattle

S<small>ADIE RODE THE</small> *Coast Starlight* passenger train from Portland to Seattle on the Friday morning before Tabitha's birthday party. She loved watching the scenery and it was especially enjoyable with all the fall colors. Her train would arrive in Seattle mid-morning and her Aunt Martha was supposed to pick her up.

While she watched the scenery go by, Sadie wondered about Aeneas. She wondered about her song choices for the music she was playing at the birthday party. She also wondered about the speakers C.J. said he'd have ready for her show. Then she wondered whether she should wear her hair down or have Tabitha braid it. Her mind, like that of all teenage girls, was pinging in a million directions like a search engine. It finally settled on its top choice: Aeneas.

Sadie had decided that she liked Aeneas as more than just a friend, though she couldn't pinpoint exactly when her feelings changed. She did know it was sometime during her two-week visit over the past summer. One evening in her cousin's backyard she was playing an acoustic version of Neil Young's "Heart of Gold" for Seth, C.J., Tabitha, and Aeneas. When Sadie looked over at her audience her eyes drifted straight to Aeneas. She noticed how lean and muscular he was under his soccer jersey. Aeneas smiled at her with his big brown eyes and curly lashes; she felt her cheeks grow warm as he watched her play. Aeneas complimented her singing which made her heart race.

Feelings started to weave together after that, but Sadie was too shy to tell Aeneas or even Tabitha. Instead, when she arrived back home she started flirting with Aeneas on Snapchat. And while she was not one hundred percent sure if he liked her, she knew she liked him. It wasn't just because he was tall and fit she told herself. Aeneas was kind and funny. The fact that he was so athletic was an added bonus.

Sadie stepped off the train, carrying her backpack, guitar case and another bag of accessories for her first paying gig. C.J. said this was a real job and he expected two sets with one intermission. Tabitha waved, walked towards her and reached in for a hug.

"Where's Aunt Martha?" asked Sadie, surprised.

"Mom said the school is so short on substitutes that no one picked up her job. She said I could meet you and we could take the bus back together!" Tabitha was elated. She'd been allowed to take the bus on her own to King Street Station and meet her cousin. This, paired with the fishnet pantyhose was a rite of passage. She was feeling grown up. The other rite of passage had happened in seventh grade, and while her mom marked this as a milestone to be celebrated, it felt less so to Tabitha. Menstruation didn't make her feel older, but this new freedom—to go somewhere without her parents—certainly made her feel older and she felt like this birthday was going to be the best one in a while.

"I can't believe Aunt Martha let you come alone!" exclaimed Sadie. Tabitha grabbed one of Sadie's bags and they began walking towards the bus stop.

"I know. It's probably the best birthday present she could've given me. Let's hurry and make the connection back to West Seattle. Mom gave me money to take you out to lunch." Tabitha beamed at her cousin. She could have floated across the bridge.

After Sadie unpacked her bags she carefully examined all of Tabitha's new clothes. Tabby's style was traditional Pacific Northwest teen. Skinny Jeans. Hoodies. A couple of different styles of shirts. Boots. Sneakers. A scarf or two. Nothing she wanted to borrow and nothing she particularly disliked either. Sadie liked vintage clothes and went to great lengths to find pieces that were stylish but unusual.

Tabitha preferred mainstream styles and didn't want to spend hours looking for the perfect vintage skirt. She found shopping a little tedious unless it was for books. Book shopping could take days. She collected antique self-help guides. She had books on fixing household appliances, cookbooks, old computer manuals from the late 80s and even books on how to make butter or butcher farm animals; they were all arranged by decade. She thought they were a fascinating record of human habits and spent hours perusing them. Tabitha walked in with some chips and hummus. They had eaten lunch two hours before and it was time for more food.

"Fancy clothes," said Tabitha with raised eyebrows, examining a light blue vintage leather jacket.

"You are welcome to borrow any of it," laughed Sadie.

"I'm good. It's a cool jacket, though." Clothes were not something the cousins shared. Music was their common thread.

"What are you playing tomorrow night?" asked Tabitha. She was very curious about how C.J. planned to make up for last year.

"Not telling. C.J. said it's all a surprise," Sadie made a lock and key motion near her mouth and winked.

Tabitha rolled her eyes. "Anything's an improvement over last year."

"Poor guy. He overthinks stuff. Shoulda just put the earrings in a nice box." Sadie shook her head sympathetically.

"I feel bad for the person who ate them. He won't even make eye contact with me at school anymore."

Sadie laughed. "Can't blame him. How awkward is that?"

Sadie eyed Tabitha closely. She'd changed since the last time they were together which made her wonder.

"Dating anyone?"

Tabitha's face tightened. "No."

"Gotta crush?"

"No! I'm still getting used to all this," squawked Tabitha gesturing to her body. Sadie laughed and threw a stuffed animal at her cousin.

"Your womanly figure," as my mom likes to say, "has arrived."

CHAPTER 11

A Convincing Conversation

"So Cassiopeia, you're claiming to be the daughter of Aeneas?" asked Harold. The skepticism in his voice amused Cassie, but she knew it would take some convincing.

"Yes I am. But I prefer to be called Cassie. You probably noticed by now my family's tendency to recycle mythological names."

Harold let a smile slip. "I find it endearing." Harold's tone became serious as he said, "But Aeneas isn't missing. I just saw him half an hour ago eating a large pile of nachos I made for that bottomless pit he calls a stomach."

Cassie laughed. "His appetite isn't what it used to be... Or so he tells us."

"Us? Who's *us*?" Harold was trying to decide if this conversation was a hoax or a hallucination.

"I don't want to tell you too much. You told me to reveal just enough," said Cassie matter-of-factly.

"I told you? When did we have a conversation?" barked Harold. This woman seemed very nonchalant about the ideas she was asking him to believe.

Cassie put her hand firmly on Harold's arm, leaned in a few inches, looked directly into his eyes and lowered her voice. "Thirty-eight years from now we will have a discussion. The older version of you and my mom aren't thrilled about me coming back to seek you out, but I had a gut feeling you might be the key to finding my dad."

Harold pulled his arm back and looked at her curiously, trying to gather his thoughts as the bus bumped along. She *did* look so much like Aeneas's mother, Miranda. Miranda had a varied ancestry, but her predominant gene pool was of African origin. She'd received, by the blessings of genetic randomness, a set of features that would put her on the cover of any fashion magazine. Harold had no doubt that Miranda's genes were looking back at him.

"You could be Aeneas's daughter," said Harold softly, nearly ready to believe her. Cassie nodded, waiting for Harold's brain to start placing all the puzzle pieces together.

"So your mother, who shall not be named, but is a friend of mine in the future sent you to me… thirty-eight years in the past? So how did you get here?"

Cassie looked out the window as the bus traveled through Seattle heading towards King Street Station. This was a complicated question and she wasn't sure how much to tell the younger version of her friend and employer. Her father Aeneas had been working on unraveling the mysteries of time travel most of his adult life. She took a deep breath. "I used an energy event to access the space-time continuum."

Harold took this in for a moment. Cassie stared back at him, waiting for his next question. The bus stopped and Harold grabbed his bags. "We get off here."

He linked Cassie's arm with his and they exited with all the other passengers. Harold wove them through the rush hour crowd with the precision of a metro-pedestrian as they headed to the next stop to wait for the bus to Queen Anne. After several minutes of silence Harold asked, "What type of energy event?"

Cassie looked at her shoes. There was so much to tell Harold, but since Harold was also part of her father's research team in the future she wasn't sure how much Harold in the past could know. This conversation would require caution to ensure she honored the shamanic rules of time travel instilled by her father's mentor, Bob North Sky.

"I traveled through time using the energy created by an earthquake."

Harold scoffed. "So, thirty-eight years into the future the human race can access the space-time continuum whenever there is an earthquake?"

Cassie shrugged. "No. Only some humans can access their timeline. It runs in families."

"Aeneas can move through time." It sounded like a question, but Cassie knew the old Harold well enough to know it was a statement which would usually be followed by lots of questions.

"What earthquake? We have small tremors here all the time, but nothing that releases massive amounts of energy. How could you predict when and where you'll enter the space-time continuum?" Harold was struggling. Predicting earthquakes was still in early phases. So far no one had created an algorithm that could be used with much accuracy.

Cassie smiled. "There's a seismically active location that's easy for time travelers in this region to access. We call it the Alaskan Way Time Tunnel, after the old Alaskan Way Viaduct in downtown Seattle."

Harold gave her a skeptical look. This was becoming way too science-fictiony for him. He wasn't sure how much longer he could humor this woman who bore a strong resemblance to his employer Miranda Entwistle.

Cassie continued, "The time tunnel isn't in Seattle, Harold. It is in southern Alaska near Anchorage. The space-time continuum is always opening due to regular, daily earthquakes in the region. Most travelers wait less than half a day."

"So, it's frequented by time travelers and used whenever they need to get somewhere in time, ASAP?"

Cassie tilted her head. "I guess you could say that's true."

Harold opened his backpack, grabbed his tablet and began scribbling notes briskly. "You can enter your timeline because you inherited this trait from your father, correct?"

Cassie nodded. Harold continued. His voice had a monotone-like quality when his brain was sorting out information.

"You decided to travel back in time because your father is missing and you think I can somehow help. Your mother and I are friends in the future, but you cannot reveal her identity because of concerns about disrupting future events."

Cassie gave Harold a thumbs-up as he resumed his mining of her story. This was how his brain worked when it was in data collection mode and Harold continued to process out loud oblivious to anything else.

"Your father must be experienced at time traveling by now having started when he was a teenager. For him to be missing, and you to be here, something must have gone terribly wrong," said Harold, all businesslike as the bus pulled up.

Suddenly Cassie's eyes filled with tears. She rarely cried. She'd experienced a wonderfully imaginative life filled with games, adventures, music, and delicious homemade food. Tears were usually because of childhood bumps and bruises. Until now she'd never experienced any deep, heartfelt pain. But as she prepared to board a bus to Eleanor's house in Queen Anne, her deepest fears for her father flooded her mind. She started to break down as Harold steered her onto the bus, placing her gently in a seat as he procured a handful of tissues from his backpack.

Harold had little experience with grief. Although he was sad when he lost his home and company, he'd never lost a loved one, and this was a bit out of his realm of expertise. He patted her back, as he'd seen others do in these kinds of situations, and passed along more tissues until Cassie was spent. As they approached his stop, Harold wondered exactly what he would tell Eleanor about Cassie.

CHAPTER 12

A Distressing Damsel

ELEANOR EASED INTO HER softest chair that afforded a view of the afternoon sun. She was sipping water after her massage. Harold had insisted she lower her medication for hip pain and try massage instead. That was two years ago. Now she hardly ever needed her pain pill; instead she got a weekly massage. She felt good and was looking forward to her evening meal with Harold.

Harold waited in front of the garden gate of Eleanor's spacious, light blue Craftsman home, unsure of how to proceed. "This is my other job, Cassie."

"Oh yes, of course. Eleanor," said Cassie, completing Harold's thought. Harold smiled. He still doubted her story, but each time she revealed details about his life, the more intrigued he became.

Cassie nudged Harold, who was standing awkwardly at the gate. "Perhaps I could stay here while we sort things out?"

Harold let out a breath. "Yes, well, I'd need to speak with Eleanor, but it should be fine. Eleanor loves visitors."

"That's a relief. You told me that it's best to stay away from West Seattle."

"When did I? Never mind," said Harold waving his hand, dismissing his own question.

Cassie explained, "You were concerned about me bumping into Miranda or Archie. Or even Persephone. Apparently, Aunt Seph developed her uncanny ability to tell when people are lying at a young age."

Harold smirked at this nugget of Entwistle family history, which to him was the present, but to Cassie an old anecdote.

Eleanor peeked out of the doorway and called out cheerfully, "Harold, please invite your guest in."

Cassie waved to Eleanor and prepared herself. Harold was a poor improviser of conversation. She knew this would be a shamble unless she covered with a lie.

"Hi Eleanor. I'm Cassie, an old friend of Harold's. My luggage was lost in transit at the King Street Station and Harold said I could stay here until they locate my things. You see, my credit cards are inside my small suitcase. I only have a little cash."

Eleanor's eyes widened, placed her hand on her heart and shook her head in sympathy. Harold's friend was a damsel in distress and of course she would welcome this lovely young lady into her home. Eleanor's motto came from her mother and she never forgot it: "A friend in need, is a friend indeed."

"You poor dear. I can see you've been crying. Well, don't worry about a thing. Come have some dinner with us and I can prepare the guest room. Maizy, my old gal dog, will want to meet you," said Eleanor kindly.

Harold stood speechless trying to recover his brain from the elaborate lie he was preparing to explain Cassie's arrival. Cassie smacked his arm and hissed, "Grab the groceries."

Harold got his bags and walked inside. His mind was a jumble. The Entwistles were terrible liars. The reason Persephone was so good at lie detection was because she learned to spot it easily as a small child. This woman, whoever she was, might have the face of Miranda Entwistle, but her mother must be a trained poker player or a formidable liar.

Eleanor introduced Cassie to Maizy and the three ladies retired to the sitting room to watch the afternoon sunshine dance through the maple trees that were scattered about the garden. Harold prepared the soup, then sliced bread for the sandwiches. His mind wandered back to Aeneas. He'd always seemed content to play soccer or pal around with friends. He was never in the lab running experiments or tests, while Socrates and Persephone did little else. Harold finished up by toasting the turkey sandwiches, and garnishing the broccoli and potato soup with grated Parmesan cheese. Dinner was served.

After dinner Cassie asked to take a shower while Harold took Maizy for a stroll around the neighborhood. He enjoyed all the houses in Queen Anne decorated with pumpkins, scarecrows, cornstalks, and spooky decor lit up in orange and purple. Harold started thinking. How could he have missed Aeneas's remarkable ability? At the moment, the only thing on his radar regarding Aeneas was all his mismatched socks! Harold wondered if it was too risky to ask Aeneas if he'd moved along his timeline yet.

Time could be a delicate thing. One missed bus. One step slower and an opportunity might be gone. Wasn't that how it worked? Harold breathed in the cool night air. The Entwistles and Eleanor were his family and it gave Harold a warm glow to think that in the future when Aeneas was grown up that he was still part of his life.

Young Harold Headache

HAROLD FINISHED THE DISHES and retired to his bedroom. He grabbed his tablet and lounged on the pink velvet Chesterfield couch, scribbling questions about Cassie's story. He was listening to a quirky song from a band he liked called Gaelic Storm. Harold thought best when amused so he kept his mind occupied with TV sitcoms, videos, music, comics, and the occasional talk show. He was chuckling to himself as he imagined catching wild goats. Cassie was passing by his door and stopped.

"What in the heck is this music?"

Harold looked up to see Cassie giving him a weird look. "I missed what you said. Can you repeat it?" Harold turned the volume down on his goat gang song.

"The music," replied Cassie expectantly.

"Oh, uh... a favorite band. Going to see them soon at the Tractor Tavern."

"Well I just wanted to say goodnight," said Cassie sleepily. She moved one hand in a gentle wave and turned towards her bedroom. Harold scrambled off the chesterfield and called after her.

"Hey Cassie, I need to know more about what happened when your... uh, Aeneas disappeared." Then added, "If you wouldn't mind, please."

Cassie walked back into Harold's bedroom, sat across from him in a green pattern upholstered armchair, a lovely relic of Eleanor's old fashioned furniture. She gave Harold a quick once over and noticed for the first time how attractive he was. His blond hair was cut short, he wore stylish glasses and a pair of trendy men's ankle boots; his jeans and blue button-down shirt fit him well. Cassie smiled as Harold sat up straight and poised his stylus over his tablet, readying himself to document her story.

"My dad vanished a week ago, April 27th, 2053. There was a 7.2 earthquake along the Birch Bay Fault line. The house suffered minimal damage... C.J. designed our house to withstand a 7.8 earthquake. Once it was over my dad was nowhere to be found. He and Mom had been home together. Dad usually reappears within twenty-four hours after an energy event."

Cassie stared pointedly at Harold, willing him to be *the Harold* who could help solve any problem. Harold decided he needed to speed up the conversation.

"How come you didn't vanish?"

"I was further from the epicenter of the quake. I saw the timestream open and I knew a significant seismic event had happened, but I had no idea of the location," explained Cassie while Harold wrote furiously.

"I was attending a conference at Wazoo, so I decided to go back to 1996. My timeline is notched to my father's, so I shifted onto his timeline which links to my grandparents allowing me to access their timelines too."

Cassie waited for Harold, who had held up a finger to indicate he needed to catch up.

"My grandmother, Miranda, was a grad student there in 1996. I found her walking back from a class and casually met her. We had coffee at the student union. I returned a few hours later because the timestream was still open for me." Cassie took a breath preparing to go on, but Harold interrupted before she could continue.

"So, you just come and go through time as you please?" asked Harold incredulously.

"What I did was fairly complex time travel, Harold. It took Aeneas years to master it with the help of an Alaskan tribal shaman. By the time I was born, he was exceptionally skilled and began my training when I was three."

Harold was still. Cassie had lost him at "meeting her grandmother." Harold's mind exploded in a jumble of questions. Lifetimes were linked or notched? Cassie met her grandmother for coffee? Was this commonplace? Did Aeneas go back in time and meet him for coffee? He struggled to think if he'd ever met a stranger that could have been a full-grown Aeneas.

Harold hopped off the pink velvet couch and spoke a little sharply, "I don't understand why you did it."

"Why I went back to see my grandmother?" Cassie raised an eyebrow at Harold.

"Yes," replied Harold tersely. He was becoming exasperated with Cassie's nonchalance towards the possible disruption of the space-time continuum.

"Aren't you worried you could change the outcome of your own future? What if you had prevented your grandparents from meeting? You'd risk your own existence as well as others?" By the time he'd asked his last question Harold was practically shouting.

Cassie abruptly stood; it was time for bed. She'd had a long day, longer than normal because she'd actually departed her present in the evening and arrived in the past just after noon. She gave Harold a defiant stare. "I don't explore the past when critical events are taking place. Besides, it's not a secret. You know about it."

"That's ridiculous. Why would I knowingly condone that? Even the tiniest changes can have an impact on the future," barked Harold, feeling agitated. The idea that he would change his mind about this was unnerving to him.

Cassie rubbed her eyes. "I need sleep. I'll explain more in the morning. I'll be up early."

She turned to leave and Harold impulsively reached for her arm to detain her. Cassie quickly spun around facing him, her nostrils flared. He dropped her arm, embarrassed. He never acted like this.

When Harold's hand made contact with her arm, Cassie felt a jolt run through her body. She tried to contain a blush she felt creeping up her neck. She edged away, which embarrassed Harold further. *Old Harold was right*, thought Cassie. *He has changed a lot.* This version of himself was nothing like she'd expected.

CHAPTER 14

Squirrel Slippers Rescue

C.J. RUMMAGED THROUGH HIS backpack. His recently acquired smartphone was flashing. He opened a message. Mom again.

Where are you and when are you going to be at Aunt Martha's?

C.J. groaned. While gloriously happy over his new technology, C.J. cursed the fact that his mother could track his movements via GPS, especially since C.J. was a dawdler. He took his time and wasn't known for his punctuality regarding return times, meaning if he went somewhere and said he would be back soon, then soon could be fifteen minutes or two hours. He was generally on time for friends but could get bogged down by his own peculiar nature. It was a well-known fact that no one, not even his other friends who were "twelves," bothered to make plans with him on game day.

Besides his special scarf, C.J. needed a variety of game snacks and foods which could only be green, blue or white. His most famous snack was a green olive and blue mushroom pizza without red sauce. The only person who tolerated his quirks was his younger cousin, Seth. C.J.'s game day rituals made Seth feel like he was a part of something special.

C.J. was determined this birthday party was going to be the best one he'd ever organized. Then he realized he hadn't thought about a toast. Toasting was exciting; it signified a special event and was a grown-up gesture that Tabitha was sure to appreciate. However, he'd forgotten the drinks. Aunt Martha spent a small fortune on the pizza each year and soda was not allowed, given a whole long list of evils she would happily tell you at the most inconvenient of times. So C.J. had Plan B. Sparkling cider. Only he forgot. And now he was trying to carry one bag full, plus three more bottles in his backpack to the Willoughbys' house.

Aeneas lay on his bed reading a soccer magazine stopping occasionally to glance at the geometry homework next to him. He wore a pair of squirrel slippers which he coveted like a pair of expensive sneakers (squirrel slippers were rather difficult to find in men's size ten, and Tabitha was pleased with herself when she located them on eBay.) Aeneas liked squirrels. They darted in front of cars and turned back at the last possible moment, more often than not managing to escape the wheels just before they became roadkill. Though sometimes their daredevil acts were not successful as the occasional carcass suggested.

A gong sounded. His smartphone notified him of a message. It read:

Help me NOW. Too many bottles. 3 blocks from Tabby's house.

Aeneas jumped into action. C.J. was about to break a dozen glass bottles on the sidewalk. Rushing out of his house, still sporting the squirrel slippers, Aeneas zipped past Tabitha's house and was observed from her upstairs window by Sadie.

"I just saw Aeneas running down the street wearing a pair of brown slippers," she remarked to Tabitha with interest.

"Is your concern that he was running or that he was wearing slippers?"

Sadie thought about this. "The slippers."

"Well Aeneas likes slippers, specifically squirrel slippers. He says that he thinks like a squirrel when he plays soccer and I suppose the slippers inspire him," said Tabitha with a giggle.

Sadie smiled. She liked the idea that Aeneas was eccentric. It suited her personality. She would not want a boyfriend who was like everyone else. She would want someone decidedly unique.

"He also has a squirrel T-shirt that he found at a thrift shop and I gave him those slippers last year for his birthday." As Sadie listened to all this she felt a shift in her stomach. A slight burning. Something was off. Her face showed her discomfort.

"What's wrong?" asked Tabitha.

Sadie let out her breath. "I'm good. Maybe some water. My stomach feels queasy."

Sadie's stomach was indicating to her that while she loved her cousin Tabitha, she didn't love it that Tabitha knew more about Aeneas than she did. She wondered if Tabitha liked him too? She'd never said anything romantic about him. In fact, a boy named Everett had been recently mentioned. Maybe this surge of jealousy was just nerves. Sadie decided to press on and not get worried over the slippers. She needed to focus on finding out if Aeneas could be her first real boyfriend.

CHAPTER 15

Time Traveling
Rule Breaker

CASSIE STOOD MOTIONLESS, SURPRISED by the electric jolt that had passed through her arm. Harold was trying to recover his composure, wondering what about this woman was making him act so strangely. Finally he pulled himself together.

"Can we talk a little longer?" asked Harold quietly, motioning Cassie back to her chair. "I just have a few more questions."

Cassie shrugged. She was flustered and exhausted, but she needed Harold's help. They resettled themselves in their same chairs. While Harold reviewed his notes, Cassie drifted off and started to wonder what it would be like to see her parents as teenagers. She'd seen the old photos, but up close and personal what were they really like?

Her mind was spinning with this idea when Harold blurted, "Why would Harold version 2.0, agree that you should come to 2015, but also avoid critical events? I can't believe that I'd have changed my mind about the ethical implications of tampering with the past."

Cassie sat up straighter and threw Harold a haughty look. "I'm bound by a code of honor which dictates that my presence doesn't impact critical events happening around me. For example, I wouldn't want to interfere with how my parents first came together."

"I take it *now* isn't what you'd call a critical event?" asked Harold sternly.

Cassie cringed a little. It was a significant time in her parent's relationship, but it was also the time that old Harold thought his brain would be poised to help her find a solution which was why she wasn't supposed to bump into her parents.

Harold's face reddened and he threw his hands up in frustration. "Are you even following your own rules of time travel?"

Cassie felt her patience waning. "Listen up, Harold. You told me this was the best time to seek you out because your brain was at its zippiest or something to that effect. You're arguing with yourself."

Fatigue was creeping up on Harold. Cassie was right; he *was* arguing with his future self and his logic was usually quite sound which is why he felt so confounded. "I need to do something else right now, Cassie. I'll read some comics or watch some old sitcoms. Then I'll sleep on it and we can talk again in the morning," said Harold wearily.

Cassie sighed. She'd omitted one small detail and knew it would probably set him off again, but it had to be addressed.

"One more thing. I've got to leave November first for Northern California."

Harold shifted in his chair, "Because...?" Harold looked at her as if she'd asked for a ride to the moon.

Harold's condescension was given a reprieve and she continued on, her immediate goal to get to her comfy bed in Eleanor's guestroom. "Because that's my energy event back. A smallish earthquake, 4.3 on the Richter scale, right off the coast, will create enough energy to open the timestream."

"We have one day?" whispered Harold, nearly apoplectic.

"Yes, Halloween," replied Cassie calmly.

"Cassie, I have several things to do tomorrow for the Entwistles and..." Harold was cut off before he could admit that he wasn't sure how to help her.

Cassie raised her voice and tossed out her trump card. "You said that one day would be enough for you to help me, Harold. You insisted that I not stay any longer."

Harold started to argue then realized that she was talking about his future self again. His jaws locked and he grinded a few back teeth. It seemed his future self, Harold 2.0, had quite a lot of confidence in the younger version's capability to drop everything and help a time traveler.

"How do you plan to get to Northern California by Sunday?" asked Harold flatly.

"I'll need to travel by car to a place called Cape Town. It's located in a remote conservation area. Then I'll head to the coast and leave from there." Cassie's surety in her plan seemed misplaced to Harold.

"That could take twelve hours or more. Why don't you just fly?"

Cassie narrowed her eyes. "I'd love to fly Harold, but seeing as how I'm not even born yet, I don't have any identification."

Harold conceded her point and they agreed to leave it there until morning. Later on, once he'd had another think, Harold secretly perked up. He could watch what happened, video it, and maybe collect some data from the area when Cassie departed. Only biology and physics weren't his strong suit. He'd need some help. He *needed* an Entwistle.

CHAPTER 16

Mindful Laundry Meditation

HAROLD WAS UP AT four. He'd slept hard and woke feeling out of sorts. He grabbed his phone and messaged all of the Entwistles. He told them Eleanor was feeling poorly and he'd not be able to come over and assist with the Halloween festivities as planned. He prepared a cup of green tea then returned and sat in the middle of his bed. Some clue eluded him, like an itch he couldn't reach.

For a while Harold had taken meditation classes. The feeling of his mind unencumbered with daily clutter was calming. And he found it useful. When he needed a solution to a problem it would often float by like a dialogue box from a comic strip. This generated considerable excitement and Harold might leap up and run from the class muttering to himself, breaking the silence and jolting his neighbors from their meditation. Not long after Harold was politely asked to practice his meditation privately.

Harold sipped the tea then set it aside. He closed his eyes, taking evenly spaced breaths, letting the rhythm clear his mind. Minutes passed. In the distance a fuzzy shape approached until suddenly a giant white cube flew up through a vast empty space until it filled his whole mind's eye. Harold gasped. It was a dryer!

Meanwhile, Maizy had crept into Harold's bedroom. She needed to go out and had been waiting patiently while Harold meditated, but now her bladder was ready to give. She gave a sharp bark startling Harold, who leaped off the bed and landed in a heap on the floor. He rubbed his ankle. It smarted a bit, but he wasn't bothered. The answer to his question was somewhere in the Entwistles' laundry room.

Cassie heard the commotion and found Harold wincing while shoving on a pair of boots.

"Are you alright?" asked Cassie, noticing his disheveled appearance.

Harold explained his mishap then he grabbed his jacket, walking gingerly on the sore ankle. "Maizy needs to go out and I need to go to the Entwistles, which is going to be a problem since I just messaged them and said I wouldn't be coming over today."

"Why do you need to go to my grandparents' house?" Cassie was annoyed. She felt constantly at odds with this Harold.

"What do you know about dryers?" asked Harold, eyeing Cassie skeptically.

Cassie shrugged. "They dry clothes."

Harold sighed and grabbed Maizy's leash.

"I'll be back in fifteen minutes," said Harold gruffly.

Cassie made a cup of chai tea and waited for Harold. She was starting to think she'd made a huge mistake coming back. Old Harold had warned her about his younger self, but Cassie felt sure together they could find some clue. Now he was obsessing over something about a dryer.

When Harold returned his cheeks were ruddy and he seemed in good spirits. Cassie eyed him curiously. His emotions seemed unpredictable, unlike the older version of himself that Cassie could read like a book.

"What now?" asked Cassie, giving Maizy a good rub down. Maizy thumped her tail and gave Cassie a few licks. Like Aeneas, Cassie loved dogs.

"It's Saturday. Miranda and Archie will be at their paintball game until one o'clock. Persephone has booked the lab later this morning and Socrates will accompany her and stay while she works, giving us a narrow window of time."

"That leaves Dad."

"Yep, but Aeneas should be with C.J. planning Tabitha's birthday party. It's supposed to be a big event this year," said Harold with a smile. He did enjoy those goofy boys and their party planning.

Harold rummaged through the hall closet and passed some items to Cassie. "Hat, sunglasses, scarf and no talking."

"Why do I need a disguise?"

"We're going to West Seattle," replied Harold cheerfully. He was close to solving the puzzle infecting his brain like a parasite.

Cassie shook her head and handed back the items. "You told me to steer clear of there as much as possible. And I'm certainly not going to my grandparents' house."

"You mentioned that yesterday, but old Harold isn't here. And I saw a giant dryer fly through my mind's eye. Trust me, there are answers in that laundry room."

Harold's steely gaze marked Cassie and she didn't argue. Young Harold seemed quite comfortable defying the older, more experienced version of himself. Cassie resigned herself to follow his lead *for now*.

CHAPTER 17

Tabitha Gets a Ping

AENEAS CAUGHT UP WITH C.J. He was sprawled in the middle of the sidewalk, leaning on his backpack with a flushed face and weary expression.

"Bro! You can't block the sidewalk," said Aeneas with some exasperation.

C.J. glared at Aeneas. "I had no intention of blocking anyone's path, but as you can see, I'm weighted down with these... beverages." C.J. gestured towards his backpack and another paper bag with several bottles of sparkling apple cider. Aeneas held back a smile. At times C.J. sounded like a pompous prince speaking to servants. He figured it had something to do with being an only child.

"We've got this. If you can manage the backpack, then I'll carry the bag. We're only a few blocks from Tabby's house." Aeneas gave C.J. his hand and pulled him up. Aeneas knew once C.J. had a plan he went with it like a speeding train. Only sometimes C.J.'s train ran short of fuel.

They headed towards the Willoughbys where Sadie was still glancing out the window whenever Tabitha's back was turned. She didn't want to be caught watching for Aeneas. Suddenly he came into view heading towards the front door with C.J. and she felt a lurch in her stomach. Butterflies. People often said that when you liked someone, you felt a flutter in your stomach, and sure enough, she felt that fluttering.

The door slammed, and Seth was heard speaking with much animation. He loved spending time with his cousin. "C.J., come see my new bowling ball!"

Tabitha looked up from her knitting. "Should we head downstairs? C.J. and Aeneas are here."

Sadie nodded, taking a quick glance in the mirror. Her recently brushed long blonde hair was shiny and silky and her eyes were dazzling with metallic blue eyeshadow and thick black mascara. Sadie wished she could brush her teeth again, but they were clean enough to say hello. Clad in black skinny jeans, a vintage leather jacket and a snug Rolling Stones T-shirt, Sadie slipped on her black boots and headed downstairs with Tabitha.

C.J. and Aeneas paused from unloading the sparkling cider when the girls entered the kitchen. "Sadie!" C.J. enveloped his cousin in a hug and sniffed her hair. C.J. liked to smell everything and he wasn't shy about it.

Once C.J. sniffed a little too close to Aeneas's mother, Miranda. She smelled like coconut and exotic spices and he found her aroma intoxicating. Archie gave him a territorial glance and since then C.J. only sniffed Aeneas's mother from a distance. Archie had long since known his wife's beauty would require these occasional glances to other males, though C.J. was a surprise being all of nine years old at the time. Sadie smelled like flowers and berries and C.J. inhaled again.

Sadie gave him a shove and a slap. "Get your nose out of my hair, C.J." Sadie regarded her cousin as an overgrown puppy.

"You know I love to smell hair," said C.J., a little hurt.

"Hey Sadie," said Aeneas with a smile.

Sadie smiled back. "Hi Aeneas. Nice slippers."

Tabitha wasn't sure this was a compliment, but Aeneas's smile back at her cousin seemed to indicate he felt that it was.

"I try to stay connected with my inner squirrel," said Aeneas proudly as he gestured to the embroidered squirrel on his slipper.

"Cool," said Sadie casually.

The tone of her cousin's voice pinged Tabitha's special sixth sense that detected subtle differences in human behavior. Something was off. Sadie was being guarded like she needed to hide something.

The air hung with quiet until Martha walked in with several bags of groceries. She immediately gave all five children a job and this sent Aeneas and Seth scurrying to her car to unload more bags, and Sadie to the refrigerator to make room for more food. The moment was broken before Tabitha could pinpoint what had shifted with her cousin.

Aeneas left before Sadie could speak to him again and this disappointed her deeply. Later, when they were upstairs alone, Sadie discreetly asked Tabitha if Aeneas would be returning later to hang out. Tabitha gave her a shrug and felt another ping. *Why did Sadie want to spend more time with Aeneas?*

CHAPTER 18

Close Encounter
Interruptus

AENEAS FINISHED HIS SNACK and wandered outside to kick his soccer ball and have a think. Something was brewing in his mind and he wasn't sure who he could talk to about it. He heard music playing and wandered in its direction. He crossed paths with Socrates and his friend Emma, walking along, holding hands. Socrates looked like a picture-perfect hipster with his funky designer shirt, a hint of stubble and his mini Afro. Aeneas deflated. It was tough being the younger brother.

"What's up Aeneas?" Socrates regarded him with a mixture of affection and condescension.

"Hi Aeneas," said Emma kindly. She enjoyed Aeneas and Persephone. They were not as annoying as her younger brothers and she often felt Socrates took this for granted.

Aeneas nodded, raising his hand and giving a slight wave. Emma made him feel shy. She wasn't a genius, but she was an expert in her own way. Emma was a dancer, tall and slender with naturally curly black hair and sky blue eyes. Aeneas had seen her dance once at a school performance and since then he couldn't talk to her without becoming tongue-tied. Socrates was slightly irritated by this, but his dad told him, "Beautiful women often leave Entwistle men speechless, blubbering fools. Uncle William was the same way around your mother. And for me, the only way I managed to get your mother's attention was to speak science to her."

Aeneas exhaled as he went in the opposite direction. Encounters with Emma left the relaxed, happy-go-lucky, middle child a little dizzy.

Aeneas stopped near the Willoughbys and could hear music adrift in the air. He cut through the neighbor's yard and found Sadie alone in the back yard practicing for Tabitha's party. Tabitha was sequestered to the house under strict orders from C.J. as he insisted the performance be a surprise.

Sadie was singing Patty Smyth's, "The Warrior," playing guitar, and working through pieces of the song with her background music. Her eyes were closed. Sadie often closed her eyes when she was practicing songs and arranging chords. She could hear more clearly and imagine the sounds she wanted her voice to make to match the music. She didn't notice Aeneas enter the back yard or arrive quietly next to her.

Aeneas smiled to himself. He was always impressed when he heard music being played. "Are you playing that song tomorrow night for the party?" asked Aeneas.

Sadie launched herself off the lawn chair and nearly dropped her guitar. Her eyes opened wide and her mouth clamped shut.

She felt her knees buckle. This was not how she wanted her first moments alone with Aeneas to go.

"I like that song. It's classic 80s, right?" asked Aeneas as he leaned in to look at her guitar.

Sadie nodded. "Yeah. I only play classic rock. The 80s are as late as I go on the rock timeline," replied Sadie tentatively.

Aeneas raised his eyebrows. "There's a rock timeline?"

Sadie laughed and relaxed a bit. "Rock originated in the early 1950s and peaked in the late 60s and early 70s, although some really great music was played through until the 80s, like this Patty Smyth song."

"So, you think Tabitha is a warrior?" asked Aeneas sincerely.

Sadie stiffened. The song was not really meant as a dedication to Tabitha. She thought the song was more about herself.

"Not so much about Tab. More about warriors in general." Sadie held back her deeper thoughts. For her, the song was more about keeping herself strong through middle school and not feeling pressured to be like everyone else.

"I like it. What else are you playing?" Aeneas's playful curiosity relaxed Sadie.

"A song called 'Cinnamon Girl' by Neil Young. I've had to change the arrangement a little, but the lyrics are the same." Sadie started to feel exhilarated by this conversation. She could talk about music easily. She continued to explain her thought process regarding the song choices for Tabitha's party.

"That song is for Tabitha. Cinnamon fits her. Her hair is the darkest auburn like cinnamon," said Sadie.

Aeneas nodded and replied, "Yeah, when she's in the sun you can see the reddish colors in her hair."

Sadie felt that same shift in her stomach from earlier. Of course Aeneas and Tabitha would notice details about each other. They were childhood friends, but it still made Sadie feel a little jealous.

Her thoughts were interrupted by Seth who arrived with a soccer ball and was frisking about Aeneas wanting to play. Much to Sadie's disappointment Aeneas's attention turned to Seth. Seth wasn't a great athlete, but Aeneas was always happy to encourage Seth's love for the sport.

C.J. came down right after him. "Seth! Aeneas! You two can't disturb Sadie's practice. She has to get ready for tomorrow night."

"I'm done, C.J. They can play," said Sadie, masking her disappointment at losing some alone time with Aeneas.

C.J. glared at Aeneas and Seth. Aeneas shrugged and smiled back.

"She said she's done, bro. Relax. Tab will love the party. It's got costumes, live music, pizza, and don't forget the fog machine!"

Tabitha exited the back door with a plate of pumpkin chocolate chip bars. Martha had baked them earlier. She anticipated having to feed children all weekend. Aeneas beamed. He would become a man whose stomach led directly to his heart.

"I'll take one of those," said Aeneas, grinning.

"Me too," chirped Seth.

"Sadie, have you tried these?" asked Aeneas, gesturing to the plate appreciatively.

"I'm not a pumpkin fan. I'll pass," she replied stoically.

Aeneas raised an eyebrow and grabbed a second bar. Tabitha grabbed a chair and passed around the plate. C.J. sniffed his bar. At times, his Aunt Martha was heavy-handed with the nutmeg.

Tabitha smiled and turned towards her cousin. "Mom says to tell you that one day you will meet a girl, fall in love and she will put nutmeg in everything."

Everyone started laughing at Aunt Martha's classic pokes concerning C.J.'s pickiness, everyone except Sadie. She was reworking the short conversation she'd had with Aeneas for any clue that he might want to be more than friends. The worrying part was she had no idea if Aeneas secretly had feelings for Tabitha. And for that she really needed to talk with him privately.

CHAPTER 19

If This Bench Could Talk

HAROLD DECIDED THAT A hat, scarf and sunglasses only made Cassie look more like Miranda and the best disguise for her would be the only one left at the party rental store in her size. She would dress as a nun and keep the sunglasses. The costume covered most of her face and hair.

Cassie wondered how many nuns would be out on Halloween in sunglasses in West Seattle, especially since it was predicted to rain. It seemed to her she would only attract attention rather than be disguised, but Harold insisted.

"You look saintly," said Harold with a smile.

"This habit smells like cigarettes. Not very authentic for a nun," said Cassie as she sniffed her sleeve.

"We'll say you're on your way to a costume party," said Harold brightly as if the day was just brimming with happiness.

Cassie frowned and gave him a look. "What's with the cheery mood?"

"I'm on my way to see that dryer." Harold beamed. Nothing was better than the anticipation he felt before a problem was solved.

Harold booked a car to pick them up at the costume store. He wasn't waiting for a bus with an incognito nun when efficiency and speed were the preferred course of action. The driver rolled up to the Entwistles' neighborhood, depositing them a few blocks from his employer's house.

"No one should be home, but I'll check first. Stay here." Harold gestured to a bench near a bus stop and headed off.

Cassie settled in with a newspaper. Newspapers were rare in her time and she loved the smell and feel of the thin sheets and crisp edges. Someone sat next to her and she kept reading as the person unloaded a backpack and lightly tapped on their cell phone, then started talking.

"Aeneas, I'm at the bus stop bench a few blocks from your house. Can you meet me here? I need to ask you something."

Cassie felt herself sink into the nun's habit, thoughts racing. *That dolt Harold has left me on a bench in West Seattle with my parents roaming about on Halloween!* Sweat prickled beneath her armpits and along the back of her neck. She felt that peculiar mixture of fear and excitement as if she were hanging her head out of the window of a speeding train. Cassie tried to appear engrossed in her newspaper, hoping to remain invisible as most adults are to teenagers. She desperately wanted to glance at the person next to her. Cassie knew her mother's adult voice, but didn't know what she might sound like when she was a teenager, so the girl's identity would stay a mystery unless she dared to drop her newspaper and take a peek. A few tense minutes passed, and Cassie heard footsteps.

"Hi, Aeneas," said the girl, getting up off the bench. Cassie released a small sigh of relief.

"What's up?" Cassie noted the casual tone that marked her father's conversation for his lifetime. The two stepped a few feet away. Cassie could overhear snippets.

"Do you like her?" asked the girl.

"I dunno know. She's... she's..." his voice faltered.

"She's what?"

"She's my friend, and..." The rest was inaudible to Cassie because Aeneas seemed to be mumbling.

"So you're just not sure how you feel?" inquired the girl gently.

"Yeah," replied Aeneas slowly.

Cassie waited a while before she lowered the newspaper. Her father was staring off in the opposite direction and Cassie wondered if he could see the timestream sparkling up ahead.

There must have been a small tremor. I know he sees that, thought Cassie, struggling between the fear of being discovered and the excitement of seeing her dad. Aeneas turned to face her just as Harold walked up. Harold twitched a little, gasped and then tried to divert attention from Cassie.

"Hi, Harold," said Aeneas as he dropped down on the bench.

Cassie was still as a statue. She gently shook her head side to side and Harold caught the gesture.

"Everything going good, dude?" asked Harold casually.

Aeneas sunk his head into his hands. "Girl trouble."

"Rite of passage," said Harold, adding, "Maybe Socrates is the best person for advice." Harold desperately needed to get into the laundry room. He hoped his suggestion would send Aeneas off to see Socrates. Aeneas didn't budge and rolled his head back and forth in his hands. Cassie knew this story from her mother, although the small details like this conversation were never part of it.

"I'm confused. I like them both, Tabitha and Sadie," said Aeneas slowly.

Harold shrugged. "Well, Tabitha has been your friend for such a long time and that's a strong bond, but then Sadie is exciting. She sings classic rock. Tough choices," quipped Harold, without a hint of empathy. Cassie cringed. It was well known that Harold gave terrible advice regarding relationships, so Cassie wondered why her father was bothering to confide in him; she wanted to look at his face and see his expression but kept silent.

"Thanks, Harold," said Aeneas and he hopped up to go, but then stopped abruptly and looked at Cassie.

"Sister, sorry to disturb your reading," said Aeneas kindly.

Cassie nodded and waved him off and Aeneas headed towards C.J.'s house.

When he was out of earshot, Harold stood up. " Whew. That was close. Let's go. No one's home and the laundry room beckons."

Cassie glanced at Aeneas walking off. "Poor Dad. When he tells this story, he seems more confident in his feelings."

"Feelings for who?" asked Harold.

"For the girl," said Cassie with a little smile.

Harold's eyebrows went up. Tabitha or Sadie was her mother?

Cassie glanced at Harold. She knew she'd slipped, but perhaps Harold had missed her meaning. However, Harold's mind thought much. Cassie was an Entwistle-Willoughby regardless of her mother, mused Harold. This meant his association with either girl was a long one.

CHAPTER 20

Caveman vs. The Birthday Party

TABITHA LINED HER EYES, added mascara, applied red gloss to her lips, and let her hair fall in curls down her back. She shifted her bosom around and smiled at herself in the mirror. Tonight she looked older, as if the distance between twelve and thirteen was a wide canyon. Somehow, she had stepped off one side and swung effortlessly to the other.

Being a year younger than everyone else in the eighth grade meant that her body was a year behind, and this to Tabitha, seemed to be the greatest disadvantage. Everyone else had a fourteen-year old body with fourteen-year old curves. Tabitha wasn't inclined to obsess about her appearance. She knew from seeing pictures of her mother Martha at the same age that her body would eventually develop a womanly figure. By her sophomore year in college, Martha was a curvaceous beauty.

Tabitha recalled her mother's memory, "One day I woke up and everything just came together, boobs and all." Tabitha knew that those genes were headed her way. But that was years off. And those years seemed like an eternity.

Tabitha's thoughts were interrupted by C.J. "Party starts in twenty minutes. Sadie is outback getting ready. Are you all set?"

"I'm all set, C.J.," said Tabitha with a smile.

"You look spectacular!" said C.J., slightly surprised. Tabitha nodded. She didn't want to say that she knew. That would sound arrogant. But she did know. Some of those pieces were coming together.

Sadie started her first set. Tabitha would be down soon. C.J. wanted her to have an entrance so he told Sadie to start a bit early. The pizzas were placed on a table, lids open, ready to go, with extra pepperoni pizzas tucked in between Martha's eclectic ones. Party guests were arriving, grabbing slices and listening to Sadie belt out, "Take it Easy." She had remixed an Eagle's classic to fit her voice.

Aeneas munched on a slice of green olive, bacon, pineapple and blue cheese pizza and watched Sadie. His face could hardly contain his smile. Sadie was stunning with her long blonde hair sliding off her shoulders as she sang. She winked at him and Aeneas laughed. Other kids gathered around. Sadie's magnetic stage presence commanded an audience.

C.J.'s improved from last year's party, that's for sure, thought Aeneas.

Tabitha came outside when she heard the music. She was standing back not bothering to ease forward; she was proud to have a party that reflected her rite of passage. Sadie was about to start a new song when Tabitha walked through the crowd.

A friend from school, Everett, shouted when she passed him, "Tabitha you look hot!" Aeneas turned, and his pizza nearly slipped from his hand. She *did* look hot.

"This song is dedicated to my cousin on her thirteenth birthday," announced Sadie as she started "Cinnamon Girl." Everyone started swaying in time with the music. Tabitha beamed a smile back at Sadie.

Everett eased next to her and whispered, "Can I have a dance with the birthday girl?" Tabitha grinned then nodded. Everett guided her away from the crowd as the song ended and Sadie eased into the first chords of "The Warrior."

Aeneas was dancing with a group of girls from school. He was a terrible dancer but was always willing to dance when other boys shied away. He was an easy-going person and wasn't embarrassed about his mediocre dance moves. He glanced over one of his friend's shoulders and saw Everett twirl Tabitha. Sadie saw it too, and so did Martha and George, who were smiling from the kitchen window. As the song ended Everett bowed and kissed Tabitha's hand in an exaggerated gesture. Tabitha started to laugh.

Sadie decided it was time for a slow song. She had remixed The Rolling Stones', "Wild Horses." It was a favorite song of hers. She was happy her cousin seemed matched for the evening since she would have no trouble in dispersing the other girls and have Aeneas all to herself, and then maybe he could decide once and for all if he really liked her.

She started to sing, and it came out rather soulfully, even sadly, and this captured Aeneas's attention until his stomach called him back to the pizzas. He tore his eyes away from Sadie and decided to get another slice and sit out the slow dance. At least that's where his brain told his feet to go, but then he saw Everett slide his hands down Tabitha's back to rest them on her hips. Suddenly he sprinted straight for Everett. Ten seconds later Everett was flat on his back with the breath knocked out of him.

When C.J. saw Aeneas drop his pizza and take off, he scrambled to follow, yelling after him, "Aeneas, don't!"

He pushed his way through the party guests gathered around the two boys, trying to get close enough to stop him.

"Get off him, Aeneas," yelled C.J., but it was no use, he was too far away to make any difference.

Tabitha had been jostled out of the way and couldn't believe her eyes. Aeneas had pinned Everett down and was nose to nose with him as Everett struggled ineffectively to push him off. C.J. finally wormed his way through the crowd, pulled on Aeneas's left arm and swore he overheard something that sounded like Aeneas threatening to give Everett a beating, which was strange because they were on the same soccer team and had been pals for years. All attention was now focused on the entangled pair as Tabitha stood by, too stunned to act. Her father George parted his way through the throng and with some effort lifted Aeneas off of Everett.

"What's wrong with you, Aeneas?" cried Tabitha with clenched fists. C.J. thought for a second Aeneas was going to get a black eye.

"You've ruined my party!" she hissed. Tabitha turned away from him to check on Everett who slowly got up, as Martha brushed the grass off his zombie soccer player costume. Sadie had stopped singing. She felt like her gut had been punched. Aeneas had snapped. Seeing Tabitha with Everett had sent his testosterone levels into caveman mode—as C.J. would later describe it.

Aeneas couldn't speak. He grunted something that sounded like goodbye to George and made his way back to his house. Everett, feeling embarrassed and confused, decided to leave, too. After politely saying goodnight to Tabitha and her parents, he headed home thinking about how he'd deal with Aeneas Entwistle later.

CHAPTER 21

Unraveling Anomalous Data

As soon as Aeneas departed the bench, Cassie and Harold headed back to the Entwistles' house. Cassie was hesitant to enter with no one home, but Harold seemed confident in his knowledge of the family's schedule and whisked her inside once he punched in the security code.

They entered a brightly lit kitchen with buttery walls and dark brown framed cabinets with glass windows. A cedar beam ran down the center of the ceiling with pots and pans hung in neat rows. Cassie sat down at the table while Harold opened the laundry room door expectantly and tapped his foot. He took a deep breath, carefully looking at each corner of the room, allowing his peripheral vision to collect details.

Harold's brain was often stimulated by things just outside his direct line of sight. He pivoted every fifteen seconds as he waited for his brain to notice something. A few minutes passed. Cassie got up and walked in behind him. Harold took no notice of her. He just kept turning. Finally, Cassie whispered, "Well, got anything?"

Harold scowled, "No. And your presence is not helpful." Harold leaned against the washer. His meditation had clearly directed him to this room.

Cassie stepped away, yawned, then asked, "I hate to interrupt again, but can I use the bathroom?"

"Sure. Take the stairs. Second door on the left."

Cassie made her way up the stairs and tiptoed over a small pile of laundry left outside the door of a bedroom. She peered in and gasped. It was her father's room. Seattle Sounders was splashed across one wall and the opposite had an older map of the world that had been laminated. The bed was unmade. A plate with crumbs on it was half hidden under it next to a pair of squirrel slippers. Cassie laughed. Her dad hadn't changed much. She used the bathroom and decided to grab the small pile of laundry, her father's leavings for Harold no doubt, and carefully made her way down the stairs. *A nun's habit isn't the most forgiving clothing*, thought Cassie as any moment she could stumble over the long dress.

Harold was right where she left him, and she presented him with the laundry. "I believe my father left you a gift."

Harold stared at the pile and narrowed his gaze at a sock on top. "My anomalous data!" he yelped and pulled down the small basket of mismatched socks.

"We're here for socks?" mumbled Cassie, rolling her eyes.

Then something clicked. She recalled old Harold and her mom had been working on a special project to keep her teenage dad from dropping into his future. It was all hush-hush, but socks were involved. She decided to keep quiet and see what trajectory this new information took.

"Yes socks, Cassie! These have no reason to be in the house. There is no piece of laundry here that I can't account for except these four socks," said Harold and he breathed a sigh of relief.

Harold sat at the kitchen table and pulled out each sock. There were four, all different colors and all with tiny patterns scattered throughout the leg. Once Harold had tried knitting for relaxation and while the patterns fascinated him, the movement of the needles was trying. He would drop stitches, or the yarn would slip off the needles. He was forever pulling things apart and starting over. This aspect of knitting was too tedious for his brain, so he moved on to another hobby.

Now, as he carefully examined each sock, Harold noticed that these were hand-knitted socks. Someone had made them. Cassie looked at him expectantly. Harold felt pressure being observed by her and the looming time limit she'd set for him to help her find her father. "I need to do something else for a few minutes," he said slowly and set the socks down on the kitchen table.

"Can I have a look at those socks too?" asked Cassie, curious if they were *the* socks her mother and old Harold had developed.

Harold nodded and set about his work. He grated cheese, scrambled seven eggs, chopped up leftover baked potato and cold salmon, diced onion, and added a healthy sprinkle of sea salt, pepper, and dried dill. He slowly cooked the raw onion first in the pan, adding olive oil and waiting for the onion to soften.

THE RESCUE

Then he added the other ingredients to warm them except the cheese. The cheese would go last after the eggs.

Harold inhaled deeply as the smell wafted up from the pan. It was amazing how such different pieces could come together to form such a delicious meal. The egg mixture slid on top and he added the cheese and waited to flip the omelet.

Cassie sat examining the socks. She recognized the pattern, but never thought much about it. Harold carefully flipped the omelet then cut it in half and set one before Cassie. She pushed the socks aside, took the fork and popped a piece into her mouth. "I love your flair with omelets, Harold, especially the ones you stuff with Bucheron goat cheese."

Harold made a mental note to purchase this cheese the next time he went shopping. He took a bite and glanced at the socks. There seemed to be two different recurring shapes, a dot and a line, although the line was a fine stitch and the dot was blocky. He turned the sock sideways, got a pair of scissors and carefully cut the sock so it lay flat on the table.

"Binary code," he whispered to himself.

Harold felt tears well up in his eyes. Someone had sent messages through Aeneas's socks using binary code. Harold wiped his eyes. It was ingenious, as if these messages were meant for him. Harold carefully cut all the socks and carried them to the scanner. He imported all the files to a program that would lift the code off the socks then converted the binary code into text. From the four socks, there were two repeating messages. Both were addressed to him.

Dear Harold,   *Late Winter 2053*

Aeneas is a time traveler of sorts, moving along a timeline that includes his life, and the life of others in his family, or so we believe. C.J. found a fourteen-year-old Aeneas a few months ago wandering around West Seattle very early in the morning when he was out walking his dog. Aeneas was headed towards Charlie and Sakura's home, although they have since retired to Sequim. C.J. lives there now with his family. Aeneas was a little shaken up. He had never traveled further than a few moments on his timeline here and there. The onset of puberty has increased his abilities and he is more susceptible to the power of the timestream at night when he sleeps. His unconscious mind does not alert him to the opening, so he simply slips into the timestream if there is an energy event. Aeneas now knows he can time travel, but he can't yet control it and his memories of it are fuzzy. When he travels forward, we have to explain it to him all over again and give him basic instructions on how to get back to his own time. Often if C.J. finds him, he sends Aeneas back almost immediately because the timestream will still be open, but now we're adding repeating binary messages in the socks hoping you'll find them in the laundry and give the kid some help. His time travel is linked to major energy events, mostly earthquakes in the Puget Sound region, but also earthquakes associated with the Cascadian subduction zone all the way from California to British Columbia.

As you receive this message, Aeneas, C.J. and Tabitha have been trying to uncover the mystery behind his disappearances *and the socks that travel back with Aeneas. Rather than tell Aeneas the socks contain messages, it's best if you assist him with learning to control his abilities. For this you'll need Socrates as you might have already ascertained.*

All the best,

Hatman

Harold smiled at the signature. He knew his future self would understand his hesitancy to believe the message. Hatman was what Harold called himself online in chat rooms during junior high. Harold's initials were HAT and the natural inclination was Hatman, like Batman. No one knew about it except a few old buddies from Chimacum and none of them were inclined to perpetrate elaborate hoaxes.

"Who is Hatman?" asked Cassie after Harold had finished reading the letter.

Harold grinned and replied softly, "Me. Harold Alexander Torkelson."

"Oh, these are messages from old Harold," said Cassie appreciatively. Clearly old Harold's influence continued to trump his.

"Should we read the other letter?" asked Cassie. Harold nodded absently. He was still reeling from what he'd read. *Time travel was possible.* Until this moment, Harold hadn't fully believed the implications of what Cassie had explained to him on the bus. Part of him was clinging to the idea that Cassie was a just beautiful lunatic that had ensnared him with a good story. But now he was poised to become a true believer.

CHAPTER 22

After Party Awkwardness

AENEAS SAT IN HIS room staring at a poster of Clint Dempsey trying to recall what had happened at the party. Sadie was singing. She looked so beautiful. But he'd decided to sit out the slow dance and get another slice of pizza. Then he saw Everett dancing with Tabitha.

There was a tap at the door. His mother, Miranda slid inside and sat next to him on his bed. "George called." Aeneas nodded.

"Anything you want to tell me?" asked Miranda gently.

Aeneas shrugged, mumbling, "Tabitha..." That was as much as he could get out. He hung his head.

"You and Tabitha have been friends for a long time, since you were small, and now she's growing up... and so are you," said Miranda with a sigh of compassion for her rapidly growing middle child.

Socrates was nearly grown, seventeen and attending college, dating girls. Soon they would all be grown. Time had slipped away from her, and while she loved Archie deeply, her children were a joy and her heart missed them already as they needed her less and less each year.

"Sadie's so..." Aeneas drifted off again, struggling to articulate his feelings.

Miranda sighed. This was a job for Archie. She wanted Aeneas to talk to her, but she could see he was a jumble of man-like thoughts that only a man could interpret. She patted his knee and went to get her husband.

A few minutes later, Archie came in with two fragrant mugs of hot chocolate. Persephone at age four was desperate to create a perfect cup of hot chocolate. One evening, with Archie's help, she reworked a recipe by carefully heating honey with cocoa powder until it was a smooth and delicious honey chocolate syrup. Then she slowly whisked in almond milk until the mixture was 145 degrees and topped it with cinnamon. It was a family favorite and none of the children could resist it. Aeneas took the mug and gulped until it was empty. Archie offered his hot chocolate and Aeneas drank that one, too.

"What are you going to do now, son?" asked Archie.

Aeneas felt revived enough to get some words out. "I dunno, Dad. What can I say to Tabitha? 'I like your cousin, Sadie, but the sight of you with Everett unleashed my inner caveman?'"

"Inner what?" asked Archie, clarifying if he heard correctly.

"C.J. said I went into caveman mode," mumbled Aeneas.

Archie snorted. Even he was not oblivious to the reference, especially coming from C.J., "Oh? Was that what it felt like?"

Aeneas looked his dad in the eye and said, "Not really. It felt like someone was squeezing all my organs into a very small space."

This made Archie smile. Aeneas was a middle child and wasn't a genius like the rest of the Entwistles. Archie often wondered if he would ever have anything in common with his son, and now he knew. He and Aeneas gave their hearts to love, fully and completely. Socrates blew through girls. There was always a new one at the dinner table. Socrates had Miranda's magnetism. He would always find a girl to date him. Not Aeneas. One girl would find him and keep him, just like how Miranda found Archie.

"I remember that feeling," said Archie. Aeneas stared at his father as if he wasn't quite sure his feelings could be commiserated.

"Oh yes, I know it well. I'd fallen in love with your mother within two days of sitting next to her in Advanced Statistical Analysis. She barely noticed me, but I became her friend and then eventually her boyfriend." Archie grinned at this memory.

"But one evening, I saw her at a concert on campus and she was dancing with another guy. I had him in a couple classes, and he was a nice guy, but I felt that same squeezing sensation," recounted Archie.

"Did you flatten him, Dad?"

"Not exactly," said Archie, somewhat hesitant to share his impish behavior. "I walked past them, and I deliberately tripped him. He fell into your mother, knocking her off balance and I caught her in my arms. Then proceeded to tell him he was an ass who had been drinking too much and that I was taking Miranda home," replied Archie sheepishly.

Aeneas's eyes were wide with astonishment. It was an unkind thing to do to someone, but he understood it. That squeezing sensation could make you do crazy, even mean things. Aeneas was eager to hear how this story ended. "Then what happened, Dad?"

"Then I told her she should have dinner with me on Saturday night and I would show her something magical," reminisced Archie with a goofy smile.

Aeneas grimaced. There were things a kid never wanted to know about their parents, and these all revolved around romance and sex. Aeneas felt that peculiar sensation of wanting to plug his ears and sing a silly song. Archie gently smacked the back of his son's head. "I borrowed a friend's car, drove her to Seattle and we had dinner at the top of the Space Needle, Aeneas."

Archie, grinning from ear to ear, nudged his son playfully. "I showed her the Olympic Mountains at sunset. It was early October. The sky was clear, the weather was dry and cool, and the view was spectacular."

"Oh yeah, Dad. That *would* be magical," said Aeneas, relieved he was spared the details. Archie stood up to leave, putting his hand on Aeneas's shoulder giving him what Socrates called "the look of responsibility."

"You know you have to make this right with both of them?"

"Yeah, I know Dad."

~

Tabitha and Sadie were quietly sipping hot apple cider in Tabitha's bedroom. Sadie loved the smell and taste of it, but tonight there was little cheer among the Willoughby teens. Sadie now knew, as she had suspected, that Aeneas had more than just friend feelings for Tabitha. Tabitha was seething. The fight ruined her party plus the opportunity for her first real dance with a boy on her thirteenth birthday. Sadie couldn't identify her exact emotions. She felt hurt that Aeneas didn't return her affections, disappointed that the night was cut short so she couldn't finish her first paying gig, and sad that Tabitha lost a chance for a boyfriend, too.

Tabitha was also confused. Why would Aeneas try to beat up Everett? Was he jealous? Aeneas had never been jealous of anyone. He lived in a house full of geniuses, his own younger sister was smarter than him, but that never seemed to cause him any concern. Weren't they just friends? Best friends even? Each girl was lost in her own thoughts.

Minutes slipped by and Sadie felt the pressure as the oldest to do, or say, something to clear the stalemate. "You should talk to Aeneas about what happened tonight."

Tabitha shook her head. She felt a sudden shift in her chest. She didn't want to cry in front of Sadie but that need was bubbling up.

"Up to you, Tab, but any guy that will wear squirrel slippers that you buy him for his birthday definitely has potential," encouraged Sadie.

"Besides I always thought Aeneas was really chill, but clearly there's more to him than that. There's depth, and you know, big feelings."

It was hard for Sadie to press Tabitha about Aeneas. Her heart wasn't broken and yet there was some soreness since she'd hoped Aeneas would be her boyfriend, but Tabitha wasn't budging. She was keeping quiet about whatever was on her mind.

"I'm going for a walk," said Tabitha suddenly. She desperately needed to talk to her best friend.

"Seriously? It's eleven o'clock on Halloween night. Aunt Martha won't let you go out alone." Sadie knew the number one rule of all mothers was never go out at night alone.

"Good point," said Tabitha, grabbing her cell phone. "I'll ask Harold."

Tabitha texted Harold who usually went out on Halloween and asked him if he could escort her around the neighborhood.

Sadie looked at her cousin skeptically. She couldn't tell Tabitha what to do, but she wasn't about to tattle to Aunt Martha either.

CHAPTER 23

Hatman Revisited, Sister Revealed

HAROLD PULLED THE LETTER from the printer and began to read. Cassie glanced anxiously at the clock in the kitchen.

"Don't worry. We've got at least another hour before anyone's back," said Harold reading her thoughts. He set the paper in front of him like it was holy relic and started to read aloud:

Dear Harold,   *Spring 2053*

Hopefully by now you have made Socrates aware of the situation and are monitoring seismic activity so you know when Aeneas is likely to be pulled into the timestream. Aeneas saw the teenage version of himself last week in 2053 trying to order coffee near his home. The boy was ahead of him in line and Aeneas left as soon as he recognized his younger self. Teenage Aeneas turned quickly to leave the coffee shop too, embarrassed as he no doubt had outdated currency and walked right past him. Aeneas rushed home immediately to ensure his life or the lives of any others in his circle, hadn't been altered. So far we have not been able to detect any adverse effects from this event. However, the long-term implications of them bumping into each other again cannot be foreseen and adult Aeneas is quite adamant that the younger version of himself steer clear of the future. This was the only reason we were given permission to send these coded messages. Teenage Aeneas needs to practice withstanding the pull of the timestream. It's simpler than it sounds. Aeneas now chooses if, when, and where he wants to travel. You and Socrates can manage it, just remember to be mindful of you know who!

All the best and a slice of apple pie,

Hatman

"Care to explain that bizarre closing?" laughed Cassie.

Harold smiled. "A silly catch phrase from my grandpa."

Cassie looked at Harold, and for a few seconds, they both smiled. It was a sweet piece from his childhood and she liked that about him.

"Who's 'you know who?'" asked Cassie, racking her brain about the unusual reference.

"Um, my guess would be Persephone. She's frighteningly observant," said Harold with a shiver. Cassie grinned. Her dad had many stories about Aunt Seph the human lie detector.

"I'm texting Socrates. We need to meet with him," said Harold, staring back down at the sheet in front of him. And just like that the comic relief between them evaporated.

"I'll pass on that." Cassie knew this was moving into territory that her father would firmly call interference. Harold's head popped up from the paper.

"I need you there to lend credibility to this, Cassie. He needs to believe me or at least entertain the idea."

Cassie closed her eyes. This was becoming a mess.

"You don't need me, Harold. You have the letters."

"I need your face," replied Harold resolutely.

"My face?" Cassie glared at Harold.

"Well, yes. It's one of the reasons I didn't hop off at the next bus stop when you were trying to convince me that you were a time traveler."

"Fine," sighed Cassie, shaking her head.

Harold gathered up the dissected socks and letters and they headed to the coffee shop around the corner. A puzzled Socrates texted him back:

I'm dropping off Persephone at a Halloween party. I'll be there soon. What's so urgent?

Harold responded: *Need to explain in person. See you soon. H.*

"Socrates is on his way. Don't tell him who you are yet," cautioned Harold. "Though I'm curious if he'll recognize you before I tell him."

Cassie nodded. Her hopes rested on whatever young Harold and seventeen-year-old Uncle Sox could come up with before tomorrow. She was beginning to think this was all a waste of time and wondered if she should've gone back and asked her father's mentor, Bob North Sky instead.

Persephone was not interested in "kids' parties," but her parents felt she needed to socialize in her age range so she was obligated to attend the occasional age appropriate event or lose her lab time. Normally, she'd have to be dragged to a birthday party, but Persephone happily donned her mad scientist costume and let herself be taken to a kids' Halloween party.

Halloween parties were an exception for Seph. This was a holiday she embraced. She'd heard there would be pumpkin cupcakes iced with dark chili chocolate, for adults only. Persephone couldn't resist a challenge. Plans were already in place to sneak a spicy cupcake when no one was watching. So, when Socrates dropped her off at the party, she walked with a spring in her step towards the front door, and Sox headed to his favorite coffee shop a few blocks away to meet Harold.

Socrates arrived and saw Harold sitting in a booth with a woman who appeared to be a nun. Socrates had known Harold for nearly three years and expected unpredictability, but this was a first. *Although*, thought Socrates to himself, *knowing Harold, she could be his date.* He ordered an espresso then sat down next to Harold and introduced himself to the woman, extending his hand suavely, "I'm Socrates Entwistle." Cassie offered her hand in return, smiling whimsically and told him her name.

"Nice to meet you, Sister Cassie," said Socrates, giving Harold a bemused look. She was the right age to be his date.

"So, Harold... everything copacetic?" He looked pointedly from Cassie to Harold to let them know he was staying out of whatever game they were playing.

"No." Harold leaned in and lowered his voice. "We have a problem and I've been told by a reliable source that you are the person to help me solve it."

Socrates replied magnanimously, "Tell me all, Harold, old man."

Harold took out two sheets of paper and ordered them by date. He handed them to Socrates and waited. Socrates was a rapid reader and shuffled through the pages like a copy machine. Cassie glanced at Harold and raised her eyebrows.

Socrates stared at Harold then sipped his espresso, his demeanor significantly subdued. "How does she fit into all this?" Socrates glanced at Cassie dubiously.

Cassie had the presence of mind to begin removing her sunglasses, veil, headpiece and wimple. Socrates looked at her and turned his head to the side, a curious movement that reminded Harold of Maizy when he would ask if she wanted a dog treat.

Cassie was stunning. She had the subtle look of Miranda, only her eyes were a deep green and her skin was lighter. Harold watched as Socrates whispered to himself, "Mom?"

Cassie smiled at her uncle. "My name is Cassiopeia Valentina Entwistle."

"Are you a cousin?" asked Socrates. But even as he asked this, he knew no cousin that looked like Miranda could be an Entwistle. Miranda was a Freeman before she was an Entwistle. Those were two different sides of the family.

"I'm your niece, though, at this time I am physically older than you," said Cassie gently.

Socrates drained his espresso. He turned to the barista cleaning up two tables over and called out, "I need a double shot pumpkin spice latte, whipped cream and extra cinnamon on top, please Tamisha."

"Sure thing, Sox," said Tamisha smiling as she sauntered off to make his drink. Cassie smiled and marveled at what she'd heard all her life. Uncle Sox was a ladies' man, or rather a man that ladies always liked.

Harold let Cassie off the hook and told the story. Socrates sipped his latte, gripping it like a life preserver. For someone slated to become a world-renowned physicist, he appeared more rattled than Cassie would have presumed.

Socrates responded with his usual skepticism. "Assuming I believe any of this and I'm not certain that I do... What do you want from me?"

"We need you to help us find Dad, Uncle Sox," said Cassie urgently. "There must be something we've overlooked."

At this entreaty from his future niece in a nun costume, Socrates leaped up, quickly excused himself and headed towards the restroom at the back of the coffee shop. He shut the door tightly then locked it behind him. His heart rate was racing. He took a deep breath then splashed some cold water on his face. While everyone assumed that he was a calm, collected, go-with-the-flow kind of guy, Socrates suffered from occasional panic attacks. And he was finding himself on the verge of one now. A woman claiming to be his niece who bore a strong resemblance to his mother had traveled through time to find her father, his little brother, Aeneas.

Socrates had often wondered if there wasn't something they had all missed about Aeneas. They'd all assumed it was a fluke, Aeneas being bright, but not a genius. Now Socrates wondered if Aeneas's brain just worked differently so he could see the space-time continuum open up. That could mean Aeneas had an undocumented kind of intelligence. But earthquakes? High energy events? Suddenly Socrates had an idea. He smiled and felt his anxiety begin to subside. He returned to the table in scientist mode.

Harold and Cassie looked up with concern as he rejoined them. "You alright, Uncle Sox?" asked Cassie.

He nodded and suppressed the urge to wince at being called Uncle Sox. "I was thinking about the kinds of energy waves that open the timestream for you and your dad."

Socrates sipped his latte and continued enthusiastically. "What if we could artificially create an energy event so you could go back, well I mean forward, but also back to the moments just before the Birch Bay earthquake and follow Aeneas?"

Cassie's eyes twinkled. She slapped the table excitedly, startling Socrates. Harold coughed to hide his laugh.

"It's worth a shot, but there's no need for an artificial event to enter the timestream. We track all local seismic activity. And tomorrow there's an earthquake off the coast of Northern California and that's my energy event back home," said Cassie brightly, feeling for the first time that her trip might yield a way to find her missing father.

Socrates exchanged a look with Harold. This was something neither wanted to miss.

CHAPTER 24

Back Alley Meet Cute

TABITHA SLIPPED OUT THE back door and checked her phone again. Harold was usually very prompt in responding to messages. She'd waited ten minutes and each minute that went by seemed to have increased exponentially. Tabitha decided to go without an escort. She knew her mother would be upset, but it was not even two blocks so she decided to cross through the neighbor's yard to make it quicker. She slipped through their gate and went around the back into the alley. The Entwistle house was in view.

As she stepped into the next yard a barking dog startled her. Tabitha stopped and mumbled to herself, "This is stupid. I should just message Aeneas."

A blue glow illuminated her face as she began to type.

"Tabitha, is that you?" whispered a figure in the distance.

She jumped back and let out a scream. This started a chain reaction of barks from nearby dogs, and soon a symphony of barking dogs had lights popping on all around her as Aeneas came bounding towards her.

He grabbed her hand and they darted towards the street. Tabitha was so surprised and had so many different feelings that she forgot to ask where they were going. The pair ended up on a city bench where that very morning Aeneas had met Sadie, who had questioned him about his affections regarding Tabitha. That morning he wasn't sure, but now he was absolutely certain.

They sat in silence for a minute. Tabitha was still seething, her head pounding. Finally she spoke.

"You're an idiot," said Tabitha, tensing up as she held back tears.

Aeneas said nothing. He felt awful about what happened. Then suddenly he realized that in his hand, he still held hers, which made a tiny smile appear on his face. He turned to look at Tabitha. "I know," he said somberly, but the smile was still there. From his pocket, Aeneas pulled out a small silver satin bag and handed it to her. "Open it."

Tabitha let go of his hand and carefully opened the bag. Two tiny items dropped into her palm, a dainty pair of sterling silver hummingbird earrings, with blue stones for eyes.

Every spring Tabitha hung feeders for the hummers. Together they'd watched and laughed at the hummingbirds, mesmerized by their speed, agility, and quirkiness. Tabitha exhaled, her body tensing up for a moment and she started to cry.

"Can we still be friends?" pleaded Aeneas as he searched Tabitha's face for some sign of forgiveness.

"No," whispered Tabitha in a tremulous voice. "I think those days are gone, Aeneas."

Aeneas was stunned; this was going all wrong, worse than the party.

"Tab, please...," he stammered, as his insides turned to jelly. He pressed his hands into his face. This was not what he had imagined. He was supposed to give her the birthday present and then tell her how much she meant to him. She was supposed to forgive him!

Tabitha leaned over, slowly pulled down his hands, and planted a warm kiss on Aeneas's lips. A proper kiss. Not a peck, but a soft, lingering kiss. Aeneas was shaking. He started to lean in again for another kiss, but Tabitha jumped up, grabbed the satin bag and sprinted off towards her house.

"Tabitha, wait!" yelled Aeneas as he jumped off the bench to run after her, but he let her go. Girls flummoxed him. There was no predicting how they would act at times, not even his best friend, Tabitha.

CHAPTER 25

All In, All Out on Halloween Night

AENEAS WALKED HOME SLOWLY. He was met at the door by a frazzled Socrates, who was hurrying to the lab to do more research. His parent's facility had its own server and was linked to various scientific databases that he thought might prove useful in his search for his brother. Only his brother was right in front of him, with a dopey look on his face and lip gloss on his mouth.

"Where've you been, Aeneas?" said Socrates with quiet authority.

"Outside," said Aeneas nonchalantly.

Socrates eyed his brother. *More like outside with someone*, he thought, getting a better view of the sparkling sheen on his brother's lips. The signs were unmistakable. Aeneas had been with a girl.

Socrates had a thought. A thought that might help him help his brother. He stood firm, blocked the entry and said, "Come with me to the lab," in a no-nonsense tone, which piqued Aeneas's temper.

"Heck, no! I'm going to bed," countered Aeneas defiantly.

"I need your help to find someone who is lost," said Socrates urgently.

Aeneas rubbed his eyes and pleaded with his brother, "Sox, I need a break. A lot's happened tonight."

Socrates nodded. He did know. And he also knew that it was time to let Aeneas know he could trust him and confide his secret. Socrates offered to take Sput out for his late night potty break for the next three weekends. Aeneas grudgingly agreed and the brothers were on their way.

When Socrates and Aeneas arrived at the lab, Socrates sat on the edge of the red vinyl couch his mother had placed in what passed for their lobby. He closed his eyes and placed two fingers on each side of his head, massaging the tension from his temples. A minute passed and Socrates opened his eyes slowly and looked up at his little brother, unsure how to proceed.

Aeneas stood expectantly. "Well, we're here. Who's missing?"

Socrates gazed at Aeneas for a moment. Then he started rattling off questions to his little brother.

"Aeneas, have you ever considered time travel? I mean, do you think it's possible that humans can access the space-time continuum, and even navigate it?"

Aeneas stood perfectly still. He felt color rise to his face. The world stopped, frozen like a Polaroid picture in one of their old albums that showed his mom as a teenager with big hair, long shirts and shoulder pads. Happy-go-lucky Aeneas had been happy because he had two great friends to share his secrets with and no fussy parents or overbearing siblings to observe his every move, collecting data and making hypotheses about him. In essence, he had the freedom to be a normal person and now that freedom was about to slip away.

Aeneas wondered if this was some kind of intervention. Would Persephone, the human lie detector, pop out any moment and start asking him questions? *Not tonight, please not tonight,* thought Aeneas. Tonight, Halloween, Tabitha's thirteenth birthday had been great, then awful, and finally spectacular. There was nothing more Aeneas wanted than to curl up in his bed with some cold pizza and watch YouTube videos of the world's best soccer skills, drifting off to sleep with a happy memory of his first real kiss.

Socrates saw the blood rush to his brother's face then quickly drain away. Aeneas's knees buckled, and Socrates jumped up to ease him onto the couch. He rushed to get some water and an energy bar and heard his brother groggily mumbling something about Tabitha. Socrates grinned the knowing grin of an experienced older brother. His little brother had finally made a move. How long had he liked Tabitha? Since first grade? Seven years?

After he'd finished the water and energy bar, Aeneas perked up a bit and felt awake enough to ask his brother a question.

"How did you find out? Was it the socks?"

Socrates gave a brief shake of his head to indicate "no." He had to be careful with his explanation; Cassie was not even born yet.

"In the future, you will go missing. A person was sent to this time because they need some help to find you."

Aeneas considered this. He'd long felt his disappearances were linked to time travel, but said nothing to Tabitha and C.J. about it. The memories were too vague to decipher for himself, much less share with friends.

"Who was sent back to find me?" asked Aeneas.

Socrates hesitated. As a physicist here is where things got murky for him. He didn't know if meeting Cassie or even acknowledging her would somehow disrupt future events.

Aeneas could see he was struggling with the question, so he answered it for him. "You can't tell me."

"No, more like I shouldn't tell you," clarified Socrates.

"Got it. Don't disrupt the past by revealing the future," said Aeneas mockingly in a deep voice. Socrates rolled his eyes.

"What I want is any information you can give me about what happens to you when you time travel," stated Socrates with a hint of formality. Aeneas detected the shift to scientist mode.

"Additionally, I want to collect physiological data to see how you or the environment around you changes."

"Okay. Here's what I can tell you." Aeneas slunk back on the red couch and made himself comfy.

"It seems like a movie, but it's not," said Aeneas, struggling to describe the complexities of the timeline.

"It's sped up and all the images are passing by me faster than I can make them out. Then I get this urgent feeling to jump into one of the scenes," Aeneas stopped and caught his brother's eye with a mutual knowing.

Socrates was fascinated. He paused and posed a question that Aeneas had no answer for. "How do you get back?"

Aeneas shrugged. "I've always ended up back home, usually in my bed. Lately I've been wearing weird socks too."

Socrates nodded. He didn't mention the coded socks. "But where do you go?"

Aeneas gave him a mystified expression. "I can't exactly remember. It's hazy. I'm pretty sure I ended up in the future. I came back once and there was this lingering dream of C.J., but he was grown, an adult, and he took care of me."

Socrates smiled. C.J., the goofiest, oddball of a friend that Aeneas ever brought home grew into a solid guy, a real friend that had done more for Aeneas than Socrates could have ever imagined. Aeneas might not be a genius, but he had the gift of choosing quality people for friends.

"Why are you smiling?" asked Aeneas defensively.

"Ah, just trying to imagine C.J. as an adult," remarked Socrates, still smiling.

"Yep. C.J. is my best friend. He's intense, but that crazy little guy is all heart. He's there for me and anyone else he cares about."

Aeneas rubbed his face. Socrates could tell he was exhausted. If Miranda found them missing, he might lose lab privileges. Mothers can hone in on the weak spots, particularly freakishly observant genius mothers, but he needed more information.

An idea hit Socrates. "Aeneas, if I reprogrammed one of those fitness bands to collect the data I needed, would you wear it? I could get real time data sent to me and I could analyze it."

"I guess so," agreed Aeneas, who was still uncertain about becoming a project for his brother. "But what should we do in the meantime?"

"In the meantime," said Socrates determinedly, "I have to go see Harold and figure out our next steps."

Aeneas sat up, unsettled by this new information. He'd been slouching on the red vinyl couch waiting for this all to be over.

"Harold knows! What the heck, Sox?"

Socrates hesitated because he was either all in or all out and he knew it. "Of course, Harold knows. He does the laundry, man. Did you think your anomalous socks would get past Harold? The socks are part of the story. They're knitted in binary code that Harold translated. They were sent back with you from the future to help us guide you."

Aeneas had reached his saturation point. His brain was full and his secret, which he'd never quite taken fully into his consciousness, was bursting out like a jack-in-the-box all over his mind. His mind, in response, decided it needed a break and for the second time that night, Aeneas fainted.

Using an app to quickly secure a ride, Socrates navigated his brother into the elevator and was pleased to see a yellow car heading towards the lab. He remotely armed the lab as the driver pulled up next to them. Socrates gently loaded Aeneas into the backseat and they rode together in silence back to West Seattle.

CHAPTER 26

Harold Gets a Glimpse

CASSIE AND HAROLD WERE back at Eleanor's home in Queen Anne and Harold felt obliged to lighten the mood. Cassie had been happy about Socrates' suggestion at the coffee shop but later became subdued during their dinner at the nearby taco truck. "You have to go back tomorrow, catch your wave in Northern California," said Harold as he made awkward waving motions with his hands. Cassie put her head down on the kitchen table.

"How about some cake?" asked Harold, eager to cheer her.

Cassie lifted her head, as a single tear rolled down her cheek. "What do I tell them?" she murmured.

"Who?" asked Harold. He was starting to feel overwhelmed.

"Mom, you, the boys..." her voice trailed off and more tears fell.

Harold wasn't sure how to answer. He only knew that when things weren't moving towards a solution, he forced himself to slow down. His yoga instructor had a life rule that he often found useful. It was only two words: *Don't rush.* The last two days felt rushed.

Then Harold stopped. This was something new. "What boys?" asked Harold gently.

Cassie hiccupped, wiped her face with both hands. "Castor and Pollux. My younger brothers."

Harold smiled. There were more. Aeneas had sons. "There are three of you? All time travelers?"

Cassie sniffed, and Harold instinctively handed her a box of tissues, then poured hot water over a bag of chamomile tea.

Eleanor had gone to bed. Cassie and Harold were seated at an old blue Formica table in the kitchen with the lights lowered.

"No. Only me. Castor, we call him Tor, is a musician. Pollux, we call him Lux, is working towards a PhD in molecular genetics. They're both geniuses."

"I'm guessing twins," said Harold, grinning.

Cassie let a little smile break through. "Identical down to the last toenail when they were born, but completely different personalities. In fact, their physical appearance is the only thing they have in common, besides their weird twin telepathy."

Harold was intrigued. He imagined the second generation of Entwistles intertwined with the Willoughbys, introducing more right-brained traits into the genetic mix.

Harold was rapt listening to Cassie's story. "Lux works with Dad on several genetics projects. They've been trying to locate the gene or combination of genes that carry the ability to sense and use openings in time." Cassie paused for a few seconds, beaming as she thought of her family.

"Tor plays several instruments. His favorite is electric guitar, though he's working on a solar powered model. He performs, too. His band is called Puget Funk."

Harold rubbed the stubble on his chin. These genius genes were strong, two twins, both geniuses. Then Cassie... What was she? She never said. "What's your job?"

"I work as a public relations specialist," replied Cassie guardedly.

"Ah," said Harold, more intrigued. "That's a very people-centric job. What company do you work for?"

Cassie eyed Harold. It was nearly a glare, but she softened her gaze and said quietly, "I work for you."

"Me?" Harold nearly came off his chair in surprise.

"That's all I'll say, but yes," said Cassie firmly.

Harold reached for the honey and added a teaspoon to his still too hot to drink tea and gave it a thorough stirring, changing the subject as he could see Cassie wasn't going to give him any more details. "We've got to get you back home. I rented a car that we can pick up anytime tonight or early tomorrow morning."

CHAPTER 27

Cache of Entwistle Secrets

PERSEPHONE WAS PACING HER third-floor bedroom. She'd been researching materials for filtration systems that could be inserted into storm drains. Persephone was deeply concerned about the effects of stormwater run-off on the Puget Sound and to her, the easiest and quickest solution would be to install filters for the storm drains. She reasoned it would be a while before transportation related chemicals like oil and brake fluid would cease to become part of modern daily life. Filters could be in use within a few years and alleviate the looming crisis for marine species that were affected by human pollution, especially salmon and orca.

Her brain was abuzz, not only because she was passionate about creating sustainable systems, but because Persephone had eaten a few too many bat dropping bars. She'd been experimenting with the recipe for some time and this year's batch of bars contained oats, dark chocolate chips, chopped hazelnuts, chocolate covered cocoa nibs and extra pumpkin spice. It was approaching midnight on Halloween and she felt extremely alert.

Persephone heard her brothers talking and glanced out her window. They were leaving together. Socrates coming and going at all hours was of no concern to her. He kept strange hours and always had, at least in her memory. However, Aeneas and Socrates rarely spent any time together unless it was a family outing, so this was unusual, something to investigate.

Persephone was spry, lean, tiny and lightning fast. The first thing most people noticed about her was that she was mostly hair, her hazel eyes set off by a golden Afro haloed around her head. Being nine years old, she was all brains, and with puberty being a few years off, she was the most brilliant of all the Entwistles. It was well known that she could spot a liar faster than an eagle spots its prey, with what could be considered a sixth sense. There was no real way to measure it, even though Socrates had proposed several tests for her, all of which were banned by his parents. In the end, Persephone came to realize the hard way that there were times when she simply didn't want to know the truth. This wasn't one of them. Socrates and Aeneas were up to something and she being the youngest, and always left out of certain conversations, was determined to discover it.

Persephone opened the GPS app that synced all the family cell phones. The only reason Miranda gave her children travel privileges throughout the greater Seattle Metro Area was because she could use this app to keep track of them. Forget your phone and plan on staying home was her mother's rule. Persephone waited and saw that Socrates was headed for the lab. She sent Socrates a text message:

Why are you and Aeneas headed to the lab so late on Halloween night?

Socrates never responded to the text and Persephone, still wired from all the bat bars she ate, occupied herself until she heard a car pull up outside their house. Her brothers had only been gone for an hour or so. She watched as Socrates ushered a groggy Aeneas silently into the house and closed the door behind him.

Outside Socrates was trying to stay calm. He'd observed enough in one day to keep his mind busy for years. He sat on the wooden bench overlooking their front yard, took several deep breaths, leaned back and closed his eyes. There was a slow prickling along the base of his neck as the panic started to creep in. He took more deep breaths, slow and steady, filling his mind with things that made him happy. Snowboarding, soft pretzels, Grandma Freeman's stories, memories of his trip to Iceland, and experiments that he wanted to design. All alone his brain wanted to run wild with fear, but with the breath and these thoughts he kept the panic at bay.

Socrates was just eight years old when it happened. His secret was one that his parents never brought up. Miranda and Archie had spent countless hours resetting themselves and Socrates after the incident. As a young genius, he was less inclined to play with other children his own age, preferring the company of adults or teens. When the family moved to West Seattle, Miranda began taking the children on outings at Hiawatha Playfield. Aeneas loved playing on his kinder soccer team and Socrates was encouraged to roam around the playfield with a pack of kids while Miranda was busy with baby Persephone.

It was an unusually warm, sunny day in May. Miranda was tucked under a beach umbrella with baby Persephone having a rare conversation with another mother of a boy who played on Aeneas's team. She looked around and saw no sign of Socrates, which gave her no concern at all; he was quite capable of navigating the playfield.

She sighed as a wiggling Persephone needed to nurse, then began to feed her third and final baby. Miranda and Archie had decided that Persephone would be the last, not because she was a troublesome baby, but because they had their hands full with their consulting firm. They agreed they'd more than replaced themselves in the global population with three children. They had both come from families of three's as well, so it seemed fitting.

Miranda burped and patted Sephie, as she called her, and placed the baby back in the sling. She lazily watched Aeneas and the other children running back and forth, lulled by the movement of children across the field, the sounds of parents chatting and of other children playing. For a mother of three young children, a few moments of peace were blissful. Miranda smiled and closed her eyes for an undetermined amount of time, as she would later tell Archie.

She was startled by frantic, high pitched yelling and the rush of conversation from a boy calling out, "a bad man has Sox." Now for any other parent on the playfield, this might have been interpreted as *socks* and their eyes might have stayed closed, but instinctively Miranda knew that "socks" was actually Socrates. She saw a few parents moving towards some trees and she quickly secured Persephone with her left arm and began running. She felt enormous pressure shooting out in many directions as her toes and fingertips became hot and prickly.

A hundred yards ahead Miranda could see that a disheveled man of uncertain ethnicity and age, wearing an old coat, had Socrates tightly by the arm and was touching his face. Socrates was putting up a fight and two other children were yelling at the man, but he wouldn't let go.

Suddenly a barefooted young woman in yoga pants leaped into the scene, airborne. In one aerobatic movement, she flew at the man. A hand went to his face and a foot to his knee, knocking him to the ground. He howled in pain then crawled to his feet, trying to get away from this superhero in yoga pants.

The yoga pants superhero had no use for him, though. She picked up Socrates and ran towards the crowd. Whether she had psychic powers or saw the tears streaming down Miranda's face, no one was to know, but she deposited him at Miranda's feet and gave her a hug. It was the longest two minutes of Miranda's life.

The police never caught the man. He had hurried away even though several parents had tried to follow him while they spoke to the 911 dispatch operator. Based on eyewitness accounts of the man's appearance and behavior the officers concluded it was most likely a homeless man who was confused and not an attempted kidnapping.

Back on the field, Aeneas had never stopped playing soccer. He never saw any of it happen and little Persephone was simply too young to know. It would be years before Socrates would ever leave his mother's side at Hiawatha Playfield and play tag with the other kids.

The panic subsided and Socrates shook away the memory. This was all in the past, and despite the occasional anxiety attack, his life had flowed in and out of manageable challenges that were supported by parents, friends and a global network of other students with which he collaborated on physics research. Now that he was calmer, Socrates decided to go back inside and investigate any data that correlated energy events and the space-time continuum.

CHAPTER 28

Meddling Mother Morning

THE SUN TRIED TO peek through the clouds, as Tabitha awoke to the first day of her thirteenth year, alone in her bedroom. Sadie was sleeping down the hall in the guest bedroom unlike previous visits. At one time, they would have cuddled together in Tabitha's bed and giggled until well past midnight, but those days had passed, and each girl was glad to retreat to the privacy of her own room. Tabitha had not told Sadie about the meeting with Aeneas, the kiss they shared, or about the gift of the earrings. She stretched her legs and decided that for now, no one needed to know about any of it.

Her cell phone was flashing, and she saw that Everett had sent her a message:

Hey, sorry about what happened at your party. Want to meet up later this afternoon at the coffee house?

Tabitha felt a tightening in her belly. Here was a question she would have liked to have posed to Sadie. *Do I meet Everett or not? We're friends, but since the kiss with Aeneas, have things changed? What should I do?*

But for some reason she couldn't ask Sadie, which was a struggle because they'd always shared their feelings. Tabitha flipped over and planted her face in the pillow, letting the feelings of first love and uncertainty wash over her.

Martha tapped on Tabitha's bedroom door, opened it gently and walked in. "Good morning, sweetheart. I've invited C.J. and Aeneas to join us for breakfast. Then maybe you and Aeneas can talk about what happened. You've always been such good friends. It would be a shame not to work things out."

Tabitha jumped out of bed. "Why would you do that without asking me first, Mom?" she shouted. Martha was speechless. Tabitha had never been disrespectful to her before.

Martha took a deep breath then replied calmly, "I'm sorry for not asking you first, Tab. I didn't realize it would be upsetting to you."

Tabitha folded her arms across her chest and fixed her mom with a narrowed-eye stare. "I'm not coming down," she said coldly.

Martha put her hands up to indicate she was done with the conversation and walked out of her daughter's room. She entered the kitchen where George was pouring them French pressed coffee. Martha reached for the cup and slid it over with a look of desperation. George raised an eyebrow as she put a drop of milk into her cup.

"It has begun," she whispered.

"What has begun, my dearest?" George sat next to Martha, eased an arm around her shoulder and kissed her cheek. He adored Martha still. She'd made his life surprising, busy, exciting and full of promise. Martha was always planning something. It was a life full of what's more to come and days filled with merriment and love for his children.

"Tabitha's teen angst has arrived. She's upset because I invited the boys over for breakfast," said Martha with a sigh.

"Oh." George's emphasis was not one of commiseration, but skepticism.

"What do you mean, 'Oh'?" snapped Martha.

"Well, you saw how last night ended. Perhaps it's best to let Aeneas and Tabitha figure things out on their own."

Martha tilted her head towards George. "What's this all about?"

George looked around for Seth, then lowered his voice. "There's something between them. It's been coming on for some time, I think."

Martha's surprise was evident. Her eyes registered genuine disbelief and she looked back at her husband. "How did I miss this?"

"You still see Aeneas as one of our children. We've fed him dinner countless times, we've taken him camping, we've had him sleep over at parties... he's been extended family," said George gently.

Martha took another sip of her coffee. "Should I call Miranda?"

George shook his head. "Not needed. I called last night and let them know—just in case something was brewing between Everett and Aeneas."

Martha nodded. "So... we just leave it?"

"Yep. Unless Tabitha wants to talk about it, we stay clear. She will come to us when and if she needs advice," replied George tenderly.

Martha let out a substantial sigh. "That doesn't seem very proactive."

George smiled. Martha was a fixer and he loved that about her, but George was an observer of the human condition and he knew that it was time to cut some apron strings and let his daughter take some steps forward in her life unaided.

Aeneas woke slowly. He stretched and stared at Clint Dempsey's poster. If his life were only that simple, playing professional soccer. Aeneas let out a small laugh. Clint probably thought his life was complicated and maybe it was. A quick glance at his phone revealed messages from Martha, C.J., and Persephone. This generated a groan. Sunday, November 1st, was a busier day than he'd imagined if three people all wanted something from him before nine o'clock in the morning.

Martha had invited him to a family breakfast. C.J. wanted to know if he planned to go to this breakfast, because in his opinion, it wasn't a good idea after he pummeled Everett at Tabitha's birthday party. And finally, a midnight text from his sister who wanted to know what he and Sox were up to. She hinted that by no means was she to be excluded if they wanted her to keep their secret. Aeneas fell back into bed. Maybe it was best if he just stayed put for a few more hours.

CHAPTER 29

Slang in the Wee Hours

SOCRATES HAD BEEN UP most of the night, searching through multiple scientific papers related to the space-time continuum. There was no hint of research that correlated disruptions in time to high energy events involving plate tectonics. There was plenty on the S and P waves and how they moved, but nothing that crossed over into quantum physics or accessing the space-time continuum. While this was frustrating to start from scratch, Socrates knew that he could begin collecting his own data, starting today when Cassie left to go back to her own time.

Harold, too, was up early checking a maps app on his phone to see how long it would take to get Cassie to her departure site. The earthquake would hit in the late afternoon. They needed to leave soon; if they got through Portland early before the traffic, there should be no problem arriving in Northern California in time to send her back.

Socrates was modifying a fitness tracker to send biometric data to his server. If Cassie agreed to wear it, he could collect data until one second before her departure. He also wanted to collect climatological data, which would require sensors near her departure site. Socrates texted Harold and told him about his idea. Harold's response was simple:

20 minutes. Bring I.D. We're flying back.

Socrates grabbed his laptop, phone, and pieces of equipment he'd been tinkering with, but it all seemed inadequate without time in his lab to program and test the sensors. He was relieved when he realized he'd be able to test and develop the sensors during the journey.

Harold woke Cassie and left a note for Eleanor explaining he had to drive Cassie home because of a family emergency. Harold's plan was simple. He would drop off Cassie and then head north to Medford to catch a flight back. He and Socrates could leave the rental car at the airport, arriving home in the early evening.

Cassie crawled from her bed and collected her things, feeling low. Nothing had been resolved. Her dad was still missing and all she could do was try to follow him seconds before the earthquake, then track him through time. She and Aeneas had traveled together before when he was teaching her how to navigate the timelines of their family. When she was eleven years old they had gone back to 2014 and watched a Sounders game. It was quite a thrill to see Clint Dempsey play. It was a special memory she shared with her dad, especially since she, not Tor or Lux, had played soccer too. All this passed through Cassie's mind as Harold drove over the West Seattle bridge well before dawn.

Socrates scribbled a note to his mom explaining that he was assisting Harold with an experiment and would be back late Sunday night. His parents would likely take away his lab privileges for this, especially since the note was vague. While it wasn't a lie, it was an omission of several facts, the truth being a large chunk of information and Miranda getting the smallest piece.

He quietly backed out of the house, locked the front door and walked right into Persephone who stood before him fully dressed and carrying her bright blue backpack. Socrates froze, having the wherewithal not to yell out and wake his parents. "What are you doing, Seph?" he whispered.

"Me?" she hissed. "You, Aeneas, and Harold are up to something."

Socrates squared his shoulders and took a deep breath gathering all the haughty older-brotherness he could muster. "I have a small experiment to conduct with Harold's help. Now, I would appreciate it if you could go back into the house without making a sound, and I'll answer any and all questions when I get back. You can even message me."

He started to unlock the front door to let her back into the house but then heard the unbelievable.

"Nope," said Persephone, putting strong emphasis on the "pe" sound to illustrate her resolve.

"What did you say?" Socrates thought for a second he was dreaming. Among her other proclivities, Persephone Augusta

Ball Entwistle despised slang. She never used anything but proper English. She burst into tears at the age of three when her grandmother Freeman used baby talk when speaking to her and refused to come out from under her bed until her grandmother apologized.

"I said nope, Sox," repeated Persephone brazenly.

At that very inconvenient moment, Harold pulled up. Persephone turned on her heels and made her way toward the car. She tried to open the car door then noticed a woman sitting in the front seat. Cassie sat perfectly still as if not moving would somehow disguise her. Persephone looked from Harold back to Cassie, the wheels of her mind normally working at lightning speed seemed to stick and she was suddenly befuddled.

Socrates walked behind her and gently removed her hand from the car door, turned her around and began to walk her back towards the front door.

"Who's that woman?" whispered Persephone. "She looks like Mom."

Socrates bent down and whispered back to his baby sister, "When did you last sleep, Sephie?"

"Well those bat bars kept me up and..." she lost her thought.

"I haven't really slept yet, Sox. But that lady really looks like Mom," said Persephone sleepily.

"I think you need to go to bed, Kitten." Kitten was a nickname Socrates had given his baby sister because her crying sounded like a kitten's mewing. She allowed this of course because kitten was a real word and not slang, though as she grew older Socrates rarely used it. It now seemed very appropriate.

He scooped her up, deftly opened the front door and deposited her on the couch. He tucked an Afgan tightly around her and told her to close her eyes. Kissing her forehead he whispered, "I think you have had a waking dream and now it's time to go back to sleep, Kitten."

Socrates' voice lulled Persephone. Confused and exhausted, she nodded her head in agreement and fell into a deep sleep.

Socrates slowly backed away and silently crept out the front door.

CHAPTER 30

Cassie Wins
Best Actress

WITH EVERYONE SETTLED IN the car, Harold headed south and cruised down I-5 with no traffic except the occasional semi. Cassie was steeped in thought. She wasn't sure that much had been accomplished by her visit to 2015 with the exception of Uncle Socrates' suggestion, but she was thrilled to have encountered Persephone.

Her Aunt Seph, so spry and tiny standing right next to her. A woman who would one day change many things in the world, least of which was to save the entire Puget Sound ecosystem from becoming a sterile place without any hope of recovery. Cassie smiled to herself because it was hard to ever imagine her Aunt Seph as a child. Aunt Persephone, a masterful innovator who was credited with many outstanding inventions that protected the environment, was to Cassie an exuberant, thrilling adventurer who shared her love of the natural world.

Harold breezed through a Starbucks north of Vancouver to procure some breakfast items. The car smelled of coffee and bread, which calmed Socrates, helping him to mull over a few ideas about the device he was preparing in the backseat. In fact, everyone was feeling so satiated that no one noticed that Harold whizzed past a state trooper, who clocked him going 85 mph in a 70 mph zone.

Harold pulled over with flashing lights behind him, struggling to get the rental car paperwork ready to show the officer. As Harold rolled down the window, Cassie tapped his arm and said firmly, "Harold say as little as possible." He nodded.

Meanwhile, in the backseat, Socrates took off his coat, tossed it over his equipment and carefully opened his second breakfast sandwich to appear to be busy with his food.

The officer walked purposefully towards the car and tapped the driver's side window. "Good morning, sir. Can I see your license and registration?"

"Of course, officer. This is a rental car. Here are the details and my license," said Harold anxiously, fumbling with his license and rental car paperwork. This was the last thing he needed.

The officer collected the documents along with Harold's license then thanked him as he headed back towards his vehicle. The officer was gone for a few minutes and returned the paperwork.

"Okay, Mr. Torkelson, here's where we are: you were exceeding the posted limit by 15 mph. I'll give you a warning for that and ask you to please slow down. The real issue is that your license expired three days ago."

Harold smacked his forehead with his palm and he started to say something, but it came out as gibberish.

Cassie turned to Harold with a mixture of surprise and irritation. "I thought you said you sent in the renewal, sweetheart?"

"I'm sorry, Officer Ferguson. I did remind him," said Cassie politely as she cut a glance at Harold that made the officer wince.

"We're headed to Arcata, California to give a university presentation on Monday and wanted to get through Portland before any heavy traffic. I'm happy to drive the rest of the way. And I'll set the cruise control to the speed limit." Cassie gave Harold a cold stare.

Officer Ferguson sensed that poor Harold was about to get a wife's wrath, since both he and the young guy in the back seat looked mortified. Officer Ferguson hated pulling over couples. He often thought these poor guys would prefer to be taken to jail rather than listen to their wives' report on their driving or lack of follow through.

"Thank you, Mrs. Torkelson," said Officer Ferguson. And then trying to sound official, although it came out apologetically, he said to Harold, "Here is your warning and also a ticket for driving with an expired license." He quickly handed all the papers to Harold and made his way back to his cruiser.

No one said much for a minute. Cassie opened the car door and walked around to the driver's side, giving Harold another withering stare. He got out slowly and walked to the passenger side. This was all in view of the state trooper as he pulled away from them heading back onto I-5.

"What was that all about?" squawked Harold.

"Your license has expired, Harold. I thought that was obvious," said Cassie matter-of-factly.

"No, Cassie. He means your... your acting," said Socrates, who was still unsure what had happened himself.

"Oh, that," mused Cassie. "As a time traveler, I have often had to think on the spur of the moment to explain myself."

Harold gave her a sideways glance. "Well, you're good at it. It was believable."

Cassie started the engine.

"You're really driving?" bleated Harold. He was still shaken up by all this subterfuge.

"Of course. Your license has expired."

"Do you even have a license?" asked Socrates. He and Harold exchanged looks of bewilderment.

"I sure do. And it's certainly not expired!" laughed Cassie.

Cassie reviewed the dashboard unsure how to operate a vehicle without the self-driving option. "Where is the cruise control? These old cars don't exactly drive themselves, do they?"

Cassie drove easily through Portland while Harold sat pensively thinking about her personality. Harold by nature was not a person who could change his feelings to suit a situation. His face, his tone of voice, revealed it all, most of the time. His brain didn't work on falsehoods. He told the truth and he was honest whenever anyone asked him a question. Cassie, on the other hand, had found it easy to create a new story, an instant identity, as if lying were simply the way she lived. It made Harold uncomfortable; he was worried that perhaps she'd been lying about other things too.

Socrates had converted the backseat into a mini lab, with pieces of wire and small tools scattered everywhere then sometime after he finished his second breakfast, Socrates had fallen asleep. Now, a normal person would have nudged him awake and reminded him to get back to work since they were only five hours from their destination, but Harold knew the value of resting the brain and letting the unconscious mind sort out the details.

Breakfast Burritos With an Extra Side of Parents

C.J. ARRIVED FOR BREAKFAST at his Aunt Martha's house just before 7:00 a.m., hoping Aeneas would be sensible and stay home. Sadie was staring into a cup of hot chocolate, looking disappointed.

He unwrapped his scarf and looked around the kitchen. "Is Tabby up yet?" asked C.J. warily.

"She's skipping breakfast," replied Sadie as she raised her eyebrow and tilted her head towards the direction of incoming parents. Martha and George were walking in from the sunroom where they'd been drinking coffee and reading newspapers.

"Oh, C.J., you're here. What about Aeneas?" Martha scanned the kitchen.

C.J. decided it was best that he handled this right away. He took a deep breath.

"Aunt Martha, owing to the events of last night, I think it would be best if Aeneas did not join us for breakfast at this time."

C.J. felt when approaching an individual with a strong personality like his Aunt Martha, it was important to be firm to have any success at all. George half covered his face, trying to control his amusement while C.J. attempted to assert himself. Martha eyed her young nephew up and down for a second making him quiver a bit. George decided to step in because he could no longer hold back his laughter.

"I told her as much this morning C.J. Best to let things cool off for a bit."

C.J. carefully edged his way towards the burrito bar ensuring that he was closer to Uncle George than Aunt Martha. There was safety in numbers when it came to dealing with mothers or aunts. In a surprising twist of his pickiness, C.J. also loved Mexican food. He grabbed a warmed tortilla, tossed on scrambled eggs, slices of bacon, potatoes cooked with green chili, onions and cilantro, loaded up the salsa and prepared to devour it. Sadie looked at him sideways. Her breakfast burrito was much smaller, and she ate it reluctantly. She was still feeling low since her evening had not gone as planned.

Tabitha heard voices downstairs and knew breakfast was in full swing. She splashed cold water on her face until she felt clean, gave her teeth an extra brushing and carefully rolled her hair into a bun. She'd never felt this self-conscious before. If Aeneas was downstairs, then she might as well face him. Besides, she was very hungry; she hadn't eaten any food last night and her stomach was loudly protesting the absence of nourishment.

C.J. was preparing his second burrito and Sadie was helping Seth make his first. Tabitha glanced nonchalantly around the kitchen. This made Sadie smile because despite Tabitha's casual effort, it was quite obvious she was looking for Aeneas.

"Hi Tab," said Sadie.

C.J.'s head popped up from the salsa container. "Tabitha, I just wanted to say..." but she held up her palm. "C.J., it was a great party. Completely perfect."

"But, but what about Aeneas and Everett and..." sputtered C.J.

Sadie hissed, "Leave it, C.J."

"Okay. Whatever you say."

C.J. gave Sadie a parting glare and dove into his burrito. Lately it seemed to him that girls were complicated, and they changed their minds so much there was no real way to gauge day to day what their reactions might be. C.J. hoped one day he would meet a girl who was a little less complicated than his cousins; he also hoped she liked Bollywood music and burritos.

Aeneas, while having only two slices of pizza the night before, was like Tabitha, finding his stomach in need of something to stop the awful noises it was making. Normally Aeneas would have eaten seven or eight slices of pizza, so he ambled into the kitchen expecting to find something hot and delicious. Instead, he found his mother staring into her phone with marked intensity and his father talking to Persephone, who appeared to have spent the night on the couch.

"What were you and Sox doing at the lab last night?" Miranda had no 'good mornings' for her middle child.

Aeneas stood very still. He couldn't get any words to come out of his mouth while his mother's stern expression held him in place.

"Well, son? We'd like to know why your brother and Harold are headed south. Based on the latest GPS update your brother is in southern Oregon, about to cross the California border."

Miranda took a breath and started again while Aeneas was just as bewildered as ever. "The lab, Aeneas?"

Aeneas decided in that moment that the best explanation would be the closest version of the truth he could muster. "Sox wanted my help with an experiment and I agreed to go with him to the lab," said Aeneas, trying to keep his voice level, "but then I started to feel pretty bad and I fainted, so we came back."

That information instantly changed the trajectory of Miranda's questioning. "Are you feeling unwell?" She slid off the stool and came to check Aeneas's temperature, testing his forehead, scrutinizing his eyes.

"Is there anything to eat?" pleaded Aeneas as he glanced hungrily around the kitchen. "I only had two slices of pizza last night, Mom."

Miranda was relieved to be able to solve a problem; she grabbed some leftovers from the refrigerator and popped them into the microwave.

Aeneas sat quietly on a stool near the microwave waiting for his food to heat up and was privy to an odd conversation about Harold and Socrates.

Archie walked in shaking his head. "Seph ate a lot of bat bars and she was up most of the night. She says that Harold and Sox left with a lady very early this morning. She said the lady looked like you."

Miranda made a face. "Not likely. There must be some other explanation." She held up her phone and showed it to Archie.

"Harold sent us a text very early this morning, saying he and Sox were helping an old friend, a researcher at Humboldt College who desperately needed assistance from a programmer and a physicist before her presentation on Monday."

"I trust Harold, but why didn't they wake us and explain the situation instead of sending a text and leaving a note?"

Archie was not a person prone to panic, rather he was mostly pragmatic and it seemed his oldest son should know by now that he expected some type of reasoning for the choices that were made, especially if that choice was to head off to California in the early hours of the morning.

As Aeneas was walking over to the dining room table with his leftovers, Persephone shuffled in and looked around the kitchen. "I'm so thirsty, Mommy."

Miranda walked over and put her arm around Persephone, giving her a hug and kiss on her forehead before heading to the refrigerator. She poured Persephone a large glass of rice milk and heated her a piece of leftover quiche. The atmosphere was quiet as the Entwistles were caught up in their own thoughts.

C.J., not needing to knock, walked in with a burrito wrapped in foil and found the Entwistles perfectly still as if they were frozen. He wasn't sure exactly how to proceed so he whispered, "Aeneas I need to talk to you about Tabitha."

Unfortunately his whisper was louder than he had intended. All four Entwistles turned in unison and looked at C.J.

Aeneas then gave him a narrow-eyed stare which was the meanest face he could muster. He'd already had plenty of interference in his life in the last twenty-four hours. Miranda and Archie exchanged looks.

"Let's go out back, C.J." Aeneas took his leftovers, grabbed his fleece then he and C.J. walked out onto the back deck greeted by the cloudy, cold morning.

"Bro, don't bring up Tabitha in front of my parents," grumped Aeneas.

"Oh, don't they know about what happened last night?" asked C.J., surprised.

"Yeah they do. George called my parents," mumbled Aeneas.

"Ouch, I should have guessed that." Privately, C.J. thought this was probably for the best. Aunt Martha was a meddler. If Uncle George handled it, then the news would be less detailed.

C.J. pressed because he had one more thing which he'd found confusing. "Well, the reason I wanted to talk to you was that when I tried to apologize to Tabby this morning, she brushed it off and told me, and I'm quoting here, 'It was a great party. Completely perfect.' And dude... unless I'm missing some teenage girl dark sarcasm, I think she was serious."

Aeneas let a slow smile escape his face. C.J. had seen this smile before a few times when Aeneas had bested an opponent, scored a goal and was later reminiscing. It was a smile that remembered a happy, cherished moment. This confused C.J., because Aeneas didn't seem happy last night. He was upset and angry, and tried to give his friend a beating.

"Why are you smiling? Are we going to see caveman mode on a regular basis?" This side of Aeneas had shocked him.

"Heck no! I was just thinking about something else," said Aeneas, recalling the kiss. And then it came out again, the smile.

"Dude, what is with you? Why are you smiling like that?"

Aeneas shrugged and then wondered. Tabitha wasn't his girlfriend, was she? But now there was this kiss that was like fireworks all over his body and every nerve cell was shouting, "She's it, buddy. You've found her!"

CHAPTER 32

Time Travel in a Driving Wind

AFTER HIS NAP, SOCRATES programmed the fitness band to collect biometric data and upload the results to his server at the lab. In the hour prior to her departure he could collect some information about Cassie's vital signs. What he really wanted to see were MRI scans of her brain as she moved along her timeline, but this would at least be a starting point.

He brought along two small weather stations that linked to a satellite and would record data for several minutes before and after the energy event. He decided to place one next to Cassie where she entered what she called the "the timestream," then place the other about a thousand feet away from her to see if there were any changes in the atmospheric conditions when the space-time continuum opened. Harold had helped him program the sensors to collect temperature, barometric pressure and humidity before arriving in Northern California.

Harold was reading a text message from Archie. He believed the story about heading to Arcata, but it was obvious Archie was not pleased at their clandestine departure. Harold was leaning against the car window watching the landscape of southern Oregon pass by and began to think about his life. Harold was only twenty-eight, still a young man, and Cassie was in the age range of women he dated.

Somewhere in the future though, Cassie was a young woman, he was an old man, and she worked for him. Somewhere in the future, he, Aeneas, C.J. and Cassie's mother, who was one of the Willoughby girls, he guessed, were trying to figure out how to get Aeneas, who was older than Harold was now, back to his own time.

The life that lies ahead of me is one where the Entwistles and the Willoughbys are still with me every day, thought Harold.

Suddenly, Harold let out a little gasp. He realized that he'd often felt the last few years seemed isolating and obscure compared to the exciting life he had lived as a young, wealthy entrepreneur when actually nothing could be farther from the truth. He was living in the best possible place and time for the exciting future he would have to unfold. This road trip with Socrates and Cassie was the beginning of that life. Harold smiled and laughed for a second.

Cassie gave him a weird look. "Okay over there Hatman?"

"Yes. I'm taking a nap to see what little jewels will surface from my subconscious," replied Harold as he snuggled against the car window.

When they finally arrived at the location near Cape Town, Socrates and Harold hopped from the car and looked around.

"Cassie, I thought you had to enter the timestream on the beach, since the earthquake was offshore?" Socrates could smell the ocean, but he was sure they weren't close enough.

"We've reached the end of the road and still have around a mile to go," said Cassie, gesturing towards the ocean. "This is a remote area, not frequented by beachcombers. It seemed easiest to leave from here without a lot of people present."

"I doubt anyone would be out here today. Look at those clouds and the wind is picking up. When is the earthquake supposed to occur?" Socrates was looking at his watch as he loaded the sensors into his backpack.

Cassie checked her notebook. "Just a few minutes past 4 p.m. We have about an hour, which should be enough time for you to set up and test your equipment, Uncle Sox. When I see the timestream, I'll head towards it then drop the sensor next to me."

"Where should I place the other?" asked Socrates, concerned about the validity of his experiment.

Cassie thought for a moment. "Further away in either direction would be my best guess. I'll show you where I'm likely to enter the timestream; you can take the other sensor down the beach away from that spot."

Socrates gave her a look of exasperation and she chirped, "Sorry! I'm not the scientist in the family!"

Cassie smiled to herself. Socrates wasn't quite the Uncle Sox of her childhood. Her Uncle Sox had taken her and her cousins (his daughters) on a special trip one spring to Oxford University when he was considering taking a position there as a visiting professor. Cassie, Athena (Thena) and Artemis

(Missi) had spent a whole day walking through the Ashmolean Museum. They rested after a few hours in the museum café, ordering a pot of tea served with milk in a tiny silver pitcher accompanied by tasty green pistachio cake, and discussed ancient cultures. All had agreed that the naming trend of the Entwistles would come to an end with them, and that their children would not have names that were based on ancient Greece. That afternoon was one of many wonderful memories from her childhood.

The trio trudged along a trail, Harold and Socrates following behind Cassie. The wind blew in from the west and the sea spray created a mist along the shoreline. Clouds on the horizon were thick and gray. It would be raining soon and not the friendly Puget Sound drizzle, but harder, windblown rain from the Pacific Ocean.

No one spoke about the next steps or the future, only of sea birds that they spotted. It was up to Cassie now to travel back to her own time, then leave again just before the earthquake to follow Aeneas. It seemed to Harold that this was an enormous task. He still didn't understand how time travel worked in the practical sense. He hoped when Cassie headed back to her current time that he might observe some useful details.

The walk was brisk and soon they were at the beach. The roar of the ocean grew deafening causing everyone to yell over it to be heard. Socrates set up the two sensors to collect climate data and tested them a few times to be sure they were recording properly. Then he checked Cassie's modified fitness tracker he'd placed on her wrist an hour ago. It was a few minutes before four o'clock when Cassie motioned them to back away from the shoreline towards a quieter spot near the trees.

"Harold, thanks for all your help. Old Harold is waiting for me when I get back, but I'll still miss you," Cassie reached in and gave Harold a hug and kiss on the cheek.

Harold choked back emotion and returned her hug. "Good luck, Cassie."

"Uncle Sox, I was glad to meet the younger you. It explains a few things." Cassie giggled and Socrates laughed heartily.

"It was incredible meeting you, too, Cassie. I'll do all I can to find out what happens when you time travel." Socrates teared up. He was just over six feet tall, requiring him to lean down when he kissed his niece on her forehead. He whispered, "We'll find your dad."

Cassie turned her face to the ocean as if she sensed something. "It's time," she said, walking towards the shoreline near the first sensor. Harold dug into his windbreaker and grabbed his phone to record her departure so they could watch the video frame by frame to collect additional data.

Seconds passed and nothing extraordinary happened except the wind and rain increased. Cassie seemed to be looking right at them, but then her gaze changed and she bent her knees, just a bit, a subtle movement then she was gone, her fitness tracker going with her into the future.

Harold and Socrates ran forward to where she had stood and looked at each other in amazement. The rain was coming down harder and they had no time to discuss what they'd just witnessed. Socrates grabbed the first sensor and placed it in his backpack while Harold ran down the beach and grabbed the second one before it was blown away by the gusting winds.

Socrates and Harold quickly made their way back to the car, the rain was pouring on them now and neither thought to bring extra clothes. Socrates, for all his accomplishments didn't have a driver's license, so Harold drove cautiously, sticking to the slow lane, with the cruise control set at 65 mph.

They arrived in Medford, Oregon and boarded a short flight to Seattle. Few words had passed between them until after the drink service. Then Socrates perked up and addressed the issue at hand. "Harold, I suppose we should get our story straight before I return home."

Harold was looking out the window. They were above the clouds and he could see the night sky, which Harold had believed infinite, but more so now since he'd watched Cassie vanish into another time.

"Sure, Sox, though I was thinking what else we might do to help the future situation." Harold paused for a moment recalling the time he and Cassie decoded the socks. "The letter from myself said we needed to teach Aeneas to control his abilities, so he won't be randomly swept into the timestream." Harold turned to Socrates and asked earnestly, "Do you think we could start working with him soon, discreetly, without your parents' knowledge and somehow escape Persephone's notice?"

Socrates smiled and tilted his head. His parents would be easy to avoid, but his sister was like a bloodhound. She could sniff out anything, and trying to exclude her only heightened her senses and increased her determination. Socrates wondered if a career in the CIA or FBI wouldn't suit her personality best. He shook off his wondering.

"Persephone is the real issue and Aeneas himself too. He's a little preoccupied at the moment." Socrates gave Harold a meaningful look. "He's smitten. Did you know last night he tried to beat up his pal Everett when he was dancing with Tabitha?"

"Ha, I had no idea the boy had it in him!" exclaimed Harold.

"Had what?" asked Socrates, giving him an odd look.

"The green-eyed monster, the bubbling bile." Harold's analogies were amusing to Socrates. Harold had a flair for the dramatic at times, but Socrates agreed. "Me neither. He's always seemed to be the least jealous person in the world."

CHAPTER 33

The Longest Sunday

THE LEAST JEALOUS PERSON in the world had meandered silently through his morning trying to let the events of the night before settle. His parents were off on their Sunday ritual, a long walk followed by a late lunch together. Aeneas had the house mostly to himself. He was supposed to stay home with his little sister until his parents returned since Socrates was gone. Luckily Persephone was asleep for now, and C.J. was walking Sput, leaving Aeneas to work in peace.

Aeneas cleaned his room and finished reading two more chapters of *Great Expectations* for his language arts class. He paced around the house and then raided the fridge for another snack, but he couldn't settle. His thoughts were jumbled, and he realized that he wanted to see Tabitha and talk to her, but he wasn't sure what to say.

Aeneas texted his mom to see when he could leave for the playfield. Miranda replied that they were two blocks from home and he was free to go. He grabbed his water bottle, rain jacket and soccer ball, tossing them into his sports bag as he pulled on a warm hoodie. He passed his parents on the sidewalk, high-fiving them both as if he were their happy-go-lucky child they knew him to be and continued his jog to the playfield.

After a short while, C.J. and Sput joined him at the playfield. Playing around with C.J. and Sput was like a tonic for him and Aeneas felt his worries melt away. An hour later C.J. called it quits as the clouds moved in and the wind picked up. He wanted to get Sput home before the rain started as his mother wasn't fond of the wet dog smell. Aeneas grabbed his sports bag while C.J. worked Sput's legs into his Seahawks doggie jersey to keep the rain off on the way home.

The boys and Sput ambled down the sidewalk and were surprised to see Everett just ahead leaving Freshy's, followed by Tabitha, who stopped on the sidewalk to give Everett a hug.

Sput barked at them and started to pull the leash, charging forward. C.J. struggled to hold him back and whispered through clenched teeth, "Sput, stay!" but Sput loved Tabitha and he continued to lunge. Aeneas was rooted to the spot and had not moved. When Tabitha looked up, she caught his eye and held it for a moment. Everett, however, started walking home and didn't acknowledge C.J. or Aeneas.

Tabitha hesitated, unsure if she should walk over, then waved casually as if nothing had happened and called, "I've got to head home. See you guys later."

Sput let out a yowl of frustration that seemed to echo the sentiments of his owners.

"Well, that was weird," puffed C.J. "This morning she acted like everything was fine and now this." C.J. gestured with his hand toward the direction the two had departed.

Aeneas was quiet, too quiet for C.J. who said nervously, "Well, let's get going and see what my mom has made for dinner. Maybe you can eat at my house since Harold isn't cooking tonight."

He gave Aeneas a tug, but Aeneas didn't budge. "Dude, no more caveman mode. Just forget about it."

But Aeneas couldn't forget about it. Tabitha had been with Everett and she had hugged him! Then the look she gave Aeneas was a very exacting glance that was supposed to communicate something, but what?

~

Early Sunday evening, Socrates and Harold deboarded the plane and walked through to arrivals. Harold turned to Socrates and started to say, "We should set a time to go over..." then stopped mid-sentence. What he'd witnessed was unbelievable, but he now believed Cassie was who she said she was. Socrates knew what Harold was trying to convey. "Yeah, for sure. I'll examine the data tomorrow and get back to you."

They silently parted with a handshake and a hug. Socrates dreaded facing his parents. He hopped into a taxi and set off for West Seattle trying to stay calm.

When Socrates arrived, not more than two minutes had passed before his parents descended on him with questions about the research at Humboldt State University and why it was necessary to depart without consulting them. After a few minutes, Miranda's questions started to wind down and she seemed oblivious to the facade Socrates put up to cover the lie. Socrates noticed the lull and hoped she would be more interested in his immediate needs. "Mom, I could really use a hot shower and some food. I haven't eaten much since breakfast," said Socrates wearily.

Miranda sighed, just relieved to have her eldest back home. "Of course, Sox. I'll heat up some leftovers while you shower."

Archie was less obliging and spoke sternly as they headed upstairs. He placed a hand on Socrates' shoulder to stop him. "Son, I want to make it very clear to you that should you ever need to leave urgently for any reason, regardless if we're asleep or not, your mother and I expect to be notified in person." Archie paused and softened his tone. "Socrates, you will no doubt become one the greatest physicists of your generation, but you're still only seventeen and you need our permission to venture beyond the city. Is that clear?"

Socrates stood a few feet away with his father's glare holding him in place like a tractor beam. He let out a long breath that he didn't realize he'd been holding, worried that he would lose lab privileges over this incident. He managed to keep his facial expression contrite as he answered, "Yes, sir."

~

The night closed up around the Puget Sound with a slow rain. C.J., clad in green plaid pajamas, sat on a Seahawks pillow in the corner of his room with a nearby lamp shining a bit of light. Each evening C.J. tried to meditate, but his thoughts were often a mixture of ideas and worries, so he ended up using this time to sweep his mind clean before bed. He started with deep breaths to relax, followed by a string of prayers, though some of them were broccoli prayers.

His broccoli prayers were the last of the prayers and they were reserved for people who had hurt his feelings or annoyed him. C.J., widely regarded as a picky eater, was not a fan of green vegetables, but his parents insisted he eat something green so he ate broccoli because he knew it was good for him. His broccoli prayers were the spiritual equivalent of eating his vegetables. And tonight, he found his cousin Tabitha in his broccoli prayers.

C.J. was angry at Tabitha because he felt she was deceiving him, but he wasn't sure how. She had a right to be upset about her birthday party, but then she wasn't upset at all. She was happy, and this was a huge relief to him, but he had a sinking feeling she was hurting Aeneas. He worried it would dismantle the friendship the three of them had shared for years.

Life had also quieted down at the other Willoughby home, which was unusual because when Tabitha and Sadie were together, the house was filled with the girls' constant chattering. Sadie had wanted to ask what had changed, but something within Tabitha had suddenly shifted and Sadie didn't feel she could approach her cousin. They'd always talked about everything, but when Sadie stopped by Tabitha's room on her way to pack up, Tabitha was reluctant to share much information.

Sadie's face was pink and freckled, bright and freshly washed. She looked younger without her stage makeup. She smiled at her cousin with eager eyes. "Tab, are you okay?"

"Yeah. I'm fine, Sadie." Tabitha topped off this comment with a few vigorous nods and went back to her book.

"Okay, it's just, you know if you want to talk about Aeneas or Everett or anything..." Sadie trailed off and stood her ground, but Tabitha wasn't ready to talk to anyone. She'd made a horrible mistake that afternoon and was too ashamed to tell anyone.

• CHAPTER 34 •

Waffles, Data, & Double Standards

SOCRATES WAS UP EARLY and met Harold in the kitchen. Harold was making cinnamon waffles and grilling turkey sausage for the Entwistle breakfast. He gave Harold a contemptuous glance. Waffles were his father Archie's favorite and he was sure Harold wanted an advantage if his dad decided to have words with him about their trip to Northern California. The coffee maker had just stopped, and his dad would be down any second.

Socrates spoke in a low voice to Harold, "I'll be working on the data this morning and later this afternoon. I'll send you the results."

Harold stopped before he poured more batter onto the waffle iron. "Socrates, how will we know if she made it back? How will we know if she found Aeneas?"

This part of the plan was never fleshed out. They'd spent so much time trying to set up data collection devices and get

Cassie to her departure spot that they never thought to ask her how they'd know if Aeneas had been found and returned to his present.

Before they could continue their discussion, Archie came briskly down the stairs and greeted Harold a little stiffly. "Hmm. I thought I smelled waffles."

"Yep, all your favorites to get your day off to a good start."

Harold cheerfully presented Archie with two fat cinnamon and flaxseed waffles, topped with a pat of butter, three links of sausage and a large cup of piping hot French roast coffee.

"Archie, I'm very sorry for the mix up the other night. We really should've awakened you before we left for California," said Harold as he gently set the maple syrup in front of Archie.

Archie was silent for a few seconds wondering whether it was worth it to lay into Harold or not. He'd made himself quite clear with his son the night before.

"I know how people can get ahead of themselves when they're trying to get somewhere in a hurry, but I would have appreciated some notice," said Archie tersely before he popped in a mouthful of waffle.

Relieved that Archie wasn't furious, Harold glanced over to find Socrates glaring at the back of his father's head. Had he been feeling more courageous, Socrates might have muttered under his breath about double standards, but he decided to let it go. You had to pick your battles carefully with your father and there was no reason to make matters worse for himself, so he shook off his frustration and made for the lab, but not before getting some breakfast.

"I have a bus to catch. Can you make me a waffle sandwich to go, Harold?" Harold gave him a bright smile as he assembled the sandwich ingredients.

"I've also packed you some quinoa salad, a tuna sandwich and your favorite spicy barbecue chips," said Harold happily. He was relieved to let his mind toil away in the kitchen after the last few days.

Socrates gave Harold a thumbs up, collected his lunch and wished everyone a good day, ensuring that he communicated to his father that he was headed to the lab, to his class at UW and then back to the lab, just for good measure.

A half hour later Socrates was sitting in the lab sipping espresso. He'd pulled the data off the climatological sensors and quickly created a table to review the results. The wind and rain were identical at both sites, but the pressure differences were significant, as well as some slight temperature changes in the air and soil that could not be accounted for by topographical changes.

Sensor two was further down the beach, but the same elevation and landforms were present. The temperatures should have been similar. The pressure was low though, and this was the biggest anomaly between the two data sets. It was so low in fact, that the same levels of air pressure were found inside the walls of a tornado or hurricane.

He encrypted the data set then sent it, along with his observations to Harold before heading to catch a bus to UW for his advanced calculus class.

Time Travel Data	Sensor 1 near Cassie ~ 6 inches from her person	Sensor 2 1/8 mile away from sensor 1	Sensor 1 near Cassie ~ 6 inches from her person	Sensor 2 1/8 mile away from sensor 1
Time (24 hours)	16:00	16:00	16:15	16:15
Temp F	56 F	56 F	63 F	56 F
Pressure	1008 mb	1008 mb	920 mb	1008 mb
Humidity	96%	96%	96%	96%
Wind Speed	SSW 12 mph	SSW 12 mph	SSW 12 mph	SSW 12 mph
Soil Temp	52 F	52 F	60 F	52 F

Harold, Notice the pressure difference between the two sites. 920 millibars is the type of pressure reading found inside the walls of a powerful hurricane. It appears that when the timestream is open there's a microclimate of sorts. I can't figure out why there'd be differences between the soil temps. See what you can make of this data. When I get back to the lab I'll pull the fitness bracelet data off the server. SE

When Socrates returned to the lab from his class he looked over the physiological data collected from Cassie just before she vanished. She'd worn the modified fitness bracelet for an hour before she left, starting around 3:15 p.m. in the afternoon, or 15:15 as Sox used twenty-four hour time. In the first fifty-seven minutes her heart rate and body temperatures were mostly consistent with activities like walking out to the beach or riding in the car. The last few minutes did have some note-worthy changes. Her heart rate started dropping and so did her temperature.

"She cools down and slows down," said Socrates to himself. He wished that there was more time to study Cassie, more time to develop better data collection tools so he could see her brain activity when she transitioned to the space-time continuum. He was curious about her biometric data as she traveled through time. If her body temperature and heart rate dropped then maybe her brain waves changed, too. He deliberated this while his eyes bore into the data table. "It's odd that her body temperature drops, but the environment around her warms up."

Time (24 hour)	16:13	16:14	16:15
Heart rate	77	62	56
Body Temp	97.2	96.4	95.5

Socrates quickly typed up his observations and stored the data in an encrypted file he created on his server. For now, this data would be kept secret from everyone except Harold.

After some research, the closest data to match the pressure at her location was a ten-year-old measurement of the inner walls of Hurricane Katrina, a powerful Category 5 hurricane. Socrates munched on his tuna sandwich and shook his head, bewildered by the anomalous data.

"Pressure drops, and it gets warmer around her, perhaps an exothermic reaction," said Socrates thoughtfully.

"Pressure that low should have created some kind of weather anomaly within the rainstorm, but the data didn't change. It's as if she was sucked into a vortex of some kind and her body slowed down for the process."

Socrates stroked the stubble on his chin. He wished he could ask Cassie if she felt cold or lethargic, but that was the trouble. He might not see her again for thirteen years and even then she'd only be a baby. Although mused Socrates with a tiny grin, he did have someone nearby who might be able to answer these questions for him. Back at Entwistle Central, a busy Harold read the text, briefly looked at the data, then responded hurriedly to Socrates' message:

Intrigued by data. We should investigate further. Must finish packing school lunches. Will leave it to you for now. HT

Harold set down the phone and a flurry of sandwich making, and snack packing ensued before the remaining Entwistles began the exits for their respective days.

Persephone was escorted by Harold five blocks away to her tutor's house for a few hours of coursework in algebra and biology; she was homeschooled for her advanced courses instead of attending high school. Afterwards Harold picked her up and dropped her off for her two electives at school. Persephone was not keen on taking PE or choir, but her parents insisted. She needed socialization with peers. As it happened Persephone had recently made a friend in her age range, a fifth-grade girl named Soon Lee, who was extremely bright, and shared Persephone's determination to eliminate storm water pollution in order to save the Puget Sound eco-system. Miranda was thrilled. She worried Seph might miss some coming of age experiences if she had no female friends close to her own age.

As Harold retraced the five blocks back from the tutor's house, he thought back on breakfast that morning, recalling Aeneas had only eaten two waffles instead of four. Aeneas had seemed unsettled, even a little agitated and Harold wondered if it was girl trouble or something else, especially since the boy had always shared his father's love of waffles. Then Harold remembered what Socrates had told him on the flight. He knew more about the future than he should already.

Later that evening Harold finished his video conference with Socrates, shaking his head in amazement. Cassie's biometric data was that of a person entering a state of hypothermia. The area around her mimicked a hurricane or tornado, yet after she had departed the area showed no signs of extreme pressure. Nothing was damaged or changed. Harold pulled out his phone and played back the video a few times looking for some detail he might have missed. Finally he decided to transfer the video clip to his laptop. He watched it over and over at the slowest speed, then frame by frame. Nothing popped out at him and he felt fatigued. Harold knew it was time for pie.

Eleanor was watching an old movie, one of her favorites: *Cool Hand Luke*. She'd invited Harold to join her, but after he googled it, Harold decided that watching an old movie with certain types of scenes with Eleanor might embarrass him. So he kindly declined her invitation, but not before making

Eleanor some popcorn and presenting it to her in a dark blue ceramic bowl that was made by one of her granddaughters.

When he passed through the living room on his way to the kitchen for his pie, she called to him again, "Harold you are missing a classic. Nothing like Paul Newman with his shirt off to give an old gal quite an evening. Are you sure you don't want to join me?" Eleanor was feeling sassy and she enjoyed teasing Harold.

Harold shook his head and laughed. When they'd first met her teasing would have made him blush.

"Thanks, Ellie but I'm in the middle of a project. Maybe next time. Just on my way to the kitchen for a slice of pie and a cup of tea."

Harold loaded a tray with a generous portion of apple, raisin, and walnut pie he'd made the night before and steeped a small pot of green chai tea. He headed back upstairs, but paused to catch a quick glimpse of the movie. Old movies had a vintage quality that he liked. Climbing the stairs Harold wondered if he could apply some filters to the video clip of Cassie, curious if altering the lighting might reveal anything new.

Maizy padded upstairs following the scent of pie and curled up near Harold, waiting patiently. They had an agreement regarding used plates which Maizy monitored closely. The pie had two bites left at best and she anticipated that her cleaning of the plate would soon commence.

After applying several filters, none of which yielded new information, Harold tried a black and white filter then slowed the video, frame by frame. He absently stabbed a bit of pie and popped it into his mouth when something caught his eye.

"Hah!" yelled Harold, startling Maizy. Not surprisingly the pie got lodged in the back of his throat. Harold sputtered like an old tea pot then hacked a small glob of pie onto the floor. Maizy shot over and licked it up. His body continued to revolt causing Harold to sneeze six times in rapid succession. He grabbed some tissues and winced as he blew his nose. Inside the tissue was a tiny chunk of walnut along with some blood. Maizy barked once then jumped up to sniff his face. Harold patted her reassuringly then gulped his lukewarm tea. One more glance at the video clip and he had his answer. Just before Cassie departed into the timestream, a shadow appeared behind her.

"How can there be a shadow on a rainy day?" said Harold. Maizy came to rest her head on his knee looking up at him pleadingly. Harold smiled. It was time for her evening walk.

CHAPTER 35

Tabitha in the Soup

TABITHA WAS FEELING UNSETTLED as she headed off to school. The thought of sitting through fifty minutes of geometry class with both Aeneas and Everett caused her stomach to tighten. Normally she, C.J. and Aeneas would have walked to school together, but today the boys didn't knock on the door or wait for her on the sidewalk. The gray drizzle made the morning even bleaker as she walked to school alone.

Geometry was the last class before lunch and as the morning passed by, Tabitha felt a growing dread of not knowing how to proceed in an awkward situation. She wished she'd just texted Aeneas right after the hug and sorted out this whole misunderstanding. Now it was taking a toll on her stomach which knotted and gurgled every time she looked at the clock.

Meanwhile, Mr. Schmidt had just put the finishing touches on his geometry review game. He thought his class needed an infusion of excitement and movement so he decided the students should play a competitive game to solve the proofs to prepare them for the unit test. Six teams were listed on the smart board when the students entered.

Aeneas had wandered in early and saw to his great relief that neither Tabitha nor Everett was on his team, yet they were on the same team. His fists clenched as he sighed in disgust. Aeneas glanced around the room for a distraction until the game started.

Fortunately, his distraction arrived in the form of Bethany Purvine. Bethany was a petite girl with platinum blonde hair and light blue eyes. She was a gymnast and had all the perky pep that comes from one who flies through the air and bounces off the ground effortlessly. Bethany had long harbored a secret crush on Aeneas and had asked Tabitha to intervene on her behalf a few months ago.

Tabitha did try several times to guide Aeneas in Bethany's direction, commenting on her perkiness, indicating she might be someone he would consider taking out for a walk with Sput. While Aeneas appeared amiable to the idea, he never finalized any plans with Bethany. To be fair, Aeneas did think Bethany was attractive, but he was far too laid back to want to spend time with anyone so energetic. However, in this instance, Bethany was just the person to have a conversation with while Mr. Schmidt finished attendance and readied the teams.

Bethany's eyes widened, and her face was all smiles when she saw Aeneas was on her team. The third team member was Annie Kim, known far and wide as a fierce competitor. Annie's twin brother Andrew was equally competitive which is why Mr. Schmidt, after careful consideration, decided to separate the twins. Their intensity was better halved than squared, he thought with a chuckle.

When Tabitha entered the class and saw she'd landed on a team with Andrew and Everett, she felt another small knot added to the growing collection in her belly. Since the twins both hated to lose, it meant she would likely be in competition with Aeneas's team straight away, dashing her plan to fade into the background until lunch when she could finally talk to him.

The tables were facing the screen and arranged in a U-shape around the classroom. Mr. Schmidt explained the rules once all the teams were settled.

"A proof will appear on the screen and the first team in the rotation will have one minute and thirty seconds to solve it."

Mr. Schmidt paused to see if there was any reaction to the amount of time given to solve the proof. "If the answer is correct, the team receives the point. If not, then the next team can present their answer and receive the point. This will continue until we have a correct proof or until all teams have had a chance to answer. Then a new proof will appear on the screen for the team to the left of the one that earned the point," said Mr. Schmidt cheerfully.

Annie Kim set the timer on her phone to match the timer in the corner of the smart board. She wasn't taking any chances. The prize, which was also posted on the screen, was five extra points on the unit test for all team members.

Tabitha was working hard to focus on the first proof, but her heart wasn't in it as her mind drifted back to yesterday. When she caught sight of Aeneas and C.J. she wasn't ready to talk to either of them so she made an excuse and left. What was it her mother called it? *Avoidance behavior.* She avoided both of them and now they were avoiding her.

"Okay, that's a win for us!" said Andrew as he high-fived Everett and held his hand up for Tabitha who was still staring at the proof.

"Tab, we got it. High five me," urged Andrew excitedly. Tabitha sat up straight and looked at Andrew, dazed. She had no idea that the round had ended and blushed deeply as her hand went up slowly to meet Andrew's.

Annie seethed a bit, but not enough for her brother to notice. Her team was up next and she squirmed in her seat. Annie knew Bethany was of no use, owing to a long-standing crush she had on Aeneas, so to give her something helpful to do Annie asked her to watch the timer and whisper the time every thirty seconds. She was hopeful that Aeneas might be useful. After all, he did come from a family of geniuses.

The next proof was tricky. At the one-minute mark Annie was almost finished, but faltered. Aeneas quickly pointed out a small error she'd made, and the proof was solved in time. Annie jumped up and high-fived Aeneas and then Bethany. She was beaming. As the rounds continued, the points were mostly awarded to the twins' teams, with some points scattered among the four other teams.

Annie was impressed that Aeneas's geometry skills were as competent as her own. Aeneas had, of course, excellent spatial awareness because he played soccer every day.

"We've got this," whispered Annie breathlessly when the last proof was about to come up.

"The team before us is struggling so they won't get the point." She continued excitedly, "We can get this last question and tie the game."

Aeneas nodded. "I'm ready."

"Me too," replied Bethany, gazing adoringly at Aeneas.

The last proof materialized on the board; Annie cringed. It was complex and worth two points instead of one. The other team wouldn't finish in time, but she worried that her team wouldn't either and if that were the case then Andrew's team would win by one point.

Annie froze as she overheard Andrew whispering to his team, "They won't get it and neither will Annie. This is a two-minute proof for sure." Andrew being her twin always knew the right button to push. The logic button. Andrew started the proof himself, working furiously, and stealing glances over at his sister.

The timer had started but Annie hadn't moved. "Annie, are you okay?" Aeneas asked quietly. Annie shook her head vigorously just as Bethany whispered, "Thirty seconds."

Aeneas slid the paper in front of himself and glanced at the proof. He knew that he had to prove multiple congruences to solve it, so he took a deep breath. He worked steadily and finished by the time Bethany whispered, "Sixty seconds." Annie grabbed the paper and scanned the proof. She was astonished. It was correct and in thirty seconds!

Mr. Schmidt called time, and as predicted, the team to the right of Annie, Bethany, and Aeneas, was not finished. Proudly Annie walked over and handed him their page. He smiled as he scanned the proof. "Way to go, team. Excellent work here."

THE RESCUE

Annie turned and gleefully threw her arms around Aeneas. Bethany glowered at Annie as she waited to sneak in a hug. Tabitha too saw this and dashed out of the classroom, knocking over a large bottle of hand sanitizer.

Mr. Schmidt called after her, "Hey Tabitha, wait!" then turned expectantly to Everett and Andrew. "Is she not feeling well?"

Andrew shrugged, and Everett made unknowing gestures with his face and hands, both surprised at being asked.

Mr. Schmidt sighed. "Bethany, please check the girl's restroom."

Bethany hurried to the nearest restroom and found it empty. As she returned the bell rang and the students burst into energy to leave for lunch. The room was emptied in less than two minutes. Mr. Schmidt was about to call the office to report a student missing when the second bell rang, signaling the next set of classes and lunch for eighth graders. Just then Tabitha shyly walked in.

"Are you alright, Tabitha?" called Mr. Schmidt, pulling a glass container from his lunch box.

"I wasn't feeling well. Sorry I ran out, " said Tabitha, gathering up her things.

"Do you need to see the nurse?" he asked delicately. Mr. Schmidt never pried as to why eighth grade girls weren't feeling well. He simply offered a nurse pass and moved on to another topic.

Tabitha shook her head. "No thanks. I need to talk with a friend then I'll feel better."

"Sounds like a good plan to me." He opened the door and ushered her out.

"Thanks for not making a big deal out of this," said Tabitha gratefully.

"No problem," replied Mr. Schmidt. "Go find your friend. I'm going to get in line for the microwave and heat up my soup."

Mr. Schmidt and Tabitha parted ways, one headed towards a soothing hot bowl of soup and the other feeling like she was *in* the soup, as her dad would say.

CHAPTER 36

Stuffed Frogs and Pheromones

AENEAS STARED AT HIS neatly packed lunch. A thermos of Harold's beef stew full of his favorite chewy, fat rice noodles, some carrot sticks, chips and hummus and three peanut butter granola bars usually held him through soccer practice. Normally he would be shoveling in the stew and working his way through the hummus, but Aeneas's appetite waned as he was more perplexed than ever by Tabitha.

The old Tabitha was observant for sure, but she always revealed her observations in conversations. This new Tabitha seemed secretive and complicated, two traits Aeneas did not find attractive. He knew some guys thought that those kinds of girls were a challenge and interesting to pursue, but he liked knowing that the Tabitha he knew was the same Tabitha to herself as she was to everyone else.

"That looks delicious. Did your mom make it?" Annie appeared before Aeneas holding her lunch and smiling with such intense happiness anyone who looked her way might have thought she was losing her mind.

Startled, Aeneas replied, "Uh, no. Our housekeeper Harold. He knows I like rice noodles."

"Can I join you?" Annie asked nicely and though Aeneas only wanted his own company, he was always a kind person.

"Sure." He motioned her to join him.

Annie was about to take a seat when Bethany also appeared at his table.

"Hi guys. Great game today." Her perkiness spilled out easily and she sat next to Aeneas as if she had been specially invited. Annie was not so keen on sharing Aeneas's company, but Bethany had decided she was going to take this opportunity and would not be outmaneuvered. Each girl was talking at the same time. Combined with the background noise of the cafeteria, Aeneas felt the beginnings of a headache.

Tabitha searched the crowd for Aeneas. She wanted out of the soup. And her dad was usually right when he said, "Taking a step in any direction will get you out of the soup. You just have to move." Tabitha smiled at the memory of her dad's strange, but useful advice.

Aeneas was at his regular table and seated on either side were Bethany and Annie. Tabitha wondered if things could get any worse. It took all the perseverance she could muster to walk in the direction of the trio.

She slowed her pace as Aeneas's expression came into view. *He looks like a stuffed frog*, thought Tabitha, trying to suppress a smile. She brought her hand up to her mouth to hold it back, but suddenly she exploded into snorts, giggles and finally tears. She was breathless, heaving and holding her chest as tears streamed out of her eyes. If she'd been jealous even for a moment, Aeneas's face of pure misery unwound all those tight feelings. Then Tabitha remembered why she liked him so much. Most people shaped their personalities to fit into whatever idea they thought other people wanted them to be. But not Aeneas, he was simply himself, completely genuine.

Aeneas finally saw her and he was on his feet. Was Tabitha crying? He didn't bother to untangle himself from Annie and Bethany. He hopped up onto his seat, stepped on the table and leaped over his lunch like a ballet dancer, landing neatly and hurrying towards her. Aeneas was not a genius, but he possessed extraordinary agility.

"Tabitha!" exclaimed Aeneas, taking her hands in his.

"Are you crying?"

Tabitha let out a hiccup. "Not crying. Laughing at the look on your face."

Annoyed, Aeneas pulled his hands back from hers, readying himself to walk away. But Tabitha reached out, grabbed his hands, pulled him closer and gazed up at him with her emerald green eyes. Aeneas was temporarily immobilized, his heart thudding in his chest.

"I'm so sorry about yesterday. I met with Everett to let him down easy. He's a super guy and I didn't want to give him the wrong impression. I wasn't sure how to tell you with C.J. there."

Instantly Aeneas felt like the happiest person alive. Happy, but starving.

"Let's eat lunch together," said Aeneas enthusiastically, feeling all was finally right in his world. Tabitha tilted her head towards the lunch table and raised an eyebrow. Aeneas had left his lunch in between his new fan club. They both looked back. Annie and Bethany were staring at them, their lunches untouched. Aeneas whispered to Tabitha that he would be back in a minute. He walked toward the girls and started to explain that he would be leaving to eat lunch with Tabitha, but they weren't having any of it. Annie was the first to leave. She stood quickly, turned on her heels and walked to another table, followed by Bethany, who shot Tabitha a menacing glare.

C.J. had been troubled all day about the disharmony of his friend group. Never in all the time he, Aeneas, and Tabitha had been friends was there any falling out among them. After school the weather had cleared a bit and was breezy and cloudy. C.J., well positioned, was leaning against a tree out in front of the school.

As he waited for Tabitha, C.J.'s mind was a jumble. *Aeneas should be headed to soccer practice and Tabby should be walking home, hopefully* thought C.J, *not with Everett. But wait,* he grimaced, *Everett has soccer practice too. This is terrible. Should I go to practice to be sure Aeneas doesn't pound Everett again, or wait for Tabby and confront her?*

Then out of the corner of his eye, he saw Tabitha leave a side door and hurried after her.

"Tabitha," he called sharply.

Tabitha turned and looked back. C.J. was headed towards her like a steam train, red faced and puffing.

"Hi," said Tabitha flatly.

"Hi," replied C.J. curtly. There was an awkward silence as C.J. gathered himself. He shuffled his backpack onto both shoulders and started in earnest.

"Listen, Tabitha. Whatever game you are playing with Aeneas has to stop. I can't sit by and watch you toy with him and ruin our friend group."

Tabitha could see that her cousin was miffed and needed an update on how things stood. Aeneas had wanted to speak with him first, which was why she was trying to slip away unnoticed from school.

"Aeneas and I are okay now. We talked at lunch," Tabitha said casually as she started walking towards the sidewalk. She didn't want to have this conversation at school.

C.J. took this in as they walked. "So, you guys are friends again and no one is mad? What about Everett?"

"Everett and I are just friends. Aeneas won't try to pummel him again."

C.J. was skeptical. "You're sure about that? He has this caveman mode. You saw him at the party. He lost it."

Tabitha stopped walking. She realized that it might be up to her to explain the new situation to C.J. when a shrill voice from behind interrupted them.

"You might've told me you liked him yourself, Tabitha. It was dishonest to keep that secret when I asked for your help."

Tabitha and C.J. spun around simultaneously to see Bethany closing in on them. Her arms were crossed and she stared at Tabitha with daggers in her eyes.

"Bethany, I'm so sorry," said Tabitha evenly. While it had been comical in the cafeteria to see her and Annie storm off, Tabitha knew that Bethany had wanted very much to be Aeneas's girlfriend. She also knew that this would hurt her.

"Whatever," scoffed Bethany. "You and Aeneas can laugh behind my back, but don't count me as a friend to you anymore."

"Excuse me," said C.J. formally. He had a feeling the two girls had forgotten he was standing next to them.

The air was thick with something and in that second C.J. recalled words from his father. "If two ladies, or girls," he amended, "are having a disagreement, it's best not to interfere." Charlie occasionally bestowed helpful advice to his son with the hopes of making his passage through life easier. C.J. remembered this because at the time of this explanation, his mother, Sakura and her sister, his Aunt Tamiko were squabbling in the kitchen. Charlie and C.J. legged it to the market for some extra groceries and his dad took his time about it so the ladies could sort out their disagreement. Unfortunately, C.J. didn't heed his father's advice because he had a burning question that he couldn't hold back.

"Excuse me," C.J. repeated.

"Tabitha, do you mean that *you* like Aeneas?" Tabitha ignored the question, but Bethany was too worked up to be her polite, perky self.

"Butt out, C.J. This is between me and her." Bethany gestured in Tabitha's direction with her thumb.

"I'll talk to you later, C.J.," said Tabitha tersely, dismissing him with a wave of her hand.

C.J. froze, stunned by this poor treatment, but then Bethany shot him a hostile glance and he hurried away, muttering under his breath, "My dad was right."

CHAPTER 37

Home Again, Home Again

CASSIE MOVED SWIFTLY ALONG Aeneas's timeline, slipping over to hers with the ease of a familiar pathway. She aimed herself like an arrow focusing on the present she'd departed a few days before in the year 2053. It glowed brightly and she felt drawn to it, as if she were meant to be there. Beyond that was the future, misty and somewhat underdeveloped. If she overshot her present, she could get tossed into her future and Aeneas had warned this was dangerous and forbade her ever attempting it. She leaned into a spot of time within the tunnel that would bring her to West Seattle and then refined her course to her parents' home. This was a key piece her father taught her, be very specific in your thoughts as you exited the timestream.

Cassie had hoped so much that when she returned her father would have made his way back, but her mother's eyes were tired and her smile forced when she rushed into the kitchen.

"Is Dad back?" asked Cassie with all the anxiousness of a person who has been holding back worry for days.

Tabitha sighed, "No, sweetheart. Did you learn anything that could help us find him?"

"A little," said Cassie, taking a towel from Tabitha.

Cassie was wet and cold from the rainstorm on the beach. She peeled off wet clothes and wrapped herself in the towel. Tabitha quickly retrieved a robe, blanket and pair of slippers then headed straight for the kettle.

Tabitha finished preparing chai red bush tea with steamed coconut milk and a heaping tablespoon of honey, which she dubbed her restorative tea, rich, sweet, a little spicy, and always warming. She handed the frothy cup to Cassie, who took a few sips before beginning her story.

"Well," smiled Cassie, tearing up, "I got to see you, Dad, Uncle Sox, Aunt Seph, and meet young Harold."

"Did you see *her*?" whispered Tabitha eagerly. Cassie need not guess who 'her' referred to because there was only one 'her' that evoked this kind of emotion in Tabitha.

"I heard her playing one afternoon. I think she was doing a sound check for your party." Tabitha nodded and poured herself a cup of the special restorative tea. Sadie had been gone for a long time, and the ache in her heart had never quite healed.

"Young Harold was a piece of work, Mom," said Cassie. "I never realized how tough it would be to connect with him and get his help. He was very peculiar."

Tabitha finally had cause to laugh. She hadn't laughed in ages and it felt like a relief. She happily expanded on the history of Harold.

"Let's just say Harold improved as he aged," mused Tabitha with a slight shake of her head. "There were several events that shaped and matured him. I was always quite fascinated by him, you know." Tabitha stared into her teacup reminiscing.

"I once met Harold's mother. She was..." Tabitha stopped. She tried to think of people in terms that were non-judgmental. "She wasn't a highly educated person and her communication style was limited." Tabitha sipped her tea before continuing.

"I think Harold grew up without a lot of nurturing or conversation. The Entwistles and dear, sweet Eleanor became his family, so in his twenties and thirties, Harold grew up again and became more like the person you know today." That was the best way Tabitha could explain that Harold's social skills weren't fully formed until he was older.

Tabitha ushered Cassie in front of the gas fireplace and urged her to share more of her journey.

Cassie smiled and looked at her mother. "Uncle Sox, once he got over his shock and had enough evidence to believe that I was really his niece, collected some physiological data that might be useful to figure out what happened to Dad."

"Your dad and brother have hundreds of data sets," replied Tabitha with a twinge of frustration. Tabitha was a highly sought-after therapist and had collected and used all kinds of data in her practice, but forty-year-old data with forty-year-old technology didn't seem like much of a start to her.

"Why would data from Socrates be worth examining?" she asked Cassie, trying to keep her voice even. She'd hoped Cassie was right and the key to solving this mystery was in the past with Aeneas's earliest time travels.

"Because it *is* forty years old, Mom. Maybe we missed something obvious, something old that we all take for granted."

Tabitha sighed and pressed her hands over eyes, but Cassie was determined to stay positive about her trip, even though she herself had some misgivings about its success.

"Harold's brain power was zippy just like he said it would be, but the real prize of this trip was that Uncle Sox had an idea that just might work to rescue Dad."

"Okay, Cass, tell me this idea," said Tabitha wearily.

"Uncle Sox thinks I should go back in time prior to the earthquake and try to follow Dad." Cassie looked at her mother pointedly. "He said when the timestream opens up I should follow him."

Tabitha shook her head. Her disappointment was obvious to Cassie.

"You were in Pullman at a conference when the quake hit! You went back in time yourself and visited your grandmother when she was a student at Wazoo," said Tabitha loudly. Her patience with the situation was waning. She wanted some tangible plan to recover her husband.

"Yes, but that doesn't mean I can't hop another energy event and come back here a few minutes before the quake and follow Dad."

Tabitha rubbed her eyes. She was exhausted from worry and didn't fully understand how Cassie, who had already gone back in time during the earthquake, could go back in time again somewhere else during the same exact moment? Was there another version of Cassie headed back to the 90s to spend time with her grandmother Miranda while the current Cassie was following her father through time to track him? The whole thing boggled Tabitha's mind.

Just then, the kitchen door flew open and Lux walked in. If Cassie looked like a mixture of Miranda and Tabitha, then Lux and Tor were a blend of the Willoughbys and Entwistles with Martha's hazel eyes, Aeneas's chiseled nose and a dimpled chin inherited from Archie. Lux wore his hair clipped short while Tor preferred a full head of curly hair. Lux also still lived at home. He was only nineteen after all, working on his Ph.D. at the UW and found it easier to live with his parents.

"Sis! You're back. So, did you find Dad?" Lux was not a worrier. This he also inherited from his father.

"Sadly, she didn't," Tabitha answered for her, trying not to tear up. Cassie was still sipping tea by the gas fireplace, trying to take the chill off.

"What's next then?" Lux was a mover of things forward. If something wasn't working he made note of what parts worked, what didn't, and moved on.

Cassie was not an optimist like Lux. Her personality was more pragmatic like her mother and Uncle Sox.

She looked up from her tea and replied, "I have another plan via seventeen-year-old Uncle Sox."

"Oh really? And what did the budding physics master have to say?" Lux was very fond of his uncle and was curious what kinds of ideas he had when he was about the same age.

"Uncle Sox suggested that I travel back just before the quake hits and follow Dad when he enters the timestream," said Cassie cheerfully.

Lux accepted some tea from his mother. He read her body language; she was skeptical, so he asked the question he thought she was likely mulling over in her head.

"When Dad enters the timestream, even if you are seconds behind him, would you be able to catch up to him?" Lux set down his tea and looked at his sister with concern. "It sounds risky to me."

Cassie gave Lux a cool glance to remind him she was still the oldest and didn't appreciate being questioned. "Dad and I have traveled together before, but we've always been physically connected... holding hands when I was little, locking arms when I was older. I'll need to observe what transpired during the earthquake but I'm certain I could follow him."

Tabitha chimed in anxiously, feeling like she had to explain again why she knew nothing about Aeneas's disappearance. "I was out back when the earthquake hit. Your dad was in the kitchen and then he wasn't."

"Then I'll arrive a few seconds before the earthquake and meet up in the kitchen with Dad," said Cassie as she reached over and squeezed her mother's hand reassuringly.

CHAPTER 38

Download, Overload, Done for the Evening

AENEAS WALKED ONTO THE pitch and looked around. He owed Everett an apology and an explanation. Everett saw Aeneas approaching as he was changing into his cleats. Still bristling about the birthday party, he made no eye contact; he tied his right shoelace and walked off to get a ball. Aeneas knew he had one shot to fix this with Everett.

Everett was a guy who saw things in black and white, so he needed a reason that was congruent with his own sensibilities. Aeneas knew he needed to state the facts, apologize, not make any excuses for what he had done, but accept full responsibility. He called after Everett, who didn't bother to stop.

Aeneas sped up and walked along beside him. "Everett, I need to talk to you, man. Please stop for a sec."

Aeneas's black, curly hair and mocha complexion contrasted Everett's fair, freckled skin and sandy hair. They were both nearly six feet, well-muscled and equally matched. Everett stopped and turned abruptly, facing him. "What do you want, Entwistle?"

Everett took a step back, fists at the ready, and locked eyes with him. Aeneas started right in before Everett decided to throw a punch. "Look man, I owe you an apology. I never realized how much I liked Tabitha until I saw you dance with her and then something in me just snapped—I kinda lost it. I was wrong and I'm hoping you can forgive me."

Everett nodded slowly and exhaled. Aeneas could see the tension in his upper body release a bit. "So how come you never asked her out? You hang around her all the time."

Coach blew the whistle and Aeneas explained as they started warm up drills jogging along with their knees up. "We've been friends since first grade. I've always liked her, but lately I've been feeling that I liked her more than just as a friend. I just wasn't sure how to tell her because it might screw up our friendship." And this was the truth, minus the part about how he'd planned to give Tabitha a special pair of hummingbird earrings, but was edged out when Everett started dancing with her, eliminating his chances of an after-party conversation with Tabitha.

"When were you going to tell her?" asked Everett.

"Hey, Entwistle, Veltcamp," interrupted their coach. "Would you two get a move on?" Aeneas and Everett had slowed down, lagging behind the team.

"After the party," Aeneas called as he picked up his pace and rounded an orange cone, breaking away from Everett.

Things made more sense now. Everett was interested in Tabitha, but he could see that Aeneas had a long-term crush on this girl. The next pass Everett made around the pitch, he made eye contact with Aeneas, gave him a smile and a nod. Aeneas gave him one back, took a deep breath and felt his energy shift. He was not the kind of person who liked to be embroiled in conflict. Everett was a teammate and while not his best friend, he was a decent guy and he deserved to be treated with respect. Aeneas had Archie to thank for instilling this sense of fairness. His father was a strong advocate of the golden rule.

~

C.J. stirred his soup around a few more times before finally pushing it away. He'd sent a text to Aeneas, but he was still at soccer practice and the wait seemed endless. Sput came up and nudged his leg and whimpered. He was reminding C.J. to drop the bowl so he could lick it clean, which of course, was prohibited by his mother. Generally, he and his dad agreed if Mom wasn't around, Sput was the middleman before the dish made it into the dishwasher and she didn't need to know about it.

"Here you go," sighed C.J., mixing the remaining soup into Sput's dog bowl making a dog food casserole, as he liked to call it. Sput was face down, munching happily, when Charlie came in, carrying his violin.

"Hi Dad," said C.J. without much enthusiasm.

"What's wrong, son?" asked Charlie, setting down his violin case.

"It's complicated," mumbled C.J.

Charlie opened a kitchen cabinet with tiny, frosted glass windows. Inside were neat stacks of Japanese soup bowls. He pulled one out and filled it with a heaping ladle of chicken and leek soup. Sakura always made soup when she would be home late. Tonight, she was playing the cello in a performance downtown and wouldn't be home until after ten o'clock. C.J. and Charlie usually ate dinner at the kitchen counter instead of the dining room table. Charlie enjoyed this time with C.J. and referred to it as their "Men's Night Meal."

"Anything I can do to help?"

"I don't think so. I'm going to work on it tonight," said C.J. absently.

Charlie nodded, then started in on his soup. He was not one to press for information. When C.J. needed help he was always quick to approach the parent he thought would be most useful in finding a solution.

"Well, there is something I wanted to talk with you about," said Charlie as he slurped soup and took a bite of his sourdough roll. C.J. looked up expectantly.

"The thing is," Charlie hesitated. He was a little embarrassed. He didn't quite know how to proceed.

"The thing is, what?" snapped C.J. He was already feeling like life was changing all around him with the situation between Aeneas and Tabitha taking twists and turns. His parents couldn't be having problems. Not now. Not when puberty was just starting, and he could expect all sorts of odd things to begin happening to him. His mom bought him a book a few weeks ago and the contents terrified him. It basically boiled down to his body getting hairy, smelly and having reactions to things without much warning.

Charlie could see he'd approached this too slowly and should have just gotten the message out quickly. He laid his hand on C.J.'s arm to calm him and said cheerily, "Your mom is pregnant."

C.J. eyed his dad critically and said nothing. Charlie was disappointed by the unwelcomed reaction. He'd hoped C.J. would be excited about having a sibling. Finally C.J. got up from his stool and threw back a frosty comment.

"Please consult me regarding any name choices for my new brother or sister. I'd like to have some input."

Then he grabbed an apple, whistled to Sput and grumbled as he headed upstairs to his room. "C'mon, Sput. Let's go watch some highlights of last week's game." The only thing C.J. felt he could count on for now were his beloved Seahawks.

CHAPTER 39

Up Your Bro-time

WHEN AENEAS CAME HOME the smell of Mexican food permeated the house. This elicited a big grin of relief and he made his way into the kitchen. Persephone was setting the table and his mom was plating up enchiladas verde from a pan. A dish of jalapeno and onion rice was on the table along with a fragrant pot of pinto beans. Aeneas had been known to eat six enchiladas in one sitting.

The family was well into Harold's Mexican feast when Socrates arrived and grabbed a plate. He'd missed seeing Harold before he left for his job at Eleanor's house, so he sent a text and asked if they could video conference later.

As Socrates contemplated the fate of his younger brother lost somewhere in time, there sat Aeneas, happily shoveling enchiladas into his mouth. It made his head swim. He wished he could say, "Hey doofus, on such and such date and time there will be an earthquake. Tie yourself to a chair five minutes beforehand and stay clear of the crack in time or else you will be lost with little hope of anyone ever finding you." If only it were that easy.

Socrates was still thinking about this when his mother asked Aeneas, "Have you set things right with Tabitha?" She hoped there was no feud brewing. She liked the Willoughbys and felt comfortable with Aeneas's friendships with Tabitha and C.J.

Aeneas gulped down a large bite of enchilada and Socrates suppressed a smile. "Yeah, we're good, Mom," said Aeneas as blood rushed to his cheeks.

Persephone glanced at her brother and noticed the small change in his coloring. "Are you blushing, Aeneas?"

"I'm not blushing," said Aeneas as he opened his mouth, waving air and making ha-ha-ha noises to distract from his embarrassment. "I bit into a jalapeno seed." Socrates and his father exchanged glances but said nothing.

Dinner was nearly finished when C.J. knocked at the front door. It was Sput's night at the Entwistles and though Aeneas usually picked him up, C.J. was eager to hear what happened at soccer practice, and even more eager to find out what was going on between Tabitha and Aeneas.

The boys settled down into Aeneas's bedroom while Sput was exploring the upstairs. Each time he came back from C.J.'s house Sput liked to take a good sniff of each family member's bedroom. He was particularly fond of Persephone's room. C.J. and Aeneas had long suspected that she kept some scent in her room to attract Sput just to vex them.

Aeneas closed his bedroom door and C.J. immediately began pacing. He usually made himself at home, but he felt uneasy and started talking rapidly.

"Bethany and Tabitha were having an argument on the sidewalk in front of the school." Aeneas's eyes bulged a little as C.J. kept going.

"It seems Bethany feels betrayed by Tabitha, who apparently likes you, but two nights ago, she was dancing with Everett!" C.J. stopped for a split second and made a bewildered gesture. Aeneas tried to interrupt but C.J. started pacing even faster.

"Then when I tried to ask a question and by the way..." C.J. stopped, ensuring he had Aeneas's full attention as he was about to impart sage advice handed down by his father, Charlie.

"Never, ever interrupt two girls during an argument, Aeneas. All that happens is they turn on you with blistering comments and shoo you away."

A forlorn looked crossed C.J.'s face. "Tabitha, my own cousin, shooed me away like I was nothing to her!" Although Tabitha was a year older than him and two grades ahead of him in school, C.J. was treated as an equal within their friend group.

"Sit down, bro," said Aeneas calmly. C.J. took a step back and flopped onto a bean bag chair, Aeneas's furniture of choice. Aeneas lowered himself to the floor. He crossed his legs and leaned against the side of his bed and spoke quietly. "The thing is, I do like Tabitha, more than just as a friend and I think she feels the same way."

C.J. pushed his bangs out of his eyes and stared bug-eyed at Aeneas.

"Are you saying you two are dating?"

Aeneas shrugged and said in an off-handed way, as if it weren't a big deal, "We kissed."

"You kissed her? When? Where was I?" C.J. was peddling himself out of the bean bag chair, trying to stand.

"After the party. Halloween night," said Aeneas casually. He didn't want C.J. to overreact, but it seemed that might be impossible.

"After she yelled at you for trying to beat up Everett?" asked C.J. nearly apoplectic and getting more animated as he once again paced around Aeneas's bedroom.

"Is this all going to get gross? Are you two going to be kissing when we're hanging out?" squawked C.J. He could feel angry tears coming on and didn't want to cry in front of Aeneas. That would make this whole thing even worse.

Aeneas hesitated. He wasn't really sure. "C.J., I don't know about any of that. I just know we like each other."

C.J. stopped pacing, hung his head like Charlie Brown and stared at the floor. His whole world had shifted in just one day. His best friends were about to start dating and his mom was going to have a baby.

A tap at the door brought Sput back along with Socrates. He looked from C.J. back to Aeneas. Something was off between them. He started to ask, but then changed his mind. He had a video conference with Harold soon. "Gentlemen, Sput needs some food. How about feeding this guy? He's been trying to unload my garbage can."

Socrates gave C.J. a smile. C.J. glanced up with sad eyes, then walked over and patted Sput as he trudged out of the room to get some dog food. Recently Socrates had realized what an important role C.J. would play in his brother's future, but things seemed momentarily strained.

"What's up with you and the little dude?" whispered Socrates, glancing back at C.J. who continued slowly towards the stairs.

"I told him that Tabitha and I like each other."

"Hmm..." said Socrates with a scratch to his ever-increasing chin stubble, making him feel even more grown up than his seventeen years.

"You probably need to up your bro-time. Reassure him that you're not ditching him for a girl."

"Bro-time?" repeated Aeneas thoughtfully.

Socrates nodded. "Make some plans with the little dude and don't include Tabitha."

Aeneas scrambled off his bean bag. "Thanks, Sox. I'll go talk to him."

Socrates sighed. He had to be careful not to influence Aeneas beyond the usual older brother's advice. He and Harold would need to create protocols to ensure they didn't interfere with the future.

CHAPTER 40

A Consensus Is Met

CASSIE POURED A CUP of coffee and buttered a walnut scone. Sometimes it felt soothing to be at her childhood home instead of her apartment in Ballard. Homemade baked goods were much missed now that she was living on her own.

Waking up ravenous was nothing new after a stint in the timestream and Cassie settled into her scone and coffee, wondering if relationships in the present had been altered. When she traveled back and visited her grandmother Miranda, she'd invented a new persona. When she had bumped into her dad on the bench Halloween morning her identity was concealed. This was the first instance when she had gone back in time and returned to the present with potential life changing consequences.

The back door opened and a clean, wet spring breeze blew into the house, warmer than winter wind, accompanied by pounding feet, which belonged to Harold knocking the muck off. He tucked his boots into a cubby in the mudroom then walked into the kitchen where Cassie stood, refreshed from a goodnight's sleep, ready for their meeting. As soon as he saw Cassie standing there, Harold's eyes misted over and he enveloped her in a hug.

"Dad's still missing," said Cassie hopelessly. "I made no progress."

"Well you convinced me and Socrates of your identity, which changed my life significantly and made me the person I am today. Your uncle was changed, too. Meeting you made him grow up during a time in his life when he tended to be more self-centered. He had to consider the future of his little brother."

Cassie hesitated, speaking slowly. "I thought I wasn't supposed to alter the past. That's what you said. You were quite angry at me," said Cassie haltingly. It took her a second to realize that, *for her*, the argument was still fresh, but not for Harold.

"Cassie, what little we know of time travel doesn't always preclude the idea that someone's destiny might be in the past," said Harold reassuringly.

His tone was so different from the younger version that it instantly evoked so many new feelings from Cassie. Her mind churned away as she thought to herself, *Why does old Harold always make me feel so comforted? The younger version was never easy for me to deal with. He was so arrogant at times.*

Cassie shook off her inner musings and said jokingly, "Don't take this as an insult Harold, but I much prefer the mature version to the younger prototype."

Harold chuckled. In his twenties he was still stuck in a life view that the world revolved around him. He had been successful so young, arrogant and full of vim that other people's welfare was not always a consideration. That changed though, and it all started with Cassie.

In the center of the table Tabitha put out some freshly baked walnut scones and set down a pot of Earl Grey tea. The scent of bergamot always cheered her up. Lux brought milk and cane sugar and placed five cups around the table.

The earlier breeze was gaining energy and the weather became blustery and rainy as the group assembled. Lux sat next to his uncle and Cassie sat next to Harold. Tabitha sat at the end of the table, while directly opposite her was an empty chair, another reminder of Aeneas's absence. Everyone took a scone and passed around the teapot while Cassie relayed the events of her travels.

When Cassie finished the last piece of her story, explaining the idea from teenage Socrates to Lux, Tabitha, Harold and Uncle Sox, there was silence. Suddenly the room erupted with questions and several people spoke at once, some to each other, some to Cassie, but the cacophony was quieted as Socrates spoke forcefully and they all stopped and looked at him.

"I remember," he said, slapping his hand on the table in excitement. He looked at Cassie and was grinning from ear to ear, his million dollar smile surprising everyone.

"I remember meeting you. I remember my idea, but I hadn't recalled it until just now. I mean, I guess I've always known it, but your story seems to have activated those memories."

"This morning when I woke up, I remembered meeting Cassie too just like Socrates described," said Harold, trying to keep his voice even.

"Cassie's been gone two days, but you met her around thirty-eight years ago." Lux looked from Harold back to Socrates. "But you just recalled it today?"

Harold raised his bushy eyebrows and looked to the ceiling. He was trying to find a good way to describe the sensation he had that morning. "Ever forget something happened then suddenly a smell, sound, word, or person jogs your memory? It felt like that." Socrates nodded in agreement as he munched on a scone.

Lux then glanced at his mother. Tabitha returned his glance, her expression critical. Aeneas had been extremely cautious about his own time travels after being trained by Bob North Sky. Aeneas passed on these rules of time travel to Cassie. As far as they knew no one had really tampered with the past in such a way as to alter memories.

"So do you remember meeting Cassie and also not remember meeting her? How does this work?" Tabitha was concerned about the implications of changing the past. Aeneas had always been very strict about this when Cassie first started traveling alone. Socrates put on his think face and Harold was rolling his bushy eyebrows around in consternation.

"I met Cassie when I was seventeen. I've no memory of not knowing she would be born or not knowing about her. I think the other past has been replaced," said Socrates, more serious now. This was something they all needed to consider and Socrates' mind was now creeping into worry mode.

"The other past must have been overwritten," agreed Harold.

Lux glanced at the small piece of rectangular glass placed near the middle of the table. It was used to record their conversation for historical documentation. It shimmered green every few seconds, which meant it was recording all programmable variables. This tiny device, known as a SAIL (Sustainable Autonomous Interconnected Link) recorded the meeting using holographic technology and tracked the biofeedback of everyone present along with environmental data. Lux was patting himself on the back at his forethought to record this meeting. This meeting contained valuable data for his thesis and would add another layer to his father's history of time travel.

Everyone was in favor of Cassie traveling back to the moments before the Birch Bay earthquake and following her father. Everyone, except Tabitha. Harold sensed her apprehension as she asked several questions concerning the feasibility of the attempt.

Finally, Cassie turned to her and said gently, "Mom, I'm coming back. If I can't follow Dad, I'm coming back." She reached over and took her mother's hand.

Socrates smiled. He'd known Tabitha since she was a child, a precocious, non-genius child that Socrates thought possessed keen observation skills that were 'genius-like' in their accuracy. She seemed to know the small pieces and parts that were hidden inside of others.

Tabitha exhaled and a wave of tears flooded her face. "I just can't lose anyone else," she sobbed.

And then Socrates saw a piece that was hidden inside Tabitha, the piece of sorrow of unexpectedly losing someone that she loved. She'd lost Sadie and now Aeneas.

Lux went to his mother and hugged her for a long time. "We'll find Dad," he whispered.

Time Tunnel Task

CASSIE WAITED QUIETLY AT Sea-Tac Airport. She was flying to Anchorage on the redeye and wanted no goodbyes or send offs. She departed her mother's house before anyone was up to keep her mind fresh for the task ahead.

The journey would take just under an hour from lift off to touchdown. Supersonic speeds were now commonplace since a clever device had been invented by a budding sixteen-year-old scientist that muted sonic booms caused by breaking the sound barrier, allowing for speeds in excess of Mach 2. Air travel was now extremely fast and essentially non-polluting with hydrogen fuel cell technology.

Cassie boarded the plane, found her pod, an enclosed reclining seat, and activated the airline entertainment menu. Each pod allowed passengers to access a hologram database of a hundred years' worth of entertainment. She recalled young Harold's proclivity to let his mind drift with something silly, so she chose a show her Grandma Martha loved: *Laverne and Shirley*. Just then, the flight attendant came by to take Cassie's drink order. Her old standby was their coconut milk mocha latte.

A few minutes later the flight attendant returned with a cartful of drinks and passed Cassie her latte. She sighed as her hands wrapped around the warm ceramic mug etched with Clear Horizon Airlines' slogan, "Quick. Cozy. Coffee all the way." Cassie sipped her latte and relaxed, knowing that an old family friend would take good care of her no matter what the outcome of her journey.

Sheila North Sky operated a bed and breakfast in the South Addition neighborhood adjacent to downtown Anchorage. She was seventy-eight years old and as spry as ever. Her father was an Alaskan native belonging to the Chugach tribe, and her mother was a Pacific Islander from Samoa. Sheila often joked she had a foot in two worlds, and one was much warmer than the other. Through a series of unusual events that seemed to be common in her family, Sheila found herself the proprietress of a B&B. Due to the regular seismic activity in the area, occasionally her patrons were time travelers who used the Alaskan Way Time Tunnel.

Sheila's father, a time traveler, served as a shaman for his tribe. Bob North Sky was in the twilight of his life, with many children and grandchildren when he met Aeneas Entwistle. Aeneas was still in high school and was on a quest to investigate areas with high seismic activity. He was working on a hypothesis that a larger part of the population might possess genetic markers for time travel, but the absence of high energy events left them unaware of their abilities. He focused his search from Alaska to California, conducting the occasional experiment with time travel along the way.

Bob met Aeneas by accident one summer afternoon when Bob brought two of his young granddaughters to McHugh Creek in Chugach State Park for a picnic. Bob and the girls were moving silently along a trail watching for birds when a nearby 4.7 earthquake opened up the timestream.

Bob was a master time traveler. He moved along his timeline with ease and purpose. As the opening formed in his peripheral vision, he breezily waved it away, immune to its pull after years of practice.

Bob's oldest granddaughter, Naqi saw what she thought was a man behaving strangely. She silently motioned to her grandfather who was about fifteen feet behind her on the trail.

Aeneas was also hiking near McHugh Creek and had seen the timestream open. He stopped and steadied himself by a tree as he peered into his timeline. As he learned to control his abilities, Aeneas paused to decide where he wanted to travel rather than be drawn in and land haphazardly somewhere along his timeline.

Aeneas neither heard nor saw Bob and his granddaughters approach as he scanned the opening in the space-time continuum. Bob's face erupted in a grin. He knew exactly what was about to happen, but he was surprised that a traveler would be so foolish as to enter the timestream on a well-worn trail where he could be seen.

Time travel was a closely guarded secret among his people and this young man needed to be cautioned. Bob was still quite agile for an old fellow. He quickly had Aeneas by the scruff of his fleece yanking him from the edge of the timestream.

"What the heck?" yelled Aeneas. He whipped around to see an old man smirking at him with two little girls standing wide-eyed behind him. "You should be more careful, son. You're not in the bush. These trails are busy in the summer," said Bob North Sky sternly.

This chance encounter on the trail would change Bob's life and the lives of many others. Later, Aeneas, too, would identify this as a pivotal moment. Until then he had been his own teacher, but now he became the student of Bob North Sky, the man who would teach him to honor shamanic rules of time travel. Meeting Bob opened up many new possibilities in his research and understanding of time travel, far beyond what he'd been able to discern on his own.

Sheila greeted Cassie at the airport with a hug. They chatted about everyday things while her bags were loaded into the self-driving electric taxi, but no real conversation occurred until they were settled in at Sheila's bed and breakfast.

Sheila's house had a cedar facade, with a sharply angled bright red roof that gave it a cheery geometric appearance. The rectangular windows were tall to let in plenty of light and the spacious six bedroom home had a ladder in the living room to access a loft that was used for her guests. The house had hardwood floors scattered with old bear hides that served for rugs, totem carvings she had rescued from a burn pile hung as wall art, as well as paintings and photographs from native artists. She served Cassie lemon balm and peppermint tea at one of the small hand carved tables set up for guests in the large kitchen.

"Your mother's call was a surprise. Your father is the most experienced traveler I've ever known besides my old papa." Sheila smiled gently at Cassie, sipped her tea and waited for Cassie to speak.

Sheila had first met Cassie when she was just five years old. All her grandkids called her Nana Shi-Shi, and so for Cassie, she was always just Shi-Shi. When she finally spoke, Cassie's voice trembled with emotion, "I've got to find him, Shi-Shi."

Sheila nodded sympathetically. "I've never heard of anyone following another when they enter the timestream, but then we've all learned many new ideas over the years since my papa began helping Aeneas study travelers."

'Travelers' was a reference to time travelers, of which Sheila was not. Sheila had three brothers and one sister and none of them could enter the space-time continuum. However, some of their children were travelers. Sheila's eldest daughter, as well as two nephews, could enter the timestream. Her father and Aeneas had been helpful guiding them, especially when they were teenagers. Sheila felt she owed quite a debt to them both for without their help she might have lost her daughter many times.

Cassie teared up at the mention of Aeneas's work with Bob. Sheila took her hand and gave it a motherly squeeze. "The timestream is often open here," Sheila said to Cassie encouragingly. "You can leave to search for your father when you are ready."

Cassie took a deep breath, wiped the corners of her eyes and decided it would cost her nothing to be brave, so she shared her plan with Sheila, willing herself to sound optimistic.

"I've seen the opening several times today, so I'm hopeful that tomorrow after lunch something will catch my eye."

Sheila smiled and gave her a stout nod of approval. "Yes, it's best you rest today and eat well before you attempt this rescue. I'll make you a hearty dinner tonight and we will go to bed early."

"Thanks, Shi-Shi," whispered Cassie gratefully. Sheila's presence always made her feel supported.

"No thanks needed. I love to cook. And I want to help." Sheila stood and walked around the kitchen table and planted a kiss on Cassie's forehead.

~

The next day Cassie ordered an electric car and arrived at her favorite sushi place just before noon. She finished off two Denali rolls and a bowl of miso soup, then headed towards Campbell Creek Trail. She walked and walked heading towards Far North Bicentennial Park. Every step made her even more sad and for a few minutes, tears slid down her face. Nothing so big had ever been asked of her. She wiped her tears with her shirt sleeve and kept moving.

The sun hitting Cassie's face brought a spontaneous smile. It broke through the trees, warming her tear-soaked eyelids. As a child of the Pacific Northwest, Cassie loved the sun on her face. She blinked away the sunlight and there it was, just to her left. Cassie glanced around cautiously. The trail was empty in both directions. She stepped left towards some shrubbery, knowing she didn't have to enter the timestream. Time was hers. A gift she would one day come to cherish.

Cassie centered herself, took a deep breath and recalled the day of the quake. She focused on her family's home in West Seattle, imagining it in her mind's eye. Cassie leaned in like an arrow, focused on the moment she needed and saw the day opening up like a gigantic flower just ahead.

Tabitha was in the garden and Aeneas in the kitchen. She made for the living room and arrived on the couch with a thump, but before she could stand up the couch started to shake violently. She leaped off the couch, gingerly making her way towards the kitchen.

The opening of the timestream was enormous, larger than she'd ever experienced. It filled the kitchen, like a curtain pulled back on another reality. Cassie felt like she was being sucked into a vacuum and it took all her energy to resist.

Aeneas dropped a cast iron skillet, clipping his big toe. He yelled, trying to stay upright, but the ground shaking thrust him towards the counter. Aeneas smacked his head on the granite edge and collapsed. He rolled into the timestream with Cassie seconds behind him.

Aeneas had lost consciousness, and his arms and legs were flailing uncontrollably. Cassie reached out to grab any part of him without success. Aeneas was slipping further back into his timeline and Cassie couldn't reach him. She grabbed at his right foot and his sandal came off. Cassie leaned into his direction, willing herself to close the distance but she was too far behind him as Aeneas merged into a blur of people and places that looked vaguely familiar. Cassie pulled back. It could be the difference of days or even weeks and she couldn't risk getting stranded.

Suddenly overcome with fatigue, Cassie faltered then steeled herself and imagined the front door of Sheila's bed and breakfast. She aimed for her present, but botched her landing because her legs gave out from under her. Exhausted, Cassie grabbed the railing of Sheila's front porch. Back-to-back trips had drained her. Sheila heard the commotion and rushed to the door. Cassie was pale and sweaty. Sheila knew from her father that prolonged exposure within the timestream was physically taxing. Add in any kind of stress and the effect was magnified, leaving the person spent, as if they had been running for their lives.

Sheila brought her into the living room and piled on several blankets. She rushed to the bathroom and ran the water for the tub, filling it with Epsom salts. Then she hurried back to the kitchen and ladled a cup of warm bone broth she had simmering on the stove in anticipation of Cassie's return.

Cassie sipped broth while she waited for the tub to be filled. Once she finished, Sheila helped ease her into the hot water, and within a few seconds, Cassie's teeth stopped chattering. She would need at least a day of rest to recover.

CHAPTER 42

Cassie the Hypno-Traveler

AFTER THE LONG BATH, Cassie sat on a cushioned stool along the polished stone counter while Sheila prepared her special homemade cereal. She wiped her hands on a towel and sat down next to Cassie with a sigh.

"Where do you think your father landed?" she asked.

Cassie sighed, closing her eyes, thinking back.

"I could see it was West Seattle because I remembered many of the same landmarks from my childhood."

"A puzzle for you to solve, eh?" Sheila smiled. Her father loved puzzles and taught her to appreciate the process of solving.

"I also saw a red Volvo station wagon and people nearby. I'm fairly certain one of them was my Grandpa Archie," said Cassie hopefully.

"So, you have a clue, one that could lead you to your father." Sheila nodded with confidence. Cassie nodded back but didn't share Sheila's confidence. She was worried about contacting her mom.

Cassie snuggled into the moose embroidered throw pillows on the bed, pulled the woodland themed coverlet over her and enabled the small rectangular device, her SAIL, to generate a full-body holographic communication portal. Once enabled, the device projected a hologram to both users. Back in West Seattle, Tabitha's face formed a rare smile as Cassie's hologram appeared in her kitchen where she was making dinner. She was relieved that her daughter had returned safely. Their conversation was brief as Cassie needed to rest. Tabitha reminded her about the report that was urgently needed by her uncle and Harold to pin down the location of her father.

Cassie quickly sent a video of herself to Harold and Socrates describing what happened. Then she drew notes along the side with detailed information she recalled, including the glimpse of the red Volvo. Once Cassie was finished, her head sunk into the pillows, and she slept for a few hours.

Later that day Cassie woke from a deep sleep. She felt rested and decided to find Sheila. Wandering around the bed and breakfast, she came upon Sheila in the tiny studio at the back of her house working to conserve an old carving.

Sheila, who had been pondering Cassie's rescue attempt, motioned her into the studio and started chatting straight away.

"Cassie, my cousin Sandra might be able to help you recall some smaller details from your experience in the timestream."

Sheila smiled and her eyes seemed to brighten. She had not been born an optimist, but life had taught her that patience and faith were the best ways to keep moving on your path.

"You said you were struggling, trying to catch your father's foot, right? Maybe you glimpsed a piece of this puzzle that shows a clearer picture of the past."

Cassie shrugged, still feeling hopeless. "What can she do?"

"Sandra helps people find lost memories," said Sheila cheerfully.

Patting Cassie's hand reassuringly, Sheila continued, "She will be here soon to help you, my dear one, but for now, let's go into the kitchen and have some good food."

Sheila began preparing the stuffed salmon, while Cassie sat at the counter watching her bustle around the kitchen assembling the ingredients. Sheila beamed as she placed the food into the Nimble Chef and this took Cassie back for a moment. She giggled and recited the commercial for the cooking device, "a revolutionary kitchen aid that can cook or cool any food to its ideal temperature!"

Both Sheila and Cassie laughed.

"I'm so grateful Harold invented this cooker! I could just kiss him every time I use it!"

Within minutes the salmon was baked to perfection. Dinner was casual and Sheila maintained the jovial atmosphere by inquiring about Lux, Tor and Tabitha.

Sandra called into the house from the front door. Both women were in the kitchen putting away leftovers and loading the dishwasher. Sheila called back, and Sandra took off her shoes and made her way to the kitchen.

Smiling as she entered, Sandra looked like a miniature version of Sheila, who was much taller owing to her mother's island genes. Her frizzy gray hair and piercing black eyes were striking. Cassie smiled as Sandra walked towards her with open arms.

"I always introduce myself with a hug, Cassie. I hope you don't mind." Cassie was a little surprised, but she smiled and returned the gesture.

With the introductions over, Sheila ushered them into a room on the first floor that served as the bed and breakfast library. The room contained three firmly cushioned sky blue chairs with antique side tables next to each. Scores of books lined the cases that were built into the walls. At Sandra's request, Sheila closed the blackout curtains and began lighting candles.

Cassie sat in one of the blue chairs and Sandra scooted the other chair next to hers and sat down, too. Sandra explained that she was a trained counselor and would use hypnosis to guide Cassie back through the event. She wanted Cassie's brainwaves to reach just below the alpha state and enter the theta state. This would allow memories gathered by her unconscious mind to come into her consciousness. Drumming would help achieve this. Once the room was ready, Sheila placed Cassie's SAIL on a table next to her to capture the event so it could be streamed to Socrates and Harold for further analysis.

From her bag, Sandra carefully pulled out a caribou hide drum and mallet. With a nod she passed them to Sheila, who was sitting a little further back in the third chair. Sheila closed her eyes and began drumming, lulling Cassie into the rhythm. Sandra stayed silent for several minutes to allow Cassie's brainwaves to sink deeper into the theta state.

Finally, Sandra spoke softly to Cassie, "Listen to the drum and let your gaze rest on the candles. Relax as your mind journeys back to the moment you arrived in your family's kitchen."

Cassie thought back, though it felt different from before when she'd tried to recall what had happened. Before it was so fast and now there was a slow-motion element to the memories and she could discern more details.

"I stopped in the doorway to steady myself. Dad was struggling. He'd dropped a skillet on his foot then fell forward." Cassie winced, but pressed on.

"He hit his head on the edge of the stone counter. My stomach hurts just seeing this..." Cassie hunched over, moving her hands to her abdomen. "The impact to his head was hard... he must be really hurt... Now he's on the floor, unconscious and the timestream is wide open."

Her voice became tremulous as she struggled to speak, "It has this weird effect on us... it pulls on us like a magnet. Normally we can resist it. It's too powerful, though... way too powerful." Cassie's breathing was shallow and tears flowed quickly down her face as she wept.

Sheila stopped drumming and moved toward Cassie to wipe her eyes with a tissue, but Sandra rapidly motioned her back and pointed to the drum.

"Go on, Cassie. What happened next," urged Sandra as the drumming resumed.

"He was pulled into the stream. I can hear Mom outside, yelling for him. She's scared. I'm following him, but he's unsteady and flailing everywhere. If he would just reach out to me..."

Cassie sniffed and choked back more tears. "If he would just lean back or if we could focus on the same time, I could catch up to him."

Sandra knew that critical information pertaining to Aeneas's rescue was imminent, so she began her questioning in earnest.

"Where are you now, Cassie?"

"Dad is flying back into his past and I'm trying to grab his foot, but the sandal came off." Cassie's face tensed up in anguish.

Sandra dropped her voice. "Okay Cassie, look beyond Aeneas to the image in the tunnel ahead. What do you see?"

"He's falling back into his childhood. I see Grandpa Archie," Cassie said with surprise.

"He's handsome, and oh... he's loading the car, a red Volvo station wagon and he's putting a baby carrier of some kind into the car... and there's an old house, and oh... that's Dad..." Cassie smiled spontaneously, so happy to see her father.

"He... he looks to be about four years old. This is his Montessori school."

Suddenly Sandra remembered the license plates from her childhood and pressed Cassie. "Look carefully at the car! Can you see the license plate?"

"Um, yes, it says 2005!" said Cassie excitedly.

"Now, Cassie," said Sandra, slowing down. "Look for other details, anything that could tell you about the date or time of year."

Cassie's brow furrowed and she wiped sweat from the side of her face. She scanned what was before her, but there was nothing helpful in the image. She could see her father was walking towards the car parked on the street, behind him the old two story Craftsman-style house had kids' pictures taped in the windows.

"I don't see anything useful," said Cassie, tiring. "There are pictures taped in the windows of stick figures, hearts and flowers but, wait..." Cassie paused as she registered details from the drawings, "all the pictures have children and their moms."

"Cassie, look at the trees," prompted Sandra. "Tell me what you see."

Cassie was struggling to focus and her voice was fatigued. "Um...they're all leafed out. Baskets of flowers are hanging on the porch."

"Cassie, I am going to bring you back now. I want you to imagine we are leaving a movie theater and climbing steps towards the lobby."

Sandra paused so Cassie's mind could engage the visual. "We are nearly to the top and when we open the doors you will slowly open your eyes."

Cassie opened her eyes and looked over at Sheila, who had just walked in with a glass of water and a cloth to wipe her face. Sheila hoped that the new information would guide them to Aeneas, but all she could see in Cassie's face was disappointment.

CHAPTER 43

Puzzling Out
the Pieces

CASSIE FLEW BACK TO Seattle the next afternoon and made her way home. She wanted to come back with a definitive plan to find her father. She wanted to relieve her mother's grief. And she especially wanted to feel that time travel meant something—that it had a purpose just beyond the novelty it had been most of her life.

The next morning Harold was bustling about in his lab when Cassie walked in with two green smoothies.

"My dear Cassie!" Harold exclaimed. "Is that smoothie for me?" he asked, grinning, bobbing his bushy old man eyebrows up and down.

"Yes, Harold," said Cassie absently. "You know I always bring you whatever I am drinking."

This was, of course, their thing. Cassie and Harold always brought each other any new food, drink, recipe, or gadget the other found interesting. It was a connection they had begun when she was very small. Harold had always taken an extra interest in Cassie and seemed to favor her over the boys, bringing her unique things to try out.

Cassie teared up briefly. How had she not realized this sooner? Had Harold known her already? Knew she would be born and what she would be like as an adult? *No*, thought Cassie to herself. *Wouldn't I have sensed the change in our relationship?*

"Something wrong, dear?" inquired Harold in between sips of his smoothie.

"It's been a hard few weeks," said Cassie, taking a long sip.

Harold's mood was quite the opposite of Cassie's. "Well, I for one am extremely pleased with the results of your hypnosis in Anchorage. We have a recognizable time frame within the year. It should be easier to plan a trip back to find Aeneas."

Cassie looked up at Harold, taken aback. "What's the time frame?"

"May, sometime before or after Mother's Day which in 2005 was on May 8th. The pictures on the window of the Montessori school were an easy clue. The merry, merry month of May is where we'll send you back in time to find your father," sang Harold with enthusiasm. Cassie recoiled discreetly as she turned her back to him. Old Harold was always cheerful and she found that annoying, even odd. Young Harold was less so. He was edgier, skeptical about life. Cassie realized that she was missing him.

"Harold, I can't spend the entire month of May looking for Aeneas," snapped Cassie. "It would be better if we had a more approximate time. Those pictures might have been up for a week before or after Mother's Day. That leaves about two weeks for me to search. Have you run this by Uncle Sox? Did he have any insights?" She threw a frosty look in his direction, but Harold paid it no mind.

"Socrates was only seven or eight at the time. After he watched the video nothing seemed to pique his memory. He recalled the Montessori school and the red Volvo, but that was the extent of his recollections," said Harold.

Cassie shrugged. "What about Grandma?"

"Cassie, I don't think Socrates or Persephone will want to tell their eighty-four-year-old mother that her son is missing," chided Harold, which set Cassie off even more.

"My grandmother isn't frail—she's still a practicing scientist and eventually she will want to see her son, Harold." Cassie met his eyes with her exacting stare, a stare inherited straight from Miranda thought Harold.

"You're right, but Archie's death was sudden and it hit her hard. She spent nearly three-fourths of her life with him and they were always very much in love," said Harold fiercely, letting go of his well-controlled emotions. Harold had never married or found anyone that he wanted to spend his life with. This was his one big regret. Cassie noticed his countenance shift and backed off her argument.

"So, you think it should be my mom?" asked Cassie, but Harold didn't answer. He seemed to have deflated and Cassie regretted her animosity towards him. She patted him on the back, assuring him she would handle it.

Later that day, Socrates, Lux, Cassie and Harold were all waiting in Tabitha's kitchen while she privately conferenced with Miranda via SAIL. Given their history, Socrates had politely declined to call his mother when Cassie asked. So it was now up to Tabitha to break the news.

As they sat around the table waiting, everyone was quiet. Finally, Lux looked over at his uncle. "Why aren't you with Mom making the call to Grandma Mimi?" It seemed only logical to Lux that his Uncle Socrates should also be in on the conversation as his father's older brother.

Socrates cleared his throat. "Well..." he stopped for a second, exchanging a glance with Harold. "The thing is, when your dad decided not to attend college, it left our parents stunned and hurt."

Harold knew what was to come next, but Cassie and Lux sat up straight as their uncle continued.

"The 'why' of his choice was more difficult to describe. Your dad patiently explained how he could travel through time to our parents. He detailed what he knew about his abilities, the connections to high energy events, the research and data he'd collected and his plan for the future. He also told them about the support he'd received from me and Harold..." Socrates looked over at Harold and a nod passed between them. They'd both taken a hit for keeping that secret, Socrates more so than Harold.

"My parents wanted proof, obviously, and Aeneas, understanding their hesitancy, was intent on providing it," said Socrates, leaning back in his chair, looking pointedly at Harold.

"Around twenty minutes passed and he returned with a neatly folded newspaper from the day he was born and a fresh loaf of bread with an eighteen-year-old sell-by date on it." This caused chuckles from everyone at the table.

At this juncture, Harold joined in the story. "Ultimately, Aeneas made a compelling case for working on his own experiments. He wanted to determine if there was a gene sequence that enabled him to see and access the space-time continuum. Even though Archie and Miranda had reservations, they supported and aided his research."

Socrates sighed, recalling the other outcomes. "My mom was hurt. She wished Aeneas had trusted them enough to share his secret. My dad laid the blame at my feet..."

Harold reached over and gave Socrates a brotherly pat on the back. "Your Grandpa Archie held certain ideas and traditions about older brothers. He thought it was his eldest son's duty to inform them, so they had the opportunity to support their younger son."

Lux and Cassie had not spoken, their faces a mixture of surprise and concern. Socrates noticed this and clarified, "Aeneas's secret didn't divide us, but it did cause small wounds here and there."

Twenty minutes or so had passed and Socrates felt somewhere in the universe he was in trouble with his dad. Just then Tabitha came back into the kitchen. Cassie and Lux both noticed she looked brighter, even her voice seemed more hopeful.

"Miranda knew something wasn't right. She'd been dreaming of Aeneas the past week and had sent him a message three days ago, but he never responded." Tabitha paused, and everyone was quiet. She gestured towards Cassie. "We watched the recording of Cassie's hypnosis. Miranda remembers that time in her life, including the old red Volvo, Aeneas's Montessori school, but she can't recall Mother's Day of that year."

Harold chimed in, "It's a small detail, but if we could determine when those drawings were put up at the Montessori school, we could narrow the time frame."

"Uncle Sox, are you sure there's not a faint memory that was evoked by the video?" asked Cassie eagerly.

Socrates hadn't contributed much to their discussion after his story. He shook his head no, staying silent. It seemed they had reached a stalemate. Everyone agreed to sleep on it and regroup the next day.

CHAPTER 44

Uncovering an
Anxiety Anomaly

CASSIE WAS GETTING READY for bed when a hologram greeting from her cousin Missi projected above her SAIL. She yelled open from across the room to accept the call. Missi and Thena were Cassie's main confidants as she had no other close female friends. The hologram opened up life-sized with Missi curled up on her couch in a pair of blue silk pajamas.

"Hey time traveler, glad to see you home and in one piece. Thena and I were a little worried about you. There was a lot of pressure with this trip."

Cassie wished she could reach into the hologram and hug her; she was still so sad about the outcome of her journey into the past. "It was disappointing. I nearly caught his foot and then he was gone... somewhere into the past of our fathers." Cassie forced herself to smile back, albeit weakly.

"Well I for one would love to visit the past of our fathers. I can't believe you saw your mom, your dad, Aunt Seph, and met 'Socrates the Ladies' Man'." Missi giggled and mimicked a smoldering look from her father she'd seen in an old photo. Her dad had dated many women before he'd fallen in love with their mother, Keniah. She was the last woman he ever dated. Archie and Miranda knew the moment they met her she'd put a much welcome end to his serial dating.

"I feel like there was something Uncle Sox was not sharing about his childhood. Has your dad ever told you any stories from when he was young? He couldn't recall much from when he was eight years old, though to be fair it was nearly fifty years ago."

Missi tapped her fingers on her chin. It was an odd gesture, but a familiar one. Her grandpa Archie and her Aunt Seph were also chin tappers. "Nothing comes to mind, except a story Mom told me and Thena. Though it's not so much of a story of then, as it is of now."

Cassie waited. It could take Missi a few minutes to come to the point. Cassie settled in for a long explanation.

"Mom mentioned on a few occasions that Dad had night terrors when they were first married. He would wake up from sleep, yelling and flailing, covered in sweat..." Missi stopped for a second and shook her head sadly. Cassie gave her a perplexed look. "She also said he suffered from panic attacks. I remember an incident that happened when I was about nine years old. Thena and I were with a group of kids and parents at the Washington State Fair."

Missi took a sip of tea and continued, "You know how we loved roller coasters." Missi gave Cassie her best impression of riding a roller coaster with hands up and mouth open, then went on.

"Anyway, we became separated from my parents in the crowd and Dad had a panic attack." Missi paused before the finale of her story. Cassie was wide-eyed and motioned her to keep going. "And this I found surprising... she slapped him in the face and told him to get a hold of himself and help her find us."

Cassie was quiet. This was the oddest thing she had ever heard. No one in her family had ever mentioned anything about the girls going missing at the state fair, much less that her Uncle Sox suffered from panic attacks. When she met young Uncle Sox a few weeks ago, he was breezy and confident. Her mind was reeling.

Missi interrupted her thoughts. "Cass, I can see your wheels turning. What are you thinking?"

"I think I need to talk to my mom. A person who has night terrors and panic attacks has experienced a trauma," said Cassie slowly.

"He saw a counselor after what happened at the fair. My mom insisted. She said she needed him to be able to cope with stressful situations without falling apart." Missi tilted her head with a knowing expression. "You know what she's like."

Cassie nodded. Her Aunt Keniah was five foot two, but every inch of her was reactive; her childhood in Chicago's South Shore neighborhood had molded a fast thinker, with nimble reflexes. She wasn't methodical like Socrates. While Keniah was also a physicist, her physics was action-based. She used physics to find solutions to problems, and two missing daughters would have been a huge problem.

"Thanks, Missi. My mom has to know something about this." Cassie was certain Tabitha would have heard the story of the girls getting lost. But after relaying the story to her, Cassie was stumped. Tabitha's shock was genuine. She'd never known Socrates to have a panic attack or that her nieces were lost at the state fair.

Cassie met Harold the next day. He'd been around Socrates most of his life. Perhaps he might have some recollection, but his response was also disappointing.

"Never knew that about Socrates, though I am not surprised," said Harold a little sadly. "Sometimes the exterior we present to the world hides a complex interior of feelings and reactions that we'd prefer not to share."

"Who else might know about this?" asked Cassie. She felt like she was onto something and needed more information.

Harold probed with his usual question set when he sensed a sticking point that might become an obstacle. "Do you need to know? Will it help your search for your father or just distract you?"

Cassie stopped to think. "Your point is taken, Harold, but my gut is telling me to follow this."

Harold pointed her to the only person he thought could uncover this, if Socrates himself was not forthcoming. "What about Miranda? If there were some trauma in Socrates' life then his mother would surely know about it."

Cassie considered this and sent a quick message to her grandmother. The response was swift; only five minutes had passed but it only furthered her suspicions.

It's best if you ask Socrates about it. All that happened a long time ago and I'm not sure he wants to dredge up the past.

She showed Miranda's message to Harold who responded with a humph. "Well that's odd—really odd. Miranda was never one to dismiss a question." Harold and Cassie sat in his office. Her feet were twitching. What she was thinking seemed a bit ridiculous to her.

"Your feet betray you, Cassie," said Harold, pointing down at her toes. "Let's have it."

Cassie smiled. Harold could read her as well as Tabitha. "It's not practical, Harold, but I have a good relationship with Uncle Sox in 2015 and he was only nine years out from his eight-year-old self. He might have a better recollection of that time."

Harold was silent. Sending Cassie back to his past made his stomach lurch. When she departed in 2015, Harold had missed Cassie terribly, more than he'd ever realized and he'd waited years and years for her to be born. Meeting her had changed his life. Would seeing her again change his life even more? He was an old man now. When they met in the past she was twenty-five and he was twenty-eight. And now she was still twenty-five and he was sixty-six. He didn't want anything to disrupt what he'd come to know as his life, but Cassie was right. Socrates at seventeen might be able to recall more of that time in his life, even have access to pictures and details from the Montessori school.

Waving her hand in front of his face, Cassie tried to bring him back. "Harold, should I take your silence as skepticism or deep pondering?"

"Well I was just thinking of the impact it might have on all of our lives if you visited the past again," said Harold quietly.

Cassie felt emboldened and reassured Harold.

"It would be a quick trip. One, maybe two days. Then, if I had enough information, I could travel to 2005 and search for my dad."

"That trip could prove to be much more difficult for you, Cassie. No one will be there for you to..." Harold stopped. He realized he would be in Chimacum, not yet old enough to drive, working his way to an early graduation and full ride to the University of Washington.

Cassie waved her hand in front of Harold's face again. "Harold, finish your thought."

"Well I was just pondering the possibilities available to you in 2005. There aren't many. For instance, what if Aeneas has amnesia and doesn't recognize you? You won't have anyone to help you. And what if there's no energy event? You might get stuck for days or longer," said Harold. He turned away from her and looked towards the sky. Something else was bothering him.

Cassie wasn't fazed. "Lux has been searching the UW archives and he found an earthquake, 2.5 magnitude, that hit Whidbey Island around 2:45 p.m. on May 18th. I have a ride home, Harold. Don't worry."

Harold nodded. Would his life change again, and if so, would he know any different? What if tomorrow things were not the same because of her actions in the past? Could he document all of this somewhere on his SAIL? Would he then be able to determine the before and aftereffects of her trip? Harold's mind was cycling all these ideas, as if a dozen hamsters on their wheels were taking their afternoon exercise.

CHAPTER 45

Not So Happy
Reunion

CASSIE WAS FORTUNATE THAT Mount St Helen's had seen an uptick in seismic activity, with swarms of earthquakes keeping the area on high alert. Lux ordered an electric self-driving car to bring them to Amboy, Washington. He'd checked the weather archive, reminding Cassie to wear very warm clothes as she would step into a cold, rainy day in early November 2015.

Lux drank a cup of coffee with Cassie in a local pastry shop while she read a real book with paper pages. While newspapers and magazines had largely been replaced with digital versions, Pacific Northwesterners held fast and hard to traditional books. Tabitha had hypothesized this had to do with the length of time the human brain could tolerate a screen, even the new holographic ones with softer lighting that allowed you to move in and out of them.

Shorter reading materials had gone digital, but novels written on paper had never become obsolete. Cassie mused over this as she held a book by her grandfather's favorite author, Ivan Doig. When Grandpa Archie had passed away, her grandmother had sent her his collection of Ivan Doig books and Cassie was working her way through the lot.

It was a welcome distraction as she was doing her best to avoid thinking about young Harold. His short cropped blonde hair and hazel eyes, framed with light brown rectangular glasses gave her a flutter of excitement. Reluctantly, she shook her head to reset her mind, and went back to reading.

Lux worked on his doctoral thesis, scribbling away on a sheet of paper, which few people did now as well. Lux loved the noise that the pencil made on the paper. It helped his brain stay focused, lulling him into a meditative state where his thoughts flowed freely.

A half hour passed, and Cassie sensed a shift. She gave her brother a peck on the cheek and walked outside the pastry shop. As she rounded the corner, the timestream was open nearby. She ducked behind a shrub and stepped inside. The infinite colors of sparkles and pink golden atmosphere were lovely and yet there was no warmth, only the coolness.

Cassie focused her mind on 2015, thinking of the first days of November in West Seattle. She zipped down her timeline until reaching the beginning, then willed herself onto Aeneas's line. She saw a cold, rainy day emerge before her and landed neatly in the PCC parking lot. No one would notice her since people were always coming and going, often looking down at their phones.

Harold was walking slowly down California Avenue. He'd been in a funk in the days since Cassie had departed, and even the Entwistles had taken note of Harold's listlessness. Earlier that morning Persephone had made a critical remark regarding the folding of her laundry as she ate Harold's apricot and cashew granola. Harold couldn't even be bothered to correct her. Miranda, however, took her daughter adroitly by the arm and had a stern chat with her in the living room.

Later, she told Archie, "We have a housekeeper to support our family, not to create entitled little tyrants who complain about their laundry."

Archie nodded in agreement. "You are absolutely correct my dear, but why didn't Harold just take her down a notch? Normally he's quick to respond to any disrespectful commentary."

Miranda looked over at her husband, "Harold has been a little off since he and Socrates came back from California." Archie nodded in agreement.

Harold looked up from his phone as he crossed into the PCC Market parking lot. Chicken pot pie had been requested by Aeneas, whose appetite continued to demand constant feeding. While his heart was not quite in it, Harold would undertake this dish because he could double the recipe and feed the Entwistles for two nights, giving him more time to ponder time travel.

Next to a dark blue SUV, Harold spotted a woman. She had been bent over tying her shoe, or so it seemed, and now she'd risen. *I'm hallucinating*, thought Harold. *That looks like...* Was it Cassie? *No, it couldn't be her,* he said to himself. She was gone. Harold rubbed his eyes for five full seconds and when he opened them she was walking towards him.

Cassie waved enthusiastically and called out, "What luck! I was looking for you, Harold."

Harold did not move. Cassie grabbed his jacket sleeve, leaned in and kissed his cheek. Harold gasped and blushed, shaken to his core. She was not a hallucination!

"Hey, it's okay," she whispered. "I had to come back. I'll explain it all over a pumpkin spice latte."

Harold followed Cassie to Freshy's where they snagged a booth next to the fireplace and ordered lattes and sandwiches. Although part of him was glad to see Cassie, *very* glad indeed, Harold also felt conflicted by her return. The story took nearly an hour. Harold was particularly interested in Shelia, her family, and Aeneas's connection to the Alaskan shaman, Bob North Sky.

Harold swallowed the last bit of his now cold latte and scratched the inside of his ear. A gesture Cassie noted that was endearing when he was an old man, but somehow less appealing for the younger version.

"I guess we need to find Socrates," said Harold absently.

Cassie smiled and replied brightly, "I was hoping to make this trip quick. If he could meet with me this afternoon, I might be able to return home today if the timestream stays open."

Harold nodded and sent Socrates a text. The conflict he was feeling was now evident. His posture sagged a bit and Cassie leaned across the table and said, "Are you alright? I know it was a shock to see me again so soon, but I was looking forward to coming back here. It's like watching a prequel," said Cassie, giggling.

But Harold was not amused. He was struggling with the fact that he had developed feelings for Aeneas and Tabitha's future daughter who was not even born yet. He knew in the future they already had a relationship firmly established in the platonic realms of grandfather-granddaughter and employer-employee. *How can I have feelings for someone who isn't even alive in my own time?* thought Harold. *And how will I ever find anyone if she keeps popping in and out of my life?*

Then Harold wondered the one question that he'd pushed to the back of his mind, a lonely part of himself that he rarely revealed: *Am I married in the future? Do I have my own children? Or am I alone because I kept foolishly hoping that Cassie and I could one day be together?* His reply to Cassie was a mixture of all these feelings combined with the pragmatic hard-wiring of his brain.

Harold looked up from his latte abruptly. "I've been thinking about the impacts of time travel and I'm not sure it's a good idea for you to keep popping in and out of a past where you're not even born yet. And I have a strong suspicion you are violating these shamanic rules you mentioned." Harold met her eyes. He could see she was taken aback by his comment.

Feeling chided, Cassie snapped back, "Harold, my father is still missing. I'm here to meet with Uncle Sox so I can find him. I won't be returning once I clear up some unusual information." Cassie slid out of the booth and started to leave.

Harold called out after her, "Hey, where are you going?"

Cassie turned to face him; her expression was cold. Harold felt this frostiness hit him right in the solar plexus.

"Socrates is headed this way. I'll meet with him privately." With that, she turned away from Harold and headed off her uncle before he could open the door.

CHAPTER 46

Altered Memory Healing

SOCRATES AND CASSIE WALKED north along California Avenue. She told him about her hypnosis and the clues she'd discovered that could lead to Aeneas's rescue. When they reached Hamilton Viewpoint Park, they settled on a bench that looked across Elliott Bay. The sun had come out for a few minutes and the city of Seattle briefly glowed in the late autumn light. Cassie was warm enough in her layers, but Socrates was underdressed and shivered in the cold November air.

"So he's lost somewhere in May 2005? Why doesn't he travel back to his present?" asked Socrates, frowning.

"We think it's likely the blow he took to his head caused some memory loss. Do you recall much about that time?" asked Cassie, watching him closely.

Socrates shrugged. "I was eight. We'd just moved to West Seattle and bought the house." Cassie scanned her young uncle's face. His demeanor was nearly the same now as when she asked his fifty-six-year-old self. Cassie sensed there was a piece of the puzzle lying just outside her peripheral vision and maybe seventeen-year-old Socrates would be more forthcoming than his middle-aged counterpart.

"Have you ever had a panic attack?"

Cassie's question was met with silence. Finally, Socrates spoke. His voice was flat, without inflection, as if speaking these words exhausted him. "I can, at times, become rattled... panicked even. And on occasion, I have been known to have a full panic attack."

Cassie ventured another question, but she did so softly without looking directly at him. "Do you know why? I mean, are there certain things that trigger your anxiousness?"

Socrates sank his head into his hands. "Generally, I become anxious or panicked when faced with information or situations that I can't control or endanger my safety or the safety of others." This statement sounded more upbeat, as if he had been taught to use this explanation to soothe himself.

This next question came straight from Tabitha. Cassie took a breath before she asked it. "Is there an event in your past linked to this anxiety? The reason I ask is because often anxiety can be attributed to a traumatic event in a person's past."

Socrates had spent years trying to forget *one day* in his childhood. And now he was sitting next to his future niece who was technically older and perhaps wiser than him at this moment. He envisioned one day he might take his niece to ride on a merry-go-round when she was still in diapers. But right now, she was here asking him very personal questions about a time in his life he'd rather not relive. He dropped his head in his hands once more and let out a long sigh.

Cassie put her arm around him, leaned in and whispered, "Socrates this might be important. Can you share a little with me? Then if it seems non-related, I'll pass on my hunch and change the subject."

It was a fair request. Socrates, like his father, Archie, appreciated fairness. Slowly lifting his head from his hands, he spoke apologetically, as if somehow he was responsible for what happened. Cassie had heard about this from Tabitha, too. Victims of traumatic events might assign blame to themselves. It was something Tabitha helped people work through in her practice.

"We'd just moved to West Seattle. Seph was a baby. Aeneas was a little guy playing soccer. I was eight years old and oddly enough, I was in the eighth grade. I was tutored in Latin too, as Mom insisted I needed it to absorb the biochemistry she was teaching me." He paused for a second. "Like Seph, my parents wanted me to interact with peers my own age and so I often went with Mom to Aeneas's soccer games and played with the other kids."

Socrates shifted on the bench then turned towards his niece. "Now, playing with other kids was a little weird because, for me, this consisted of less conversation and more physicality. I knew I couldn't start talking about physics." A slight eye roll crossed his face, which made Cassie smile.

"They were all Buzz Lightyear fans and my analysis of the movie *Toy Story* left them a little skeptical, so we mainly played hide-and-seek, threw a football, or searched for insects."

Socrates hadn't told this story to anyone before and it was harder than he thought.

He sighed, then continued, "Anyway, I was hanging around the soccer field and this strange homeless guy came up to me, grabbed my arm, and touched my face like this." Socrates stopped, reached over to Cassie and placed two hands gently to either side of each cheek before resuming his story. "Then he started to cry and tried to drag me away with him. It scared the crap out of me."

"Why was he pulling you?" exclaimed Cassie.

Socrates let out a breath. "I've no idea. The police thought he might have been on something or mentally ill. They decided it was not a deliberate kidnapping attempt, but it scared all of us, me, especially and it took a long time before I felt safe again." Socrates rubbed the sides of his arms to keep warm. He was cold and starting to feel tired.

Cassie was quiet. Did she really need to know more? Yes, she did.

"Socrates, this man, do you recall what he looked like?"

"Yes—the police sketch artist gave me a thorough quizzing. The man was older than my parents, tall, graying hair, and possibly biracial like me." Socrates furrowed his brow, trying to recall the exact image. "He was clad in a strange assortment of clothes, like homeless people wear."

Cassie pushed herself off the bench and took a few steps forward. Her heart was racing. Her face erupted in tears.

"Cassie, what's wrong?" asked Socrates, leaping off the bench.

Cassie was spinning around like a dog trying to get a comfy seat. She stopped abruptly then gasped. "Was it Dad? Did he recognize you?"

Socrates felt his knees weaken. He steadied himself with the bench and whispered hoarsely, "Call Harold" then sat down with a thunk.

The weather had gotten considerably colder and they needed a place to scrutinize the witness statements from the police report. Harold met them back at PCC Market and they all nursed cups of hot soup at a square table and commandeered another for Harold's laptop.

"Archie had me digitize and save files last year and these police documents were included," said Harold quietly.

Socrates ate some cheddar broccoli soup. His appetite surprised him. Normally when he thought about this incident, his insides felt like knots, but that seemed to have subsided and he filled in the details for Cassie and Harold without any anxiousness.

"Dad decided if this was some kind of scheme to blackmail or scare him into giving up some of his patents, he wanted the files handy to be able to make any connections," said Socrates as he stirred his soup.

Cassie pointed at the screen. "There's a statement here from one of the boys you were playing with at the time this man approached you."

"He says that the man went straight for you as soon as he saw you, but prior to that moment he was looking for something in a garbage can," said Cassie matter-of-factly.

Before Socrates could respond, Harold interjected, "If there were so many other children about, then why choose you, Socrates?"

Socrates had the good humor to scoff and say, "I've been wondering the same thing for the last nine years." He dunked a piece of cornbread into his soup and took a large bite. This made Cassie smile. How would Socrates' life change if the man who tried to kidnap him turned out to be his brother? His brother who may have been living on the streets for weeks with a concussion or amnesia, but his brother, nonetheless.

"After this incident no one ever saw him, correct?" asked Harold, trying to contain his excitement. He felt a hypothesis forming.

"Not for lack of looking. Some parents followed him, but he disappeared just outside the playfield. Dad even hired a private detective, but the guy seemed to have vanished, at least in West Seattle," said Socrates with another mouthful of soup and cornbread.

"Weird how that would happen, don't you think?" asked Harold, trying to guide Socrates towards his hypothesis.

"What are you saying, Harold?" Cassie could tell when he was holding back. Harold delicately chipped away at details with small questions until he tossed out the idea that was zinging back and forth in his mind.

"I'm saying he likely disappeared because Cassie here is going to travel back and bring him forward into his present."

"But that hasn't happened yet, Harold." Socrates said slowly buttering another piece of cornbread.

Harold smiled. "Hasn't it?"

Socrates contemplated this and gave Harold a sideways glance. "Perhaps." And that was his last word for a while.

Socrates finished off his soup. Today his life had changed because the terrifying event that had happened to him as a child was now something entirely different. The *bad man* was his brother Aeneas, who, hungry and confused, had recognized him and wanted his help.

After dinner that evening Socrates stopped by Aeneas's bedroom and bid him a goodnight and even gave Sput a good petting. Once his door was closed and his lights were out, Socrates nestled himself into bed and felt tears slide down the sides of his face, and they kept coming for several minutes. Finally, he rolled over, let loose and sobbed into his pillow until he was spent.

~

Eleanor welcomed Cassie back with open arms.

"My dear, how is it you are back with us?" asked Eleanor, who was quite pleased to see Cassie. She thought this was just the kind of young woman who could appreciate her sweet Harold, quirks and all.

"I'm only here for a day or so on business. Harold said you like company and suggested I stay here instead of a hotel," Cassie said with ease as Harold stood behind her completely gobsmacked. He'd forgotten to formulate an explanation for her return and the conversation Cassie referenced never happened. It was another example of how easily she could come up with a plausible explanation right on the spot.

After a lovely dinner of smoked pork tenderloin and roasted winter vegetables, Eleanor was dozing in her chair while Cassie and Harold were looking over the police report from May 16th, 2005 in the kitchen. Suddenly he found himself questioning his previous hypothesis.

"Have you considered that it might not be Aeneas?" asked Harold. It was the one thing he was worried about. Cassie would be going back further in time to a place where she had no one to support her efforts.

"Aeneas was thrown back sometime in May, near or after Mother's Day," said Cassie who got up from her chair, and stood behind it, stretching her legs. She felt antsy since they had been sitting for a while.

"For all we know he could have been living on the streets for a couple weeks. I know from my own observation that he took a blow to the head and was unconscious. The likelihood that it's him is plausible. In fact, I would ask you to consider Occam's razor." Cassie said this smartly as she resumed her seat and her face took on the look of one who has proposed a watertight argument.

Harold snorted, "Really? Occam's razor? I'm certain there are many scientists who would cry Occam's razor to explain away your father's disappearance after the earthquake rather than consider the fact that he's capable of entering the space-time continuum."

This sunk in for a second and Cassie blushed. Old Harold would have probed Cassie's thinking with some questions that would have allowed her to see the flaw in her argument. Young Harold eviscerated her argument without even considering her feelings.

"Damn it, Harold," hissed Cassie. "I know it's him. I feel it in my gut and I'm going back to 2005 to find my father and bring him home. And for the record, the older version of you is not such a jerk, so there's hope that you'll improve with age."

Harold threw his hands up in the air and yelled, "I can't believe I would ever hire someone as stubborn as you to work for me!"

They stared at each other for a few seconds. Harold felt an urge to pull her to him, dip her backwards and kiss her passionately, just like in those old movies that Eleanor watched. But Cassie quickly gathered the papers she'd been sorting and headed up stairs to the spare bedroom with Harold in her wake.

The raised voices woke Eleanor. She shifted, opened one eye, looked at Harold with a sleepy grin and said, "She's quite spirited, isn't she?" Then closed her eye and went back to sleep.

・ CHAPTER 47 ・

Force of Mother Nature

CASSIE WAITED FOR THE timestream to reopen. She and Harold had barely spoken that morning except to finalize details regarding her travel back to 2005. Prior to her return, Lux had checked several databases and it was easiest for her to simply wait, as there were many small earthquakes, from 1.5 to 2.0 on the Richter Scale that she could choose from to continue her search.

She cautiously visited West Seattle. Cassie wanted to stop by The Swinery and have another one of their lunch specials, but it was risky. Persephone had seen her once and so had Aeneas, though she was in disguise. In the end, her Entwistle appetite prevailed and Cassie settled in at a small corner table eating a smoked turkey and pickle sandwich, reading a newspaper. Although her peripheral vision occasionally caught the movement of other patrons, she paid no attention. Then she heard a familiar voice.

"Hello," said Tabitha cheerfully to the lady behind the counter. She recognized the woman from when she and Aeneas had come with Harold to get salami. "My mom sent me to get some different deli meats to make tiny triangle sandwiches for a potluck," said Tabitha politely. Tucked in the corner table just behind Tabitha, Cassie saw her mother and froze, holding her breath.

"Hi yourself. Nice to see you again." The congenial proprietress smiled back, contemplating for a moment. "How about a quarter of a pound of the smoked turkey, the salt-cured ham, the seasoned roast beef and maybe some spicy salami too?"

"Sure. Sounds great," said Tabitha, relieved that the proprietress knew just the right choices.

All of thirteen and she walks into a shop, so confident and friendly, thought Cassie. She felt tears come to her eyes and quickly wiped them away. Tabitha finished up her order and Cassie, not able to help herself, continued to watch as Tabitha collected the order and left.

Still awe-struck at seeing her teenage mother, Cassie quickly finished her lunch and made a hasty exit. She walked on with her newspaper, securing her backpack over both shoulders. Keenly aware that at any second she could leave West Seattle and enter the timestream, she stayed prepared to travel back to 2005.

Cassie headed towards the PCC parking lot and saw Martha and Tabitha loading the car with groceries. Again, she couldn't help herself and continued to watch them.

Tabitha had noticed the woman watching her at The Swinery. Now she seemed to be watching her again! Tabitha told her mother that she'd prefer to walk home and they parted ways. She noticed the woman's backpack was unusual in its style and colors, but something familiar about the woman's face piqued Tabitha's curious nature.

Tabitha decided to follow her. Although Tabitha did entertain the possibility that the woman had *not* been watching her, she was determined to test her intuition.

Cassie was heading towards a bus stop. She knew Harold would be back in Queen Anne by now and was feeling bad about how she'd left things. *Maybe I should go say goodbye just to him in case the timestream opens soon*, thought Cassie.

While Cassie made her way onto the bus, Tabitha entered soundlessly from the back and waited until the bus started moving. Her plan was to sit across from the woman, then wait to see her reaction. She could always get off at the next stop. It was risky behavior and not something Martha or George would condone, but Tabitha decided there were a sufficient number of passengers to witness anything suspicious, should it occur.

Cassie had purchased *The Seattle Times* and was busy reading it when Tabitha positioned herself diagonally opposite the mysterious woman who'd been watching her. Engrossed in the newspaper she had no idea Tabitha had noticed and was now following *her*.

Cassie read the opinion section for a few minutes and giggled quietly to herself. So much had changed. Then she continued with her favorite part of reading the paper, opening the pages wide, folding the paper in half and folding it over again to read the bottom of another page. As she glanced over the top of the folded page, Cassie saw her mother sitting across from her. She quickly arranged the newspaper to cover her face. Flushed, she started to panic. She'd been foolish to watch her mother a second time. Tabitha, even at age thirteen, was a force of nature.

The facial expression and newspaper shuffle were evidence enough to Tabitha that her presence had caused this woman significant consternation. As the bus stopped, Cassie grabbed her things and bolted towards the closest exit. Tabitha headed towards the same door and watched as the woman stepped off the bus, walked towards a hedgerow and vanished.

～

"She just disappeared?" said Aeneas with his feet propped in Tabitha's lap, lounging on the living room couch.

Martha and George had gone to a concert leaving Tabitha and Aeneas to look after Seth, who was playing a game of tug with Sput in the hallway. C.J. was working at the long granite bar that separated the kitchen from the living room. He was busy making kettle corn using a recipe he got from Persephone while listening intently as Tabitha described her encounter.

"Yes. She vanished! I doubt anyone noticed though. People were busy coming and going, most with their faces stuck in their phones." Tabitha frowned. She'd spoken out often to C.J. and Aeneas that their generation was at risk for becoming the least observant and most socially inept in human history.

"Describe her again, Tab." C.J. called out from the kitchen. He'd not completely warmed to the idea that his best friends were dating, but since Seth was around and Aeneas had promised there would be no kissing in front of him, things were less awkward and C.J. was enjoying himself as usual.

Tabitha moved Aeneas's feet to the left then stood, stretched, and decided a blanket would be nice. As she walked to the linen closet to get one, Tabitha tried to convey a clearer image for C.J. "The woman had greenish eyes, lovely curly brown hair, and she might've been multiracial. Her skin color was like milky coffee, and oh, she had these funny shaped ears." She could see C.J. cringe ever so slightly as she threw the blanket over herself and Aeneas.

"Funny how?" asked C.J. who was dusting the kettle corn with a bit of cinnamon sugar and placing it in bowls.

"Well at the top where most people's ears are rounded, hers had a tiny kink, meeting at a ninety-degree angle. I've never seen that shape of ear before." Even though she'd just gotten settled, Tabitha threw off the blanket and walked towards the kitchen, pulling Aeneas along as her model. She turned his head to the side and pointed to the location on his ear to show C.J. what she was talking about.

Aeneas rolled his eyes as he stood patiently then asked, "Why were you looking at her ears anyway?"

Tabitha spun him around playfully to face her. She leaned in nose to nose with him and said, "Because she had her face buried in a newspaper for a while so I looked carefully at what I could see, which were her ears..."

"So, her ears were pointy like an elf?" Seth had dropped into the conversation.

Tabitha turned to Seth and smiled as she and Aeneas walked back to the couch. "Not exactly like an elf, but yes, kind of pointy."

Seth glanced in the kitchen and shouted, "Hey, is it time for popcorn?" But C.J. was nowhere to be seen. Seth came around the corner and saw him sitting on the floor with a wild look on his face.

"Are you, okay, C.J.?" Seth walked into the kitchen and squatted down next to him. He was a friendly child and C.J. was his favorite cousin. He was always ready to lend a hand or an ear if anyone needed it.

"Can you get me a glass of water?" C.J. whispered. Seth nodded and brought him a drink.

C.J. experienced a revelation that he could tell no one. For years, he had studied Miranda Entwistle because she was a stunningly beautiful woman. He felt that better than most, he could recall all the details of her entire face, especially her ears which were unique. They were kinked at the top. None of her children inherited this trait. When he was younger he used to imagine she was part fairy.

Sput came to check on him and C.J. drew him in close and whispered, "Sput, a woman with kinked ears like Miranda that can vanish like Aeneas."

C.J. shivered. He wondered if this unusual woman was somehow related to Aeneas, especially since there was more he knew about Aeneas's disappearances than he'd yet shared with his two best friends.

CHAPTER 48

Time Travel
Extraction

Cassie knew she could leave at any moment, but she'd hoped her mind would be clear and focused, not a jumble from nearly being confronted by her teenage mother which, by the look on Tabitha's face, was what was coming next. Fortunately, as she exited the bus, the timestream bloomed in front of her and without much forethought, Cassie entered.

The closing of 2015 was a relief. The colors and faces flying by gave her a certain comfort. This reset her focus as she maneuvered further back on Aeneas's timeline. Thanks to her Uncle Socrates, she knew the date and time he thought a homeless man had tried to kidnap him.

In her mind's eye, she saw Hiawatha Playfield, a warm Sunday a week after Mother's Day. She flew through the timestream, aiming herself like an arrow as the day she wanted became clearer and more defined.

Cassie saw a spot to land near a clump of trees beside the tennis courts. She hurried towards the playfield where groups of children in brightly colored shirts were lining up to begin their pre-game warm up. In the distance, she saw mothers and fathers on the sidelines in chairs and amongst them she spotted her grandmother under an umbrella with a baby in her arms. On the field, she saw a little version of her father kicking the ball back and forth. It took enormous control to not run up and scoop him in her arms. She'd missed her dad so much.

Cassie scanned the area and saw a group of kids playing. Making her way towards them, she spotted a homeless man digging through a garbage can across the street. She wanted to call out to him then remembered her dad might have amnesia.

She smiled as Socrates ran past her, playing tag with boys his own age. He was happy and would remain so because the traumatic event that haunted him for so many years was about to be thwarted.

A sudden discomfort in Cassie's stomach caused her to halt. Questions ballooned in her brain at lightning speed. *Was Socrates' personality and thinking shaped by this traumatic event? Might he not marry Aunt Keniah? Would Missi and Thena not be born? Would he make different research choices? Was this meant to happen? What if Harold was right about someone's destiny being in the past?*

She sighed then wondered out loud in a barely audible voice, "Should I let this happen before I take Dad back?"

Cassie exhaled. Her gut told her to stand by. Aeneas was approaching the group of boys and Cassie purposely moved herself behind the situation, so she could grab her father as he was retreating from the red-haired superhero in yoga pants who would come after him. It unfolded just as Socrates had told them. Aeneas hurried away limping after the altercation.

Cassie caught up to him, interlocking his arm firmly into hers. "Dad, it's Cassie. I'm gonna bring you home, but we need to hide, fast. Come with me," she said urgently.

Aeneas had tears running down his face. He nodded and kept pace with Cassie as they made their way on the sidewalk towards a side street that ran along the back of PCC Market.

Realizing she might need to disguise Aeneas if the police had been called, Cassie gave her father a bright blue hoodie and black baseball cap that she carried in her backpack. Once inside the market, she bought him a chicken dinner and a large bottle of water. They sat at a table near the market deli and Aeneas devoured the entire meal before speaking.

"When are we?" groaned Aeneas as he eyed the hot food buffet.

"We're in 2005," said Cassie gently.

Aeneas seemed surprised. "How did I get here?"

Cassie was not sure how much to tell her father just yet. "It's quite a story, Dad. I'll give you the highlights."

Cassie glanced over at the doors, but it seemed she and Aeneas had escaped anyone's suspicion, so she began.

"There was a powerful earthquake along the Birch Bay fault line... it was significant. The timestream opened larger and more powerful than I'd ever experienced. You were swept in on a Sunday morning while making pancakes. You dropped the skillet and then smacked your head against the granite counter. It all happened fast..." Cassie trailed off for a few seconds, overcome with emotion. "You entered the timestream unconscious. I tried to follow you, but you were flailing around. I saw you slip back into your past, but I couldn't determine your exact exit point."

Aeneas rubbed his head. The knot was still tender.

"That little boy. Was that...?" Aeneas stopped as he lost his thought. He was intermittently regaining his memory.

Cassie smiled, answering, "Yep. It was Uncle Sox. You gave him quite a scare."

"So, my mom or dad were nearby, too?" Aeneas looked around the market, wondering if he would get to see Archie again.

Cassie kept smiling because she missed her dad so much, more than she'd allowed herself to feel. "You were playing soccer. Grandma was with Aunt Seph under an umbrella. I saw them. I saw you too, but I didn't see Grandpa."

Aeneas glanced over at the bakery. Cassie read his mind. "Need some cake?"

Aeneas smiled and nodded back at his daughter.

Cassie stood up to get the cake, planted a kiss on her dad's head and said, "I guess you could use some fattening up. Carrot cake it is."

Cassie walked over to the baker's rack, grabbed the biggest slice of cake then took it to the register and paid. Through years of time travel, Aeneas had stockpiled cash from different time periods and Cassie always brought hard currency to pay for things.

Aeneas finished his dessert in silence. Seeing Socrates had shifted something in his brain and his memory restored itself quickly. Every few minutes more and more information came flooding back to him. Cassie left him to his thoughts and called a cab to drive them to Mukilteo so they could catch the ferry to Whidbey Island the next day.

CHAPTER 49

Restore, Rehash, Return

IT WAS LATE AFTERNOON when they arrived in Mukilteo. The once sunny sky was now layered with low grey clouds. The smell of cool, clean rain mingled with salt air was cheering for them both. In the distance they could see a squall passing over Whidbey Island as they exited the cab and arrived at a lovely new hotel next to the ferry terminal.

Aeneas sent Cassie next door to Ivar's for a quart of clam chowder, a large order of fries, oatmeal cookies and several bottles of water. He had been weak, but the hot shower and food fortified him. With Cassie resting on her bed and Aeneas on his, they both sank into a food coma while they watched old television shows.

Suddenly Aeneas lifted his head and asked, "When's our opening?"

Cassie was snuggled under the covers. She finally had some peace. "Tomorrow. If we time it right we can leave from the ferry."

"Hmm. I've never entered the timestream from a ferry," said Aeneas, smiling.

Cassie laughed, so happy to be back with her dad. "Me neither, what fun!"

Aeneas looked over at Cassie. "Cass, baby, how did you find me?"

Cassie knew he would ask eventually.

"I knew you'd want to hear this story. Ugh. I suppose I'll have to move now," said Cassie, giving him a playful sideways glance as she pulled back the covers, got up and walked over to the seating area.

Aeneas returned the playful sideways glance and gestured to himself in his bed and cried out, "Have you seen me lately? You are definitely the one that has to move!"

Cassie laughed as she dragged an armchair between the beds, then sat down. She looked pointedly at her father. He rearranged the pillows to sit up straight. He knew his daughter well enough to know when a story was about to unfold and he was looking forward to it.

"You'd been missing for nearly a week. Harold and I were talking and he made a comment about how well his young brain used to work. It gave me the idea to go back and talk with him. Besides, it was about the time you became aware you could time travel. Maybe there was something obvious we'd missed."

"What did you think of young Harold?" Aeneas smiled at the memory of all the wonderful food and terrible advice Harold had given him.

Cassie's face grew warm and she sputtered, "He wasn't anything like old Harold. A bit of a handful, but we got along once

I convinced him of who I was. I had to convince Uncle Sox, too. Harold said we needed his help and in the end he came up with a simple suggestion, which I suppose if I hadn't been so distraught, I might've thought of myself."

"Sox and Harold? No one else?" asked Aeneas. He was probing and Cassie knew he wanted to know how much she had altered in the past.

"Well, you once sat next to me on a bench. Harold had disguised me as a nun when I was in West Seattle," said Cassie sheepishly.

"I don't remember that," said Aeneas, stopping to think back. "Though it was a very long time ago for me."

"It was the day of Mom's thirteenth birthday. I only heard part of the conversation, but I think you were talking to Sadie about something." Cassie waited to hear his response, or if he even remembered the conversation. Aeneas gazed out the window, his face fixed. Finally he murmured, "I haven't thought about Sadie in a long time."

Cassie was quiet and Aeneas continued to gaze out at the window at Whidbey Island in the distance. A few more seconds passed and Cassie pushed the conversation along.

"Anyway, when I returned home, you were still missing and Mom was, well I suppose still is a wreck." Aeneas broke free from his memories and took note of Cassie's weary expression. This had been an epic ordeal for all of them. He let out a long breath. "Oh Tab. She must be so worried. How long have I been gone?"

Cassie let out her own long breath, "We won't know for sure until we return back, but when I left again, it had been close to three weeks."

Aeneas shuddered. He'd never been gone more than two or three days from his present. Then he raised an eyebrow. "What do you mean left again?"

Cassie wiggled her way out of the chair, feeling the sudden need to stretch her legs. She paced back and forth across the room as she continued her story. "Well I came back from 2015 and we all met—Uncle Sox, Harold, Mom, me and Lux and it was decided that I would arrive just before the earthquake to see what had occurred and hopefully determine where and when you were lost. This was the simple suggestion from Socrates the younger version."

"Sox the what?" asked Aeneas, his face half smiling at what he knew must be a humorous reference about his brother.

"Seventeen-year-old Uncle Sox gave me the suggestion and we all agreed it was worth a shot. At least I might find some clues as to when you were lost," said Cassie brightly. She was feeling less edgy for the first time in weeks. She stopped pacing and returned to her chair.

Aeneas grabbed a cookie and smelled it. He had been so hungry. Cassie paused while he took a few bites, not minding at all that her father was tearing into the cookie like a wild predator.

"I went back to the day of the quake, then back to 2015 again after that. We couldn't figure out the correct day for me to enter 2005, even though Sheila's cousin Sandra hypnotized me and I journeyed back through my subconscious to search for clues," said Cassie casually. She felt so relaxed now.

"Cass, you went to Alaska?" Aeneas shook his head in disbelief.

Cassie grinned. "Yep. I needed to enter the timestream fast. It was the obvious choice."

"Sweetheart you've worked so hard to find me." Aeneas started to cry, all the while still munching on the cookies Cassie bought him.

Cassie went over and sat next to her father and he sobbed into her shoulder, globs of wet cookie sticking to her shirt. *He's lost weight and is exhausted,* thought Cassie. *The sooner we get back, the sooner he can get some medical care.* Then she remembered there might be one small hitch.

"Dad, there's one more thing and it's important." Cassie turned to face her father.

Aeneas sniffed. He grabbed a box of tissues and blew his nose several times. He felt dizzy.

"Go ahead. Sorry 'bout that, kiddo. I'm not quite myself."

"Uncle Sox thought you were trying to kidnap him. After that incident in the playfield he suffered from panic attacks for years and had to attend therapy sessions. He was only eight years old, Dad," said Cassie solemnly.

"Sox didn't recognize me. Hell, I don't recognize me—I guess he thought I was some scary homeless guy. My parents never mentioned he had panic attacks. More family secrets," mumbled Aeneas shaking his head.

"I guess it was all hushed up. But the thing is, when I returned to 2015 the second time, I had to confront Uncle Sox to figure out what was causing these panic attacks. Grandma Mimi was tight on information. Something weird was going on and I followed my gut." Cassie got up and started pacing again. She'd felt stymied by the reluctance of her grandmother to share information.

"Your mother would be so proud," interjected Aeneas, teasing his daughter.

The pacing led her to the window. Cassie opened the curtains as the sun was setting beneath the clouds then looked back at her dad covered in cookie crumbs. He *was* feeling better. She returned and sat across from him again ready to carry on with the rest of the story.

"When Uncle Sox remembered, it became clear to us that you were the guy in the playfield he thought had tried to kidnap him, so that day in his past changed from an attempted kidnapping to a different kind of memory."

Cassie thought she could keep it together but her eyes became clouded with tears as she struggled to continue. This part of the story made her feel ashamed. Inhaling deeply, her voice choked as she tried to explain.

"The thing is Dad, I could have prevented his interaction with you, but I was worried that it was a mistake to not let him have that experience."

Cassie looked to her father for reassurance as the tears cascaded down her face. Aeneas taught his daughter that time travelers had a responsibility to not manipulate events for their own benefit, but this was an unusual circumstance he'd never considered. He got up from the bed and brushed the cookie crumbs off his hoodie into a small garbage can then paced around the hotel room, pausing at the window.

"After the Birch Bay quake, Socrates had spent his life, which was some fifty or so years, believing that he'd nearly been kidnapped as a child. You went back in time nine years after the event, and after some dissection of new information, you and he concluded that it was me, his brother lost in time and not a kidnapper." Aeneas slowly shook his head as he walked back over to Cassie. This was one he wished he could ask Bob about. There was no clear right or wrong.

"How much would that have changed things, Dad?" whispered Cassie. She was so afraid that upon her return Missi and Thena wouldn't be part of her life. Aeneas was thinking the same thought. He grabbed the last cookie and whispered back, "I have no idea, Cass."

CHAPTER 50

New Additions
to the Mix

Lux was cooking a pot of green chili while he chatted with Tor who was traveling around Japan with his band. A loud thump in the living room startled the boys out of their conversation. Lux ran to the living room. The hologram system sensed his motion and followed him.

"Dad!" cried the twins in unison.

Aeneas laughed, hugged Lux and thumped his heart twice and pointed to Tor's face on the hologram hovering nearby.

"It's good to be home, boys," said Aeneas and he sniffed the air quizzically.

"Lux is making green chili, old man. I bet you're hungry. I would virtually eat some if that were possible, but I guess I'll eat more Japanese food, if I have to," said Tor feigning suffering. Tor loved all food just like his father.

"So, you're in Japan? Band on tour?" asked Aeneas brightly. He was so happy to talk to Tor.

"Yep," said Tor.

"Home soon?" asked Aeneas hopefully.

"Two more days and you'll have me wrestling you to the floor, if you're up for it," cried Tor with enthusiasm.

"Well, I'm sure your mother will have me checked over from head to toe before I can be officially cleared for wrestling," replied Aeneas with a wink.

Cassie wanted to be cheerful but she was apprehensive. She had to know if anything had been changed.

"So how is everyone?" she asked hesitantly.

Tor shrugged and looked over at Lux who said, "Same as when you left, I guess."

"Update us, would you boys? Include all the details." Aeneas was looking at his sons pensively, so Lux replied, "Did anything happen?"

Aeneas was noncommittal but Cassie heard the undertone of worry in his voice. "Yes and no, so please just fill us in on everyone."

"Okay," said Lux with an eye roll that made Cassie want to pinch him. Growing up with twin younger brothers there were moments when they simply needed to be pinched.

"Mom's fine. Worried, but hopeful. Uncle Sox is good. He's been checking on Mom. Aunt Keniah has come by a few times to take her for walks to get her out of the house."

Cassie exhaled. She was so relieved. "And Missi and Thena? Are they doing okay?"

"Yeah, as far as I know." Cassie teared up; she hadn't lost her cousins. They were her best friends and losing them would have been unbearable.

"You didn't ask about Nia," said Tor, giving her a weird look. Aeneas's head jerked up at the mention of this new name, and he turned to Tor and spoke like he was reading off a biographical sketch.

"Of course, Nia. Harmonia Louisa Entwistle, youngest daughter of Socrates and Keniah. She's just eighteen, correct?"

"Uh huh," said Tor looking at his brother with a glance that Lux returned quizzically.

Cassie snapped to attention as memories of her cousin Nia shuffled into her mind like cards being added to a deck. Nia was younger and so associated more with Tor and Lux, but suddenly Cassie could sense Nia's presence in her memories, but she could also remember a past without her. It was disconcerting and she made a note to talk with her father about this.

"Oh, and the Torkelsons are all fine too," said Lux cheerfully.

"What do you mean, *The Torkelsons*? It's just Harold," said Cassie, disgruntled. Lux and Tor exchanged another quick glance.

"So, you've never seen this wedding picture of dad, Uncle Sox, our grandparents and Aunt Seph?" said Tor gesturing across the room to the wall of family photos.

Cassie walked over to the wall and the color drained from her face. A wedding photograph of her father's family along with Harold and his bride, was backed by a clear blue summer sky and the Cascade Mountains. Aunt Seph was a flower girl. Uncle Sox was the best man.

And then those memories came back. Meg. Harold's wife from Montana. A geologist. A sassy lady with a sparkling smile who always planned fun outings. Meg and Harold had dogs, cats, goats, chickens and a small pot bellied pig, but no children of their own, so they often included Cassie and her brothers in their adventures.

Lux and Tor exchanged information just beneath the realm of everyday human communication. The next glance that passed between them was brief, but Lux knew what to do next. The twins had watched Cassie their whole life. She was their first form of entertainment and their first learning about human interaction that was not parental. Being Tabitha's sons, they inherited her keen observation skills which she insisted they put to good use. Tabitha referred to the twins as 'intuitive geniuses.'

Tor was not bodily present, but he took control of the situation. "Old man, you need to get into bed while we contact Uncle Sox. Lux will bring you a bowl of chili and juice some greens to aid in your recovery."

Aeneas made a slight nod and headed for his bedroom. He thought he needed more food and a nap before Tabitha came home and asked him too many questions.

Lux gently steered Cassie away from the pictures and sat her on the couch. Tor hovered nearby and lowered his screen so he was eye to eye with his sister.

"Hey, so you and young Harold..." and let his face and hands ask the rest of the question.

"No," hissed Cassie, glaring at him. "Don't be ridiculous, Tor."

Tor was emboldened, especially since he was nearly five thousand miles away. "I'm not. What about it, sis? He was only a few years older than you in 2015."

"Three, I think, Tor. Just three years older," quipped Lux, who then became the recipient of his sister's intense gaze.

Cassie swiveled, sweeping a fierce glare between both brothers before she said hotly, "Bring me some food. Then leave me alone."

And like the intuitive geniuses their mother knew them to be, they did just as their sister asked. Cassie was left alone to sift through the changes her travels to the past had created.

After Cassie finished her chili she retired to a hot bath, where she could let emotions come to her without the scrutiny of her brothers. Though she recognized that she had feelings for Harold, it all intensified when she saw his wedding picture and her heart hurt a little. The second visit to 2015 shifted the future and now two more people existed in her present, one of whom was Harold's wife. But why had he decided to marry? Cassie quickly dried off and headed downstairs. She would need time to process all the changes and she wanted to see her mother.

Tabitha had been fussing over Aeneas for a good ten minutes so when she saw Cassie, she walked briskly towards her, wrapping Cassie in her arms, kissing her forehead and her cheeks. "Thank you, my brave girl," she whispered through a controlled sob.

Cassie let her tears come too, but her tears were more complex. She was sad and confused at how the present had changed. She needed to talk to someone about it, but the priority now was her father's recovery.

CHAPTER 51

They're All
Terrible Liars

INFORMING HIS FAMILY THAT he would need a few days to recuperate, the clinic admitted Aeneas for dehydration, intestinal parasites, adrenal fatigue and a concussion. Cassie wanted to talk with her father about what happened, how the present had changed, but she knew he needed to rest. The spur of the moment decision made that afternoon in Hiawatha Playfield was preying on her mind and she realized that she owed her uncle an explanation. She called him and he agreed to meet her in West Seattle.

"Uncle Sox!" Cassie walked to him and they exchanged a long hug. After their coffee arrived, Cassie found herself lost for words.

"Was it him?" asked Socrates eagerly.

"Yes," said Cassie slowly. "He recognized you."

Socrates leaned in closer, ready to hear the conversation he'd waited for since he was seventeen.

"So you managed to escape the police?" asked Socrates, gently prodding, trying to infuse some momentum into Cassie who had become unusually quiet.

Cassie perked up. "Yes. We hurried into PCC Market. I'd brought along a bright blue hoodie to disguise Dad and we sat in the cafe while he ate a chicken dinner. He was so hungry."

"Did you arrive in time to see what happened?" Socrates desperately wanted to know the end of this story.

Cassie chewed on her bottom lip. She swallowed, or at least tried to. Her throat tightened up. It had been such a hard choice.

"Uncle Sox," began Cassie. Her hands were shaking. She took a deep breath, trying to steady herself.

"I was worried that if I altered your past, I might change the future, so I let it happen. I let your eight-year-old self think someone was trying to kidnap you. I know you must've been so scared. Can you ever forgive me?" Cassie put her face in her hands and sobbed.

"Hey, shh... shh..., don't cry, sweetheart. If I'd been there I probably would have made the same choice," said Socrates gently.

Cassie wiped her eyes and proceeded earnestly. "The thing is, I told you when you were seventeen, so from that point onward your perception of that event was altered."

Socrates tilted his head and let a small smile escape. "That's true. But the future wasn't altered, Cassie. Everything is as it should be."

Cassie looked away. Like all Entwistles, she was a terrible liar when confronted directly, especially by people she knew. Landing in a different time and making up a cover story was pure survival. Lying then never fazed her, but she couldn't lie to her Uncle Sox.

Sox caught on immediately. "What's changed?"

"Nia and Meg," said Cassie in a tiny voice.

"What about them?" asked Socrates urgently. He had no idea where this information was going, but suddenly he was worried.

Cassie shook off the tears and sat up straighter. It wasn't bad news, but it was significant. "When I left to return to 2015 the second time I had no cousin named Nia and Harold had never married."

"Huh," was all Socrates could utter. They sat in silence for a few moments as Cassie summoned her inner resolve to finish this conversation she had been dreading.

"It was the same for Dad, too. They didn't exist for him, either. When we returned we quizzed Lux and Tor, and as soon as they mentioned Nia's name, all the memories of her were immediately restored. It was odd—I'd never experienced anything like it."

"Nia was never born? Meg and Harold never married?" murmured Socrates in disbelief. Now he was shaking. He had no memories of his life without them. When Cassie went back to 2015 the second time, all his memories must have been replaced.

"I'd been so afraid that I might lose Missi and Thena. It never occurred to me that there would be more cousins, instead of less." At that, Cassie sunk into her chair. She'd felt so guilty about what happened and now that the truth was out, she felt relieved.

Socrates shook his head and clarified. "So you're saying when you came back from 2015 the first time, Nia and Meg were not part of your present?"

Cassie nodded her head, yes.

"It was the second visit then that changed things?" Socrates cupped his chin and leaned his elbow on the table, still working on the information.

Finally he spoke, but it was far from what Cassie wanted to hear. "I think I understand why your second visit changed me, but I have no idea how it changed Harold. Maybe you should ask him."

Cassie teared up again. "It was such a long time ago for him. I doubt he recalls why he decided to get married."

Socrates raised an eyebrow, the precursor to refuting a statement made by someone else. "Cassie, I don't know what passed between you and Harold the second time you visited 2015, but you and I both know Harold has an eidetic memory," reminded Socrates.

Cassie broke eye contact from her uncle. All the Entwistles were terrible liars.

CHAPTER 52

An Alteration
Is Requested

TABITHA RESTED HER FOREHEAD in the curve of Aeneas's neck just above his back. He smelled like sandalwood soap and the familiar scent comforted her. Aeneas was home and she never wanted to be parted from him again. He was sleeping deeply as she started to sob softly into the back of his neck. Her tears were old ones from a time in her life she didn't fully understand.

Aeneas shifted and Tabitha reached for the edge of the sheet to dry her face. She slipped from bed and walked into the living room towards the wall of family pictures. There was Sadie. Her long blonde hair hung to her shoulders. There was a slight smile as she tuned her guitar. C.J. had taken this photo the day before her thirteenth birthday party and later this one picture had been a cherished item for Tabitha. She took it down and held it close, crying until she fell asleep on the couch.

When Aeneas awoke he was surprised to find Tabitha not next to him. He'd been home recovering after spending a few days in the clinic, and since then he and Tabitha had been inseparable. The fact that they had nearly lost each other for good had not been taken for granted by either.

Aeneas figured Tabitha would be in the kitchen cooking breakfast. He'd left about eighteen pounds behind in his past. Tabitha had been feeding him as much as he would eat, only the kitchen was empty. He glanced into the living room and saw a figure lying on the couch.

Aeneas tiptoed into the living room. "Oh no," he whispered. He saw the photo and knew that this could only mean one thing. His beautiful, witty Tabitha was about to slip into her dark place again. He slowly backed out of the living room and scribbled a note and left it on the counter. *Gone for a walk & didn't want to wake you. Be home soon. Love, Aeneas.*

Aeneas grabbed his shoes and headed to the one place he had gone his whole life when he needed to talk something out.

C.J. was taking an early morning walk with his dog, Pete, an aging terrier that seemed to have as much energy as his namesake when he was the same age in human years. Aeneas caught a glimpse of them on a side street and he smiled. Who could have ever asked for a better friend than Colonel Johan Willoughby?

"Hey, C.J.! Bro, let's get breakfast!" While the term 'bro' was now hopelessly old fashioned and Aeneas had dropped it from most of his conversation at the insistence of his sons, C.J. was always referred to as 'bro' as a term of endearment.

C.J. smiled, waved back and hurried Pete along to meet Aeneas. A few minutes later they were settled in front of two steaming cups of coffee waiting for their breakfast with Pete tucked under the table patiently anticipating his sausage link.

Aeneas slowly wrapped his hands around the warm cup, then shared his concern. "I found her on the couch this morning holding a picture of Sadie. You know the one."

C.J. nodded and blew out a sigh of commiseration. He couldn't imagine what might come next. Tabitha's mental state had been fragile the last few weeks. "We can't let her fall back into that dark place again," said Aeneas gravely.

C.J.'s eyes caught sight of a shadow that fell across their table and swallowed hard as he looked beyond Aeneas. Tabitha's hair was twisted into a bun and she looked like she'd passed a rough night. How she found them wasn't surprising. This was their place, the place they had always gone. When they were young it was called Freshy's. As years passed it expanded into a farm-to-table bistro called Westies. Aeneas and C.J. thought Tabitha had a sixth sense, but for her it was simple logic. People go where they feel comfortable.

She took the seat next to C.J., facing her husband. Silence hovered around them even though the bistro was bustling with Sunday morning breakfasters. Pete whimpered, sensing something was amiss and C.J. reached down to pet him. Tabitha reached over and took Aeneas's hand. He waited, worried at what she might say, though he never expected what finally passed her lips.

"I want Sadie back. She never should've died."

Acknowledgements

The BULK OF THIS story was written between 2015 and 2017 but it needed streamlining. I began working with Davindia Steele to fine tune plot alignment, character development and timelines (for the story, not for time travel). Without her help, we wouldn't be here now. I am deeply grateful for her patience and endurance to wrangle all the details of time travel I imagined and put them in writing. My dear friend Maggie Pierce is my biggest fan and tireless cheerleader. Without her support, book two would've never been finished and book one wouldn't have been launched.

The quirk and warmth I encountered in West Seattle is a continued source of inspiration for this series. Many thanks to Mrs. Laura Handy-Nimick's 8th grade class of 2018 for being my first reader feedback group. And finally thanks to my friend Pachomius Schmidt who makes an appearance as the only real-life person in this story. There was no other choice but him for the scene I was writing.

About the Author

SHER STULTZ IS A science teacher and writer who lives in Western Washington. She loves to hike with her mini-Aussie, go birding, kayak, play ping pong and board games. A non-singing music lover, a haphazard gardener, and a proud mother of an amazing daughter, Sher likes being out in nature, appreciates peace and quiet, but also loves to dance in the kitchen while she cooks. An ardent conversationalist, Sher enjoys listening to people's life stories and finds inspiration from her students. *The Rescue* is her first novel in The Timestream Travelers Chronicles series.

Made in the USA
Monee, IL
14 February 2024

53509638R00177